I0613068

Theodore Bacon

Delia Bacon

A biographical sketch

Theodore Bacon

Delia Bacon
A biographical sketch

ISBN/EAN: 9783337028763

Printed in Europe, USA, Canada, Australia, Japan

Cover: Foto ©Raphael Reischuk / pixelio.de

More available books at **www.hansebooks.com**

DELIA BACON

A BIOGRAPHICAL SKETCH

> " What a wounded name,
> Things standing thus unknown, shall live behind me!
> If thou didst ever hold me in thy heart,
> Absent thee from felicity awhile,
> And in this harsh world draw thy breath in pain,
> To tell my story."

BOSTON AND NEW YORK
HOUGHTON, MIFFLIN AND COMPANY
The Riverside Press, Cambridge
1888

AN ACKNOWLEDGMENT.

THE letters written by the subject of this volume to Nathaniel Hawthorne were, at the cost of diligent search, found by his daughter, Mrs. Rose Hawthorne Lathrop, carefully preserved among his papers, and were entrusted to me for the use which has now been made of them. The oversight by which this helpful service failed to be mentioned in a marginal note in the body of the book is the less regretted that it has given occasion for this more conspicuous acknowledgment, that Hawthorne's patient kindness to one who received so much from him was not exhausted in his lifetime, but passed by inheritance to the generation that follows him.

THEODORE BACON.

ROCHESTER, N. Y.,
November 17, 1888.

CONTENTS.

————◆————

THIS is the story of a life that was neither splendid in achievement or adventure, nor successful, nor happy. It began deep in a New World wilderness, in the simplicity of a refined and honored poverty; it continued for almost fifty years of labor and sorrow, and ended amid clouds of disappointment and distraction. Neither the subject of it, nor those to whom in her lifetime she was very dear by ties of kindred, would easily have consented that the world should know more of her than could be learned from her gravestone: that she was born, and died. Yet because she was of rare intellectual force and acuteness, of absolute sincerity and truthfulness, of self-annihilating earnestness and devotion in whatever work she entered upon; and because the world is determined that it will speak of her as if it knew her, supplying its lack of knowledge with conjecture or with fable, I purpose to tell it something of Delia Bacon: of what she was, from inheritance and environment; and what she did.

DELIA BACON.

I.

OF what ancestry she may have come, earlier than the six generations through which it is easy to trace her descent from an English colonist, there is no reason to believe that she ever asked or greatly cared. The whim which some have been pleased to indulge, that her opinions may have had their source in some fancy that she was herself of common blood with the greatest Englishman who had borne her family name, is utterly without substantial foundation. Even less, while she lived, was known than can now be told of the plain yet honorable race of which she was born; nor had any one pretended to trace for it a connection with the great Norfolk family which had become illustrious so shortly before the Puritan exodus began. Except so far, therefore, as knowledge of her descent through two centuries of New England Puritans, and pride in such descent, made her so strong a New Englander that she brought to Elizabethan English thought and literature a sympathy keener and warmer than that of most Englishmen, and in making her such a New Englander gave direction to her studies and imaginations, she received from her family name neither prepossession nor suggestion. But as the influences which made her, unconscious of them as she was, were operating long before her birth, something may properly be told of them.

Within twenty years after the first disastrous venture at Plymouth, within fifteen after the colony upon Massachusetts Bay was begun, there was living at Dedham in that colony, in 1640, one Michael Bacon. He was a man of more than ordinary substance, and of such social dignity as was implied by the rank, which he had held before his migration, of captain of yeomanry. From what part of the dominions of Charles I. he had come, no one now seems able to tell. His first name, which has not been a common one in England, was repeated in several generations after him, and might afford a clue to his English kin, if it could be assumed to have been a family name before him. Late researches, indeed, have disclosed the fact that the great Chancellor's half-brother Edward had among his many children a Michael, born in 1608; and for a moment it had seemed possible that this younger son of a younger son might have been the captain of yeomanry seeking better fortune in the New World. But when it was discovered that the Lord Keeper's grandson Michael died while yet a child, even this shadowy link of connection to a great family, a

link of which Delia Bacon never so much as heard,
disappeared in the light of fact.

These Puritan Bacons seem to have prospered
and contented themselves for several generations
in Dedham, and Stoughton, which was a part of
Dedham, and Billerica, and Woburn, before they
were set in motion again by the westward impulse
of their Teuton, English, New England blood. In
1764, however, Joseph, great-great-grandson of
the first Michael, went into the wilderness, and in
the border town of Woodstock, which just in those
years was passing out of the jurisdiction of Massachusetts into that of Connecticut, he married Abigail Holmes. Though they lived a little while in
Stoughton, before 1771 they had fixed themselves
in Woodstock, among the original proprietors of
which the name of Holmes was found almost a
hundred years before. In that absolutely rural
community, containing in its population (presuma-
bly of from one to two thousand) no man, perhaps,
who was not a land-holder and a land-tiller, not
excepting its parish minister of the established
Congregational order, its physician, and possibly
a general trader and an artisan or two, there was,
nevertheless, strong and high thinking with plain
living. There, in 1761, was born (himself afterward a clergyman of distinction and an author of
merit) the father of Samuel Finley Breese Morse,
inventor and perfecter of the electric telegraph.
There, in 1763, was born (also to become, in due

time, an eminent divine and author) the father of
Oliver Wendell Holmes. And there, in 1771, was
born to Abigail Holmes (whose consanguinity to
those who have made her maiden name famous
was not too remote to be traceable) a son David,
the father of Delia Bacon.

It was an unsettled life, after all, into which this
child David was born. In several New England
towns his parents lived, a while in each, during
his childhood and youth; not prosperous in business, it seems, yet able to train their children with
such education of mind as well as of morals that
they need not shrink from any station into which
the simple democratic life of those communities
might bring them. An older son became a physician of great eminence. This one, becoming inflamed in the last years of the century with that
fire of self-devotion which forced from the mis-
sionary-apostle his cry of "Woe is me if I preach
not the Gospel!" set himself to the work of study
for such service, that he might give himself especially to the instruction and civilization of the
Indians in the northwestern wilderness.

How this laborious training went on: with what
courage, when it was completed, this enthusiast
confronted the perils of a wilderness as remote in
those days, and almost as savage, as equatorial
Africa is now: with what fortitude and serenity he
suffered hardship in many forms until death took
him from weariness and disappointment long be-

fore old age, it is not necessary now to speak. The story is a beautiful and a moving one, but it has been fully written by a competent filial hand.[1]

At the beginning of this century the interior of America, from the Hudson River westward, was almost an untried wilderness. There were, it is true, the ancient Dutch settlements along the Mohawk; and some rich valleys of eastern New York had received the first touches of colonization. But beyond were unknown wilds, except that the great lakes and rivers had been rudely mapped. A hundred years before, indeed, the wise fore-thought of French military statesmen had estab-lished a trading post and fort on the strait be-tween Lakes Huron and Erie, which was to be one in the chain of strongholds from the St. Lawrence to the Gulf of Mexico by which English power on this continent was to be restrained. That post, now the splendid city of Detroit, in 1801 held a motley population of a few hundred. But at "Buffalo Creek" this young missionary, waiting for days for a vessel to take him westward, found nothing but an encampment of savages on the site of the great city of Buffalo, which now numbers almost a quarter of a million inhabitants.

There at Detroit, at the even remoter post of Mackinac, upon the Maumee River, and else-where, for five years the Connecticut evangelist struggled in competition with the frontier rum-

---

[1] *Sketch of the Rev. David Bacon.* By Leonard Bacon, D. D., LL. D. Boston : Congregational Board of Publication. 1876.

sellers for some effectual influence upon a wild
and violent race, with which communication was
enormously difficult from diversity of language.
With him he had taken his young wife, a delicate
girl of eighteen, whose refined and gentle dignity
in old age there are some who remember still.
Children had already come to them when, chang-
ing somewhat his earliest plan, but still devoted to
the spread of the religion of which he was a minister, he determined, leaving the employment of
the Connecticut Missionary Society, to establish in
the Ohio woods a colony of New England men,
after the New England type.

From east to west, across the northern part of
what is now the State of Ohio, stretches the belt
of land which, included between the north and
south lines of the colony of Connecticut prolonged
westwardly, was within the terms of the original
royal grant to that colony; for that grant was limited on the west only by " the South Sea." The
sovereignty which by virtue of this grant was
asserted by the colony was, upon the establishment of a national government, ceded to it by the
State; but proprietary rights were reserved, and
the tract to which they attached was long afterward known indifferently as " New Connecticut,"
or the " Western Reserve." In this region, then
a dense and almost unbroken forest, the adventur-
ous missionary chose for his new enterprise a tract
of five miles square, some thirty miles south of
the point where now the great city of Cleveland

looks out upon Lake Erie ; and there, having himself laid out with eminent skill and judgment the
roads and public places of the future community,
he built of logs the little cabin which was its first
house, and established in it his household.

In this town of Tallmadge, in the log cabin which
began the town, was born to David and Alice Bacon, on the 2d of February, 1811, their fifth child.

Many years afterward the child recalled, and put
into words, her vague impressions of the scenes
which surrounded her infancy. She was speaking
of the forces which drove Sir Walter Raleigh westward, and made of him the pioneer of the New
World ; and especially of " the new power of the
religious Protestantism." " It was that too," she
says, " which would begin erelong to pierce the
great inland forest with its patient strength,
sprinkling it with bright spots of European culture, but culture already beginning to be modified
by the new exigencies, going deeper and deeper
with its little helpless household burthens that the
tomahawk and the scalping-knife must long encircle, going deeper and deeper always into its
old savage heart, and breaking it at last with
those soft rings of patient virtues and heroic faith
and love. It was that which was working still,
when in its fiercest heart, — in the valley of the
old Indian 'River of Beauty,' where the mission
hut had pursued the tomahawk, and the 'Great
Trail' from the Northern lakes to the Southern
gulf went by the door, and wild Indian faces

looked in on the young mother, and wolves howled lullabies, the streets and squares of the town were pencilled and the college was dotted on that trail, and the wild old forest echoed with Sabbath hymns and sweet old English nursery songs, and the children of the New World awoke and found a new world there, old as from everlasting." [1]

In the rural town of Mansfield in Connecticut, where the father of this child had sojourned for a while before departing upon his western mission, there was among his friends a lawyer named Salter. Student-at-law with him was also a friend of the student of divinity, Thomas Scott Williams, afterwards chief justice of Connecticut. Removing, soon afterward, to Hartford for the practice of his profession, the future chief justice married the daughter of one who had himself been chief justice of the United States, Delia Ellsworth.

Remembering, in the wilderness, these friends of his younger manhood, the missionary combined their names in that of his child, and called her Delia Salter. Almost to the close of her life she continued to use both names thus given her in baptism; but when she began to contemplate closely the publicity which she was to confront, she seems — though it was never spoken of by her — to have thought of a certain ludicrousness in the sounds thus brought together, and then, for the first time, she dropped out of use the second name.

[1] From *A Study of the Life of Raleigh*, unpublished.

II.

THE enterprise which had been undertaken by this frontier missionary, wise as it has been proved by its results after not many years, in the establishment of an agricultural community unsurpassed in America for comfort, prosperity, intelligence, and morality, was, nevertheless, too great for his unaided strength. Without capital of his own, he had undertaken the purchase upon credit of the broad tract of land upon which he had traced the roads and allotted the farms of the future colony. The sale of the farms to the Connecticut men, whose emigration he himself solicited, was to enable him, he hoped, to meet the liabilities he had incurred. But close upon his purchase, in full peace with all nations, came the Embargo which closed the ports of New England to the world, and which was more ruinous to the prosperity of New England than even the war with Great Britain, which followed close upon it. The plan which founded the town ended, so far as the founder was concerned, in utter and heartbreaking disappointment within a few months after this little Delia was born. But the town itself went on growing in numbers and wealth and beauty ; and it remembers and honors its founder. The site of the cabin, which was its earliest house, was marked by the townsmen in 1881 with a great granite bowlder — an " erratic " block — with an inscription upon its face that tells of the gathering there of the First Church in Tallmadge, " in the house of Rev. David Bacon, January 22, 1809."

For almost a year of the little girl's babyhood, her father had been in Connecticut, engaged in a last endeavor to restore an undertaking already ruined. When that, too, had failed, as his eldest son has written, " with difficulty he obtained the means of returning to his family, and of removing them from the scene of so great a disappointment. All that he had realized from those five years of arduous labor was poverty, the alienation of some old friends, the depression that follows a fatal defeat, and the dishonor that waits on one who cannot pay his debts. Broken in health, broken in heart, yet sustained by an immovable confidence in God, and by the hopes that reach into eternity, he turned away from the field of hopes that had so sadly perished, and bade his last farewell to Tallmadge and the Western Reserve." In May, 1812, with his almost girlish wife and their brood of little ones, of whom the oldest was but ten, he began his slow journey of six hundred miles through the wilderness to his old home. There, in Old Connecticut, for a little while he lingered, preaching and teaching : in Litchfield, Prospect, Middletown; and at last he laid down his weary life, in its forty-sixth year, in August, 1817.

It was a very helpless family that he left behind him. By what management or magic this young widow, absolutely without inheritance other than the resolute and devout spirit which had come through many generations of English Puritans, contrived to feed and clothe her six children and herself; to supply them all with the highest education and culture which that simple community afforded ; and to enable the two sons to pass through Yale College and into learned professions, no one now living can tell. It was, however, a painful part of the process that it became necessary to accept a home for this little Delia, six years old, in the family of her namesake, Mrs. Williams, in Hartford. Here, for several years, she was cared for as a daughter of the house, while yet she maintained, by all means of communication, frequent intercourse and warm affection for those of her own blood from whom she was parted for a while. There can be no doubt of the calm and constant kindness of patronage which the fatherless child received here ; but its calmness may have been somewhat stern and grim.

It was not long after Delia had thus found an asylum in Hartford that a school for girls was opened there which made no small mark upon the

generation then coming on. It was that of Catherine Beecher, whose father, Lyman Beecher, was
a minister of the Congregational churches which
were just then ceasing to be " by law established "
in Connecticut, and one whose fame for homiletic
and polemic power is far from extinct. Into this
school Delia entered as a pupil, and with her was
the teacher's sister, Harriet, a year her junior,
who was destined to attain extraordinary renown
and success in literature, not long before her
schoolmate's life of unsparing toil ended in disappointment and failure. Through all her life, however, she retained the constant friendship of both
sisters, the teacher and the fellow-pupil. Nearly
thirty years afterward Catherine Beecher thus
described the child who now came under her
charge :

" If the writer were to make a list of the most
gifted minds she has ever met, male or female,
among the highest on the list would stand five
young maidens, that were then grouped around
the writer, in that dawning experience of a teacher's life. And never did a teacher watch the un-
foldings of intellect and moral life with more
interest and delight. Of this number, one was
the homeless daughter of that Western home missionary.

" Possessing an agreeable person, a pleasing and
intelligent countenance, an eye of deep and earnest expression, a melodious voice, a fervid imagi-

nation, and the embryo of rare gifts of eloquence in thought and expression, she was preëminently one who would be pointed out as a *genius;* and one, too, so exuberant and unregulated as to demand constant pruning and restraint. With this was united that natural delicacy and purity of mind, which frequently not only protects the young maiden from all coarseness and indecorum, but, even to full womanhood, renders it impossible for her even to conceive what impurity may be.

"In disposition she was sensitive, impulsive, and transparent, possessing a keen longing for approbation, a morbid sensibility to criticism or blame, an honest truthfulness, and an entire freedom from all that could be called management or art."

"In this period of her mental history, had her future career been anticipated by the data of her natural endowments and probable circumstances, it would have been predicted that her genius, her confiding frankness, her interesting appearance, her gifts of eloquence, and her sincere aspirations after all that is good and pure, would make her an object of attention, and probably of excessive flattery. On the other hand, her keen sensibility to blame or injustice, her transparency, sincerity, and impulsiveness, the dangerous power of keen and witty expression, and the want of the guidance and protection of parents and home, would make her an object of unjust depreciation. . . . . .

The persons who were objects of her regard, and to whom she confided her thoughts and feelings, would almost inevitably become enthusiastic admirers, while those who in any way came into antagonism would be as decided in their dislike."

The sketch thus drawn by the clear-minded teacher, strong and sharp as it is, needs yet some filling up of its outlines. I cannot speak irreverently of the terrors with which the prevalent religion of New England, from the beginning down to very recent times, sought to persuade men to live purely and think rightly. Half a century hence, when it has been proved that better, stronger, and truer men and women have been nurtured under the relaxation of those old-time rigors than those whom the seventeenth, the eighteenth, and the first quarter of the nineteenth century in New England produced, scorn and indignation at the ancient Puritan errors will at least not be untimely. But even the most loyal New Englander may doubt the wholesomeness of the exercises of self-examination and introspection into which devout parents and teachers guided their infant charges. It touches close upon sacrilege to invade the confidence of a young religious soul, seeking for illumination under the menace of eternal wretchedness; but the woman whose story is told cannot be known without knowledge of the girl. There is extant a letter from her to her brother, then a student of divinity, when she was a child of ten. It covers one side of a half sheet of foolscap, yellow with age, and ruled with penciled lines. "Your sister," says this little child, " has resisted the Holy Spirit and He has departed from me. O what a deplorable state! what a dreadful situation! When I think of it I tremble; but my fears are of short duration. Like Felix I say, go thy way for this season; but oh! what will become of me when I shall leave this vain transitory world and rise before my God in judgment! Cease not to pray for me; I have neglected the offers of salvation; I have despised my dear Redeemer; but still there is mercy with him who is able to save." (Sept. 29, 1821.)

From time to time appear, among her brother's most sacredly treasured papers, letters showing continual like struggles and miseries, with alternating hope and despair, resulting at last, at some time before her fifteenth birthday, in a formal " profession of faith," in the First Church in Hartford.

From the spring of 1826 the shelter and support which she had for years received in the Williams household were to be hers no longer. With a very sad young heart she looked out upon the world in which, at fifteen, she was to begin a lifelong struggle. At the close of February she writes to her eldest brother, who, young as he was, stood in a father's place to her : " I have but nine weeks more to remain in my present home," and then, "I shall have no home in all the wide,

wide world I can call my own." "The future seems very dark to me, and I cannot imagine what I am to do. I know I am to depend upon my own exertions for subsistence, and were there any field for these exertions I would not fear. But there seems to me none, and every way I turn I am disappointed and perplexed." (Feb. 26, 1826.)

At last, after much inquiry in various directions for a place in which a school could be maintained (the only resource in those days for women who would help themselves), after some small work in a school in Hartford, this child, with a sister but little older, began a school in the village of Southington, Connecticut.

Almost at the beginning of 1827, when Delia was not yet sixteen, the Southington enterprise was begun. It seems to have been for girls of ages up to the highest school limit; yet here, and in the other places where new experiments were made, the head of the school was Delia, and her elder sister was subordinate.

It would be profitless to reproduce from her letters the assiduous toil, the continuous struggle of pinching economy with dire poverty, in which these years of girlhood were worn away. In Southington, only the time from January to September was needed to demonstrate the failure of their project. At Perth Amboy, in New Jersey, they had learned by May of the next year (1828) that the sanguine hopes with which they had been

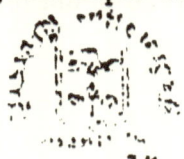

attracted thither by the townspeople were unwarranted, and they had fallen a little further into debt than when they came. At Jamaica on Long Island, twelve miles from New York, the prospect set before them was still more glowing than before. Their undertaking was to be larger. Not only were they to teach a greater number of young ladies, but they were — these two girls — to maintain a household of which some of the scholars should be inmates.

The encouragement which inspired them in beginning here, in May, 1828, was certainly substantial. There was a refined and cultured society there, which appreciated and welcomed the refinement of the girl teachers. Especially did they find support in the cordial friendliness of John Alsop King, whose father, Rufus King, had been one of the most eminent statesmen of the post-revolutionary period, and who became himself governor of New York in later years. But even here, two years sufficed to prove their powers inadequate to their task; and in the summer of 1830 an end came, in disappointment, exhaustion, sickness, and hopeless insolvency, to this last attempt. And in telling the fatal story to their eldest brother, Leonard, who was all they had for counselor, comforter, and helper, Delia begins by saying: " Our letters must still be what they always have been, a tale of blasted hopes, realized fears, and unlooked-for sorrows."

III.

THERE were no more daring enterprises in establishing and carrying on schools, with all the responsibilities, cares, and hazards of proprietorship. Here and there, however, Delia was able now to maintain herself by teaching in the schools of others. At Hartford once more, immediately after the Jamaica disaster; at Penn Yan, in Western New York, after which she frankly declares, "I will never live again in a place with such a heathenish name, unless I go on a mission" (June 16, 1832); perhaps in the rural village of West Bloomfield, not far from there, where at any rate she was for many months with her married oldest sister; and perhaps elsewhere. But during these years she was getting into her mind notions of better means of self-support than teaching school.

In the thickest of the toil and trouble at Jamaica she had prepared for the press, if a publisher could be found, her first adventure in letters. It was not strange that the history of the Anglo-American Puritans should strongly hold the attention of one who was so completely theirs by descent and by sympathy; and the series of short stories which were to make her book was founded upon incidents in their history. In the spring of 1831 there was published in New Haven, by A. H. Maltby, "Tales of the Puritans," a duo-decimo of three hundred pages. The author's name was not given, but such credit as belonged to it was soon awarded to Delia Bacon. Nor was it by any means without merit, especially, as she herself said of it shortly afterward, "considering it as written without experience, without knowl-edge of the subjects of which it treated, with scarcely a book to refer to beyond the works made use of in school." (Dec. 12, 1831.) The three stories contained in it were "The Regi-cides," "A Fair Pilgrim," and "Castine," which she had at first called "The Catholic." The first was an adaptation, far from unskillful or uninter-esting, of the romantic story of the three judges of Charles I. who found shelter in New Haven, and of the pursuit of them after the Restoration, ingeniously defeated by sympathizing officials and people. The next seems to have been suggested, but little more, by the fate of the Lady Arbella Johnson, daughter of the Earl of Lincoln, who came to die in the wilderness, at Salem, in 1630; and the subject of the last was the French settle-ment of the Baron Castine upon the Penobscot, late in the seventeenth century.

This experiment, attempted in the stress of poverty and debt in the hope of retrieving the

impending losses from the school, seems to have
achieved for her little more than the *succés d'es-
time* which was quite unquestionable. The credit,
indeed, which the girl got for it, in those days
when the girls were rare who saw themselves in
print, may have done little good in sharpening
the hunger for literary success which shrewd Catherine Beecher had already discerned in her as a
child at school. "From her childhood," her oldest
brother wrote of her long afterward, "she has had
a passion for literature, and perhaps I should say
a longing, more or less distinct, for literary celeb-
rity." So it was not long before she was at work,
in the intervals of teaching here and there in
schools, or (this she liked much better) select
classes of young ladies in her own apartments,
upon a new venture based upon an incident of
American history. This was to have been a drama,
and at first ambition had inspired the hope, at
which indeed her Puritan soul was rather aghast,
that it might be acted upon the stage. Friendly
criticism, however, and especially, as her letters
show, that of her brother, convinced her, after she
had exhausted herself with labor upon it, that it
lacked essential dramatic qualities; and at last,
when she had rewritten and greatly altered it, the
form of dialogue being yet retained, it was published in New York, late in 1839, by S. Colman.
Its title was "The Bride of Fort Edward: A Dra-

matic Story." It was based upon the pathetic story of Jane McCrea, a beautiful American girl whose lover was a loyalist officer in Burgoyne's army, just before its surrender at Saratoga. Captured by a party of Burgoyne's Indians, she promised them, in her terror, a large reward if they would take her safely to the British camp. "It was a fatal promise," says Irving. "Halting at a spring, a quarrel arose among the savages, inflamed most probably with drink, as to whose prize she was, and who was entitled to the reward. The dispute became furious, and one, in a paroxysm of rage, killed her on the spot. He completed the savage act by bearing off her scalp as a trophy."[1]

This episode and its effect, which was certainly very great, in stimulating the patriotic rage of the revolutionary army, are the theme of the book. The dialogue is mostly in prose, with passages interspersed of blank verse, not always correct; and it continues for almost two hundred pages of rhapsody and apostrophe and curiously mistaken familiar speech of common people. That partial theatrical friends — her letters even mention Miss Ellen Tree, one of the most famous of her day — should ever have fancied that it contained so much as the germ of an acting play, is inconceivable when one reads it now; and even the read-

[1] *Life of Washington*, iii. 153.

ing of it is far from being a recreation. It was a failure, every way; it brought debt instead of money, and no renown; but it did the great service of ending, for a time, her attempts at literary work, and turning her back to study and instruction.

IV.

In all these years, beginning with a severe and prolonged course of an epidemic fever at Jamaica in 1828, the girl, maturing into womanhood, had been waging a sharp though intermittent warfare with ill-health. Sometimes, indeed, the high spirits and animation which seem to have been natural to her indicated a vigorous physical state; but often there were intense, prolonged, and prostrating headaches, or agonizing attacks of neuralgia. Against this, however, she carried on with high courage her struggle to be something and to accomplish something. She writes to her brother of being "resolved to correct the defects of her early education, so far as it is possible for earnest and patient effort to accomplish it;" and so of her reading on vegetable physiology, on political economy, on the elements of ideology. (Dec. 12, 1831.) At another time she is renewing her school acquaintance, such as it was, with Latin; and again, with little help from teachers, she is trying to learn Greek.

But in the midst of it all — sickness, studying, writing of stories and plays that cannot be played — she carries on the work of instruction, from

which alone, in those days, a woman could earn
her living, if she could not work with her hands.
This she did, not in the perfunctory fashion which
seems alone to have been known to the pedagogy
of the time, but in a way of her own devising.
She gathered about her, in her own apartments,
or in some larger room.when her own proved insufficient, young ladies whose school-days were
ended, and many, even, who were no longer
young. These she taught, in literature sometimes, but above all in history. One who seems
to have thought it a privilege to be her pupil has
written thus of her instruction :

"She imparted to them new ideas ; she system-
atized for them the knowledge already gained ;
she engaged them in discussion ; she taught them
to think. 'What books do you use in Miss Bacon's class ?' A question often asked and impossible of answer. Her pupils had no books — only
a pencil and some paper. All they learned was
received from her lips. She sat before them, her
noble countenance lighted with enthusiasm, her
fair white hands now holding a book from which
she read an extract, now pressing for a moment
the thoughtful brow. She knew both how to
pour in knowledge and how to draw out thought.
And there are few listeners, I think, who can give
keener and more critical attention than the former
members of Miss Bacon's class.

"In many of the Eastern cities" these historical

lectures " called out deep interest and enthusiasm. Hundreds of the most cultivated flocked to hear them. Graceful and intellectual in appearance, eloquent in speech, marvelously wise, and full of inspiration, she looked and spoke the very muse of history. Of these lectures she wrote out nothing — not even notes. All their wisdom came fresh and living from the depth of her ready intellect. And for that very reason there is now no trace of what would be so valuable." [1]

Since these pages are written only to tell those who care to know what Delia Bacon was, it may be well to adduce further the testimony of this pupil.

" Delia Bacon was a woman of a genius rare and incomparable. Wherever she went, there walked a queen in the realm of mind. To converse with her was to be carried captive. The most ordinary topic became fascinating when she dealt with it, for whatever subject she touched she invested with her own wonderful wealth of thought, and illustration, and association, and imagery, until all else was forgotten in her magical converse.

" In personal appearance she was of middle stature, graceful, fair, and slight. Her habitual black dress set off to advantage the radiant face, whose fair complexion was that uncommon one which can only be described as pale yet brilliant.

[1] Article "Delia Bacon :" by Sydney E. Holmes [Mrs. Sarah E. Henshaw]: *The Advance* (Chicago), Dec. 26, 1867.

Intellect was stamped on every feature. Genius looked from brow and eye. The hair was a pale brown, gold tinted [1] — fit shading for such a countenance. The eye blue-gray, clear, shining, and passing rapidly through all expressions, from the swimming softness of tender sympathy to the flash that revealed the inspiration within.

"Meeting her in a crowd, you glanced over and thought — 'a graceful woman.' But your eye unconsciously sought her again, and the second time you felt rather than thought — 'a remarkable woman.' 'Who is that lady?' asked a newly appointed college official, — 'that lady whom I meet occasionally in the street.' He went on to paint her. There was no mistaking the description. 'That,' was the reply, 'is Miss Bacon.' 'That Miss Bacon!' he exclaimed. 'I knew it was some one remarkable! — I never saw such an eye in my life! and how young she is!'

"No one could know and appreciate Delia Bacon, without placing her in his estimation among the most highly endowed women whom he ever saw or heard of. Was philosophy the subject of her discourse? She dealt with abstract truth as but one woman does in generations. Weighing, balancing, analyzing, and comparing, she knew all systems, and had their resemblances and their

---

[1] This detail is certainly erroneous. The hair was of a brown which was nearer to black than is often found with blue or blue-gray eyes. — T. B.

differences clearly defined, distinctly remembered, and ready at her call. Her mastery of the subject astonished you; you were sure she had given her chief time and thought to that alone.

"Was it history? She was equally at home, and showed an insight that illustrated her great intellectual powers. Chronology, geography, narrative — all its facts were familiar to her. Knowing what she knew of these, most people would have considered themselves thoroughly versed in historic lore. But history to her was not these — these were to her only the beginning. They were the husk, the rind, the outward covering of a philosophy, which she delighted to educe for duller minds to recognize. So with poetry and art. By her own originality and genius, she set forth each with new thoughts, or with old ones in new combinations. And a deep veneration for what is good, a clear recognition of God and his providence, underlay all her teachings. This is no high-sounding praise. Let those who knew her best make answer."[1]

For some years together — exactly when the period began or ended it is hard to say — these courses of instruction were given by her with great approval. In New Haven, where her brother was minister of the ancient "First Church," and was also in official relation to Yale College, she had certain marked advantages of acquaintance and

---

[1] Article "Delia Bacon" : *The Advance, ubi supra.*

introduction; and here her classes are said to have numbered one hundred, while they included beyond doubt all that was most refined and cultivated in the society of that university town. In Hartford, the home of her childhood, her success was gratifying to her reasonable pride. In Boston, in Cambridge, and in New York and Brooklyn — these last, in 1852 and 1853, seeming to end the list — she continued this congenial but exhausting labor of oral instruction, and even found the new sensation, in the last season of this period, of earning money enough to make substantial payments upon the debts incurred in former years.

It was in Boston that she became acquainted with one of those who have recorded in public the impression she made. In " Recollections of Seventy Years,"[1] of which the first of several editions appeared in 1865, Mrs. Eliza Farrar, who had come to know her well before she died, devotes her closing chapter to the story, so far as it had been within her knowledge, "of a highly gifted and noble-minded woman " (p. 331).

" The first lady whom I ever heard deliver a public lecture was Miss Delia Bacon, who opened her career in Boston, as teacher of history, by giving a preliminary discourse, describing her method, and urging upon her hearers the importance of the study.

[1] Boston : Ticknor & Fields.

"I had called on her that day for the first time, and found her very nervous and anxious about her first appearance in public. She interested me at once, and I resolved to hear her speak. Her person was tall and commanding, her finely shaped head was well set on her shoulders, her face was handsome and full of expression, and she moved with grace and dignity. The hall in which she spoke was so crowded that I could not get a seat, but she spoke so well that I felt no fatigue from standing. She was at first a little embarrassed, but soon became so engaged in recommending the study of history to all present, that she ceased to think of herself, and then she became eloquent.

"Her course of oral lessons, or lectures, on history interested her class of ladies so much that she was induced to repeat them, and I heard several who attended them speak in the highest terms of them. She not only spoke, but read well, and when on the subject of Roman history, she delighted her audience by giving them with great effect some of Macaulay's Lays.[1]

"I persuaded her to give her lessons in Cambridge, and she had a very appreciative class assembled in the large parlor of the Brattle House. She spoke without notes, entirely from her well-stored memory; and she would so group her facts as to present to us historical pictures calculated to

[1] It should be remembered that the "Lays" had then but just appeared, and were not yet commonplaces. — T. B.

make a lasting impression. She was so much ad-
mired and liked in Cambridge, that a lady there
invited her to spend the winter with her as her
guest, and I gave her the use of my parlor for
another course of lectures. In these she brought
down her history to the time of the birth of
Christ, and I can never forget how clear she
made it to us that the world was only then made
fit for the advent of Jesus. She ended with a fine
climax that was quite thrilling.

"In her Cambridge course she had maps, charts,
models, pictures, and everything she needed to
illustrate her subject. This added much to her
pleasure and ours. All who saw her then must
remember how handsome she was, and how grace-
fully she used her wand in pointing to the illustrations of her subject. I used to be reminded by her
of Raphael's sibyls, and she often spoke like an
oracle.

"She and a few of her class would often stay
after the lesson and take tea with me, and then
she would talk delightfully for the rest of the
evening. It was very inconsiderate in us to allow
her to do so, and when her course ended she was
half dead with fatigue" (pp. 319-321).

The instruction, however, which for almost a
decade of years she was thus giving by oral discourse and conversation to classes of ladies, while
general history was perhaps oftenest its subject,

was by no means restricted to the history of events. She taught, in like manner, with high enthusiasm and with great acceptance, the history of literature and the arts, and the history and principles of criticism. More and more, indeed, through all this period of exhausting toil for self-support, under the burden of sickness and penury and debt, her interest and her inclination were turning toward pure literature and literary criticism; so that when, in 1852, her historical lectures in Boston and Cambridge were ended for the season, she seems to have hoped that they would never be, as in fact they never were, resumed.

V.

THIS was not a normal or healthful life for a girl and woman of an exquisitely sensitive nervous organization, of fine intellectual powers, of strong affections. With the warmest instinct of domestic love for the family into which she had been born, and in which privation and hardship and separation had only strengthened the mutual attachment of its members, she yet had never known a home, except the stern and conscientious hospitality which sheltered her for the few years before she became fifteen. With a keen sense of admiration, and with personal attractions so marked, that although she did not seem conscious she could not have been ignorant of them, her girlhood was grimly shut out from even the temperate social joys that Connecticut Puritanism allowed. Out of such social life, had not the necessity that was laid upon her forbidden it to her, there might have come in her womanhood the home which she was never to know, and the ties and the occupations which would have turned the current of her life into a placid, serene, and undistinguished domesticity. But there was no room in her crowded life for the passages that lead to marriage. Such addresses as had been openly paid to her she was observed to receive with amusement rather than seriously, and then to decline. Afterward, indeed, when she was mature in age, she underwent a most cruel ordeal, and suffered a grievous and humiliating disappointment. So keen was the exasperation, and so deep the humiliation to which her highly sensitive and already overwrought nature was subjected in the face of a wide and critical circle of acquaintance, that it would not have been strange if the new strain had broken it down completely. Exquisitely sensitive as she was, however, she was no less proud and brave; and if from the sharp and prolonged distress of the years 1846 and 1847 her mind did in fact undergo some permanent harm that took open effect in later years, there was little sign of it then. Sustained by the womanly pride that was born in her, and by the religious principle in which she had been so diligently trained, she was able to write, not long afterward, to her brother from Ohio, almost from the very spot where she was born in a missionary's cabin: " I begin to look upon the world, and its toil and strife, somewhat as those do who have left it forever. Objects which once seemed very large to me appear now, in the mental perspective which this distance creates, absurdly little. . . . In that calm of heart and soul to which God by his providence and by his grace has at length conducted me, I can afford to wait until 'the lying lips are put to silence.' "

More than ever before was the tender and watchful care of those to whom she was especially bound by ties of nature or affection centred upon her during these years of suffering and of threatened prostration, and the years that closely followed them. Cheered though they were, however, by her courage and fortitude, there were those among them who began already to discern upon her, even if they sounded no note of warning, the approaching shadow of a dark and dreadful cloud.

VI

STUDYING and teaching for many years not merely the history of events, but the history and criticism of literature, it is not strange that the strongly English mind of this New England woman became gradually fixed upon the greatest work of English letters, the drama of the Elizabethan and Jacobean age. So complete, indeed, was the spell of fascination under which she fell in the study especially of the plays which bear the name of Shakspere, that after the beginning of 1853 she could no longer endure the burden of her historical lessons, in which she seemed to have achieved a permanent success, sure to bring her, if only she should continue them, prosperity and credit.

To whom it first occurred to doubt the title of William Shakspere to the authorship of the plays commonly bearing his name is a question which will not be much discussed in this sketch.

Certainly no dispute of authorship was rife in his lifetime. A good reason for this was that there was no assertion of authorship by any one. It is true, that as early as 1589, when Shakspere was twenty-five years old, he had become a play-actor, and one of the sixteen owners of the Blackfriars

play-house. It is even guessed that as early as
that, one of the plays which were afterward called
his had been performed, in that house or elsewhere; although it is hardly surmised that any
one of them was printed earlier than 1594. And
inasmuch as the general agreement seems to be
that half of all that go commonly by his name, including many of the noblest, were never printed
at all while he lived, or until seven years after his
death, since there was no assertion of authorship,
contention could hardly arise against it.

Nor was it until very long after an author was
first openly nominated for these plays in the publication of the folio edition of 1623, that either literary or historical criticism could easily turn itself
to a discussion of the claim, if any one had thought
of suggesting such a discussion. It might, indeed,
be said that for a century afterward neither literary nor historical criticism existed in England;
and there were other reasons why the intellectual
activity of England concerned itself little, for
many years, with the plays of Elizabeth's time or
their authors. When the folio of Heminge and
Condell appeared, the great political struggle of
the seventeenth century, to prepare the way for
which the acted plays had already done so much,
was on the point of passing from its first stage of
discussion and lawful agitation into open and revolutionary outbreak. Two years after, the death of
James I. and the accession of his son gave new

intensity to the conflict already engaged; and
from that time onward to half of England a play,
a play-house, or a play-writer was sinful; while
for all England there was graver work than reading plays or speculating upon their authorship.
Then, when the anti-Puritan reaction came with
the Restoration, the dramas of a past generation
had little chance of a hearing in competition with
the witty abominations of Congreve and Wycher-
ley; and the stiffening classicism of the time of
Anne and the Georges afforded little tolerance for
" Fancy's child," by whatever name he might be
called, if he warbled to it only " his native wood-
notes wild."

And yet it is not altogether untrue to say that
the authorship of the Shakspere drama has always
been in controversy. From the beginning until
now, while almost all men were agreed that Shakspere wrote plays, it was hard to find two who
agreed what plays he wrote. The folio of 1623
contained thirty-six plays. Of these, eighteen were
then for the first time printed. Yet, while the
aim of the editors is to present a complete collection of his plays, they wholly disregard at least
seventeen which during the author's lifetime had
been published under his name, without any dis-
avowal by him so far as is known. Upon these
last therefore, at all events, men's opinions differed
in Shakspere's time and afterwards. They differed,
also, upon the play of " Pericles," which the folio

omitted as not his; but which modern editors
judge to be his, either partly or wholly. Then
the wisest critics of to-day, with the keenest sensitiveness for Shakspere's name, do not fear to discuss, as though they were not laying profane
hands on the ark of the covenant, the question
whether one and another of the Shakspere plays
are really his: as the three parts of "King Henry
VI."; as "Pericles"; as "Titus Andronicus"; so
that one critic has been able to satisfy himself that
but five can be rightly called his, and that all
others are falsely or mistakenly imputed to him.

While there was hardly a play of them all to
the authorship of which Shakspere's title had not
been at some time either wholly ignored or sharply
questioned; while there were many more plays
which in his lifetime or for sixty years afterward
were openly imputed to him, so that the authentic
canon of the Shakspere drama has always been, is
now, and perhaps ever will be the subject of fierce
contention; yet none of the critics went so far as
to sum up the several disputations of all the critics
by maintaining that all were right, at least in part,
and that the play-actor wrote none of them.

Many readers, indeed, from the time when criticism began a century and a half ago, found themselves confronted with difficulties elsewhere unknown. The personality of this dramatist glowed
through his work with a force and brightness
found nowhere else in literature. It seemed, in-

deed, a multiplied personality. There was in it not only marvelous insight, but exquisite cultivation and refinement, profound learning, and a practical knowledge of men, of the world, and of affairs such as all men were apt to say had never before been joined in any one man. When Coleridge called him the " myriad-minded," he simply put into a felicitous phrase what all men had long been thinking. Many, indeed, had declared their wonder that any one mind could produce creations so diverse in character as " Julius Cæsar" and " The Merry Wives of Windsor," as " The Comedy of Errors" and " Macbeth." In general, however, a single student would content himself with a demonstration which, alone, might have served to solve the difficulty found by every one, but which, when involved with like demonstrations by others, only multiplied perplexity. To prove from the plays that their author must have been a lawyer, as Lord Campbell did, was far from difficult, and would have been very helpful if the demonstration had stood alone. True, there was no historical record of Shakspere's ever having seen a law-book, a court-room, or a lawyer's chambers ; and there was some trouble in imagining how the play-actor and theatre-manager, who was writing immortal dramas before he was thirty, and died, after voluminous authorship, at fifty-two, could have acquired what Lord Campbell calls " the familiar, profound, and accurate knowledge he displayed of juridical principles and practice." It was only making a wonder more wonderful, however; and the new wonder was established by demonstration, and by the authority of a great lawyer's name. But when the eminent Dr. Bucknill, not controverting the argument of Lord Campbell, proved as clearly that Shakspere "had paid an amount of attention to subjects of medical interest scarcely if at all inferior to that which has served as the basis" of the proposition that he "had devoted seven good years of his life to the practice of law," he hindered rather than helped to understand the real life of the dramatist. So when another proves that in the few years before the play-writing began the poet, so well versed was he in warfare, must have served a campaign or two in the Low Countries; another, that he must have been a Roman Catholic in religion, while another shows him to have been necessarily a Puritan; another, that his prodigious wealth of allusions to and phrases from the then untranslated Greek and Latin authors proves his broad and deep erudition; the understanding consents to one demonstration after another, but may possibly be staggered if called to accept them all together. It might well be that weak souls, invited to believe so much of one man, sought refuge and repose in refusing to believe even what would not otherwise have overtaxed credulity.

There were other things, besides, that had

seemed strange in the relations of this man to these plays. No word or hint seems ever to have escaped him to show that he cared for, or even owned, the miraculous offspring which had fallen from him. There is no word or syllable in all the world to indicate that the man whose multifarious learning is the wonder of the third century after him ever owned a book, or ever saw one, although he brought together and left behind him a fair estate. Nor is there to be found in all the world, of this profuse and voluminous author, of this bosom-friend of poets and printers and actors, so much as the scratch of a pen on paper, except the three signatures upon his Will, wherein, by an interlineation which shows that he had at first overlooked the wife of his boyhood, he leaves her his "second-best bed." Yet of his less famous contemporaries there are autograph manuscripts in abundance. Even of his forerunners by centuries there are extant writings infinitely more plenty than the scanty subscriptions to a legal instrument. Petrarch died two centuries and a half, Dante three centuries, before him; yet the manuscripts of both abound, while of him who was greater than either, and was almost of our own time, there is nothing but the mean and sordid Will to show that he ever put pen to paper.

But while the difficulty of fixing the canon of the Shakspere text had long been such as to involve the authorship of every part of the text in

more or less doubt; while all men had wondered
that so little should be known of the actual man
Shakspere, and that what little was known should
be so far remote from any ideal one could form of
the author bearing the name: so that Coleridge
should exclaim: "Are we to have miracles in
sport? Does God choose idiots by whom to convey divine truths to men?" and Emerson: "I
cannot marry this fact to his verse. Other admirable men have led lives in some sort of keeping
with their thought; but this man, in wide con-
trast;" yet avowed disbelief went commonly no
further. Once, it is true, there was a public assertion that Shakspere's alleged authorship was impossible. In 1848 there was published by the
Harpers, in New York, a light and chatty account
of a voyage to Spain, entitled "The Romance of
Yachting," by Joseph C. Hart. The incidents of
the voyage are interspersed with discussions altogether foreign to it; and upon a trivial pretext
the authorship of the plays is considered, with no
small acuteness and vigor, upon the pages from
208 to 243. It is summarized, however, in a few
of the earlier sentences: "He was not the mate
of the literary characters of the day, and none
knew it better than himself. It is a fraud upon
the world to thrust his surreptitious fame upon
us. He had none that was worthy of being transmitted. The inquiry will be, *who were the able
literary men who wrote the dramas imputed to him?*

The plays themselves, or rather a small portion of them, will live as long as English literature is regarded worth pursuit. The *authorship* of the plays is no otherwise material to us than as a matter of curiosity, and to enable us to render exact justice ; but they should not be assigned to Shakspere alone, if at all."

If there be any merit, therefore, in having been the first to doubt this authorship, it cannot be awarded to Delia Bacon. There is no reason, however, to believe that the speculations which have just been quoted ever came to her knowledge. The ideas, or fancies, which soon after this possessed her, were, as she profoundly believed, her own discovery — indeed, she would rather have said, a revelation direct to her.

Revelation, discovery, or fancy, however, — whatever it was, an utterly subordinate part of it all, though an essential part, was that which concerned merely the authorship of the plays. If they were indeed, as they had been commonly received, a casual collection of stage-plays, knocked together by a money-making play-actor, playwright, and theatre-manager for the money there was in them and to be got out of them, it was a trivial question by what name the playwright should be called ; it should not tax credulity to " marry this fact to his verse," however fine the verse might be, if they were nothing more than verse. But to her, studying the plays with a keenness of natural insight and a burning intensity which have not often been applied to them, much more than splendid poesy began to gleam within them. Finding in them a higher philosophy, even, than in the "Advancement of Learning," a broader statesmanship, a profounder jurisprudence, and, above all, a bolder courage than in all the avowed writings of the great Chancellor, she only obeyed the teachings of that Inductive System which he had expounded, in seeking an adequate authorship for so magnificent a creation. But that all these things were in the plays — this was the main fact that concerned her; this was what she cared to discover first for herself, and then to communicate to the world. If indeed she found them there, it could not but follow, as the night the day, that some better paternity must be admitted for the plays than that of Lord Leicester's groom.

Nor was it enough for her to discover bits and gleams of philosophy and political science in the plays, however frequent or brilliant. To her eager inquiry they came to be revealed at last, not as fortuitously collected though mutually unrelated plays, but as an entire dramatic system, in which the New Philosophy was to be inculcated in unsuspicious minds, under the vehement despotism of the last Tudor and the dull pedantic oppression of the first Stuart. If the plays were really such a system of philosophic teaching, not only was it difficult to accept the competency for it of the

Stratford poacher and London horse-boy; it was
hardly less trying to credulity to impute so vast
an enterprise, added to all the gigantic intellectual labors which he avowed, even to the greatest
Englishman of his age. She judged, therefore,
that as there had been collaboration before and
since in literary work, so here the most brilliant
and philosophic minds of the Elizabethan Court
coöperated in the work which was too great for
one, and consented together, for their common
safety, to the imputation of their united work to
the theatre-manager who brought out the plays,
and whose property they were because they had
been given to him.

Reasons why these courtiers and politicians —
Bacon, Raleigh, Spenser, and whatever others
made up the illustrious coterie — should not have
wished to acknowledge the work of which they
might well have boasted, were not far to seek. It
comported ill with dignity of rank and place to be
known as a writer of plays : but to be known to
such a queen as Elizabeth, or to such a king as
James, as author of such plays as " Coriolanus "
or " Julius Cæsar " — the eager ambition of Bacon would have been quenched by it long before
the day when his office was wanted for Williams ;
upon Raleigh, living for fifteen years under his
unexecuted death sentence, the headsman's axe
would have fallen earlier than it did.

But while Delia Bacon thoroughly believed that

such a worthy coterie, and not the unworthy player, produced the Elizabethan drama, and hid in it the philosophy which it would have been fatal to publish openly ; and while she was no less sure that in some cryptic form there was truth involved in these works which was yet to be surrendered to faithful and intelligent study, it is scant justice to her memory to say, that, as the mere authorship of the plays was to her but a small part of the truth concerning them, so she never devoted herself to whims or fancies about capital letters, or irregular pagination, or acrostics, or anagrams, as concealing yet expressing the great philosophy which the plays inclosed. Her mind, it now appears, was already overwrought; before many months it gave way completely; but its unsoundness, whenever it may have begun, never assumed that form.

VII.

It is not easy — and perhaps it is not important — to determine just when disbelief in the accepted authorship of the Shakspere plays established itself absolutely in her mind. Certainly in 1852, while she was delivering her instruction in Cambridge with singular success, she had startled some of those who knew her best by her audacious utterances on the subject. To Mrs. Professor Farrar, whose reminiscences have been already quoted,[1] she then expressed a desire to visit England, not, it seems, for historical study, but, as Mrs. Farrar remembers, " to obtain proof of the truth of her theory that Shakspere did not write the plays attributed to him." The intimations thus thrown out met, indeed, only with compassionate discouragement there. The two or three ladies who alone seem to have heard them were wholly without sympathy for them, and regarding them even as indications that might in time become monomania, sedulously avoided all speech with her upon the subject thereafter.

In the same year, 1852, however, she entered upon an acquaintance and correspondence which

[1] *Supra*, pp. 28-30.

acted far otherwise upon her fancy and her purposes and hopes than the chilling avoidance of the
subject by the two or three ladies of Cambridge,
friends and admirers though they were.   Just by
what formality of introduction she first communicated with Ralph Waldo Emerson does not appear;
but Cambridge was not far from Concord, even
upon the map; and it was still nearer in spirit, at
least in those days.   The letter with which she
opened correspondence, if it existed, would be her
earliest writing on the subject.   It must have been
just before the 12th of June, 1852; but as in August she asks him to return it to her, speaking of it
as a "voluminous note," it is not among her other
letters to Emerson.[1]   The answer to it, however,
was certainly not such as to silence or repel her.

CONCORD, 12 June, 1852.

MY DEAR MISS BACON, — Your letter was duly
received, and its contents deserved better leisure
and apprehension than I have at once been able to
command.   The only alternative was to let it wait
a little, for a good hour.   And now I write, only
that I may assure you it has been received and
is appreciated.   In the office to which you have
in the contingency appointed me, of critic, I am

---

[1] I beg leave to acknowledge the courtesy of Mr. Emerson's family,
and of his literary executor, Mr. J. Elliot Cabot, in delivering to me
all Miss Bacon's letters to him, neatly folded and docketed by his
own hand, and in formally acquiescing in the publication of all his
letters to her, after inspection of copies of them. — T. B.

deeply gratified to observe the power of statement and the adequateress to the problem, which
this sketch of your argument evinces. Indeed, I
value these fine weapons far above any special use
they may be put to. And you will have need of
enchanted instruments, nay, alchemy itself, to
melt into one identity these two *reputations* (shall
I call them ?) the poet and the statesman, both
hitherto solid historical figures. If the cipher approve itself so real and consonant to you, it will to
all, and is not only material but indispensable to
your peace. And it would seem best that so radi-
cal a revolution should be proclaimed with great
compression in the declaration, and the real
grounds pretty rapidly set forth, a good ground
in each chapter, and preliminary generalities quite
omitted. For there is an immense presumption
against us which is to be annihilated by battery as
fast as possible. And now for the execution of
the design. If you will send me your first chapter, I will at once make my endeavor to put it
into the best channel I can find, " Blackwood " or
" Fraser " I think the best. But this, taking it for
granted that you decide on trying your fortune
in a magazine first, — which, I suppose, is fame,
rather than fortune. On most accounts, the eligi-
ble way is, as I think, the *book* or brochure, published simultaneously in England and here. I am
not without good hope of accepting your kind invitation to visit you in Cambridge, though I very

rarely get so far from home, where I am detained by a truly ridiculous complication of cobwebs.

With great respect, yours faithfully,

R. W. EMERSON.

MISS BACON.

P. S.   What is the allusion in the " Literary World " of last week to criticism on Shakespeare ? Does it touch us, or some other ?

What the " theory " was which had been set forth in the missing first letter can be determined only inferentially.   But though it would seem from an expression in the foregoing letter to have emphasized especially the supposed relation of Bacon to the plays, it is fair to believe that her theory was here, as everywhere in her writing and speaking afterwards, a theory of plural author-ship, so far as mere authorship was concerned. This is her next letter, so far as appears, to Emer-son :

CAMBRIDGE, August 4 [1852].

DEAR SIR, — Confirmations of my theory, which I did not expect to find on this side of the water, have turned up since my last communication to you, in the course of my researches in the libra-ries here and in Boston.   But I am going to leave Cambridge in a few days, and if it is not too much trouble, I wish you would be so kind as to inclose to me, by the next mail, my voluminous note to you on this subject.   I think it is possible that I

may be able to make some use of it, while I am
quite sure of its being good for nothing to you.

Very truly yours,. DELIA S. BACON.

MR. R. W. EMERSON.

But while she was forming such new and helpful friendships as this one, kindly tolerant, if not
more, of her great idea, she was finding, as she
thought, foes of her own household. A letter to
her oldest brother, dated that same month, makes
it plain that she had broached her theory to him
also; that his grave, cool judgment had refused to
entertain it, and that frankly and with force, as
his nature was, he had so declared, dissuading her
from cherishing it, as a delirious fancy. But his
remonstrances had only the effect to estrange her,
for the few remaining years of her life, from that
relative who had always been her most helpful,
judicious, and affectionate friend.

From the village of Cuba, in Western New
York, where she was visiting a sister, she wrote to
Emerson, September 30, 1852 :

"It is certainly very extraordinary that the
generous expressions of sympathy and interest
which your last two letters contain should remain
so long unacknowledged, and that, too, when I
have all the time been so deeply sensible of the
kindness which dictated them. . . . I know very
well what a presuming step it was to intrude

these speculations upon such time as yours, and what an embarrassing responsibility it was to throw upon one so preoccupied. For I suppose that no previous familiarity with the Shakespeare writings would qualify one to decide this question satisfactorily without much revision and scrutiny, not only of these works themselves, but of all that appertains to the subject. I think most persons in these circumstances would have dismissed the question without much consideration; and I do not believe there is any one else in the world who could have met it, under all the disadvantages which attended its introduction to you, as you have done, — with such brave decision, — with such generous discrimination. . . . I have been constantly wishing and intending to adopt your suggestion in reference to a summary statement on the subject, but since the arrival of this last quite unexpected proof of your regard I have not been well enough to accomplish even this.

"I had intended to remain here in this rude little town, which you never heard of before I suppose, until I had quite finished the statement I had before commenced, for I have a sister here, whose home, be it where it will, is always mine. But I find I cannot persist in this resolution, for it would be merely suicidal. This study is so very absorbing, and it consigns me to such complete solitude, that I find all my progress in it is made at a most ruinous expense to my life and health;

while those which I pursue with my classes have
just the contrary effect upon me. Indeed but for
this resource I think I should have died long ago.
I cannot tell you with what reluctance I relinquish
it again. My only consolation is that I cannot
help it. The choice is not mine. I am not discouraged, but sometimes I think if I can only
succeed in committing the work effectually to
stronger hands it is all I ought to think of.

"In the course of my researches last summer I
found, quite unexpectedly, a very clear historical
basis for the conclusions which my Shakspere
study had forced upon me. I found, too, the most
astounding corroborations, to the minutest particulars, of new versions of contemporary events,
which I had rejected in the cipher, on account of
their disagreement with what I supposed to be
well authenticated historic fact. Be assured,
dear sir, there is no possibility of a doubt as to the
main points of my theory. What was wrong in it
came from my attempts to patch over, and recon-
cile with what I knew before, things which seemed
to me impossible. Whether I live to accomplish
it, or not, a little investigation in the right direction will demonstrate that these marvelous phenom-
ena, so unlike all other human works, are after
all not wholly miraculous — not of the air merely.
Properly traced, according to that law of investigation which requires causes for effects, they will
prove the index to a piece of history which glis-

tens out even now very plainly from the contemporary historical documents, though it has not yet found its way into the story constructed from them. . . . Most gratefully yours,

DELIA S. BACON."

At the close of the following November she began, at the Stuyvesant Institute in New York, a course of historical instruction — "*lessons*, rather than lectures" — to ladies. A copy of the printed prospectus, with commendations from Washington Irving and George Bancroft among others, is found carefully indorsed and preserved among Emerson's papers. This was followed, upon most flattering solicitation, by a similar course of evening lessons at the same place, on "The Origin of the Oriental Element in our Civilization"; and to this, gentlemen, as well as ladies, were admitted. Upon like invitation from Brooklyn a series of lessons began there, "at Professor Gray's Lecture Room, 90 Montague Place," February 17, 1853; and when this ended, her life among men and women was closed.

In the midst of this, however, there are signs that she is intent upon the work to which she was prepared to dedicate what remained to her of life and strength. Among the warmest and most admiring of the friends she had made at Boston and Cambridge was Miss Elizabeth P. Peabody, whose sister was the wife of Nathaniel Hawthorne. It is to her that the following note, which soon found its way to the subject of it, was addressed.

Concord, 26 March, 1853.

DEAR MISS PEABODY, — I send you a letter for Mr. Putnam, which, if you like, you shall send, if you dislike, and want another, you shall burn, and tell me so. I talked with Hawthorne who did not seem to think that he was the person; but if Miss Bacon would really come to Concord, and board with Mrs. Adams, as, I doubt not, is practicable, we would make him listen, and she should make him believe. With my kindest salutations and respects to Miss Bacon, your ever obliged servt.

R. W. EMERSON.

At the end of this letter Mr. Emerson adds:

"I can really think of nothing that could give such *éclat* to a magazine as this brilliant paradox."

VIII.

If there were none of her own blood to receive with favor the strange notions which she had now begun to avow, there was elsewhere no lack of sympathy, encouragement, and aid. To Mrs. Farrar she had already intimated her strong desire to prosecute in England researches in support of her hypothesis which would be impossible elsewhere. The help, indispensable for this purpose, which her own family neither could nor, to her strong resentment, would afford was offered during her last season of instruction in New York by a gentleman of large wealth and high standing in every way, whose name, however, was long unknown to her relatives, Mr. Charles Butler.

On the 2d of April, 1853, she announced to her brother, in a letter of not unkindly tone, her expectation of " going to England as soon as I can get myself ready," but with no intimation of her purpose in going, or of the source of her means for going. " All that I can say is that the money I appropriate to that object could not be honorably appropriated to any other. I have ample means placed at my disposal, and shall go so supported as to be able to command whatever attention I may

need. . . . I cannot tell how long I shall be absent; perhaps five or six months. My plans do not reach beyond England at present."

Emerson's letter to Mr. Putnam the publisher, over which he had given Miss Peabody such broad discretion, she had evidently " liked " and " sent." For on the 14th of April Delia Bacon wrote to Emerson from Brooklyn: " Your letter to Mr. Putnam was all that I could have desired. It was indeed most truly kind. I cannot be satisfied without attempting to thank you for it, but I do not know how to do it adequately. I can only hope that you will find your generous interest in the subject justified by the result." And then she shows him how his letter to Mr. Putnam, and Mr. Putnam's proposal induced by it, — a proposal, indeed, which she had felt obliged to decline, — had so impressed a friend that he had resolved to provide her with the means for her journey. Emerson's answer and the letter of farewell that followed her to the steamer are these:

CONCORD, 13 April, 1853.

MY DEAR MISS BACON, — I was cordially gratified by the good news your note contained, that you were going forward with your studies, and really decided to prosecute them in England; and I was not a little flattered by being made however accidentally and insignificantly a party to the transaction. I am glad also that you will trust me

farther with insights of your results. By all means,
let it be so! And, by all means do you go forward
to the speediest completion! Now let me not fail
of my communication. I grieve very often —
seldom so much as now — at the disheartening
infirmities and invalidity of my wife, which makes
it most part of the time quite out of question to
invite any worthy mortal to visit my house. I do
not know that I can come to New York, — and
yet I am not sure but I shall make the time to do
so, if there is no other way. But, if you are coming
to Boston or Cambridge before your departure,
have the goodness to apprise me now of the fact,
and when, and where. In assured hope and with
constant respect,   Yours,

R. W. EMERSON.

MISS BACON.

CONCORD, 12 May, 1853.

MY DEAR MISS BACON, — I wrote to Sumner,
but have as yet no answer. Perhaps he has
directed his answer, as I suggested, to Mr. Butler.
I enclose a letter to Mr. Martineau, to whom, if
you have good opportunity, I think I would frankly
open the general design of your inquiries; but you
will judge best on seeing him. I send a letter
also for Carlyle, to find Spedding. I think I will
write myself again to Carlyle, as I shall need, perhaps, in a few days. I enclose a letter to John
Chapman. Perhaps you will find his house a good

home for you, in London.   I took rooms and board there, and was well accommodated.

I have not yet written, for want of time and a little mountain to get over to write to him, — to Helps.   Leave me your London address, and I will yet write.   Mrs. Emerson is mortified at her heedlessness in putting you to sleep in a chamber certain to be disturbed by too-early-rising washers in the night.   She never remembered it would be so, nor thought of it till next day.   But Fare well and fare gloriously !   With best hope,

R. W. EMERSON.

MISS BACON.

On the 14th of May, 1853, she sailed from New York in the steamer " Pacific," and arrived in Liverpool on the Queen's birthday, the 24th.

IX

ENGLAND must have been a very strange land to the lonely woman who then first touched its shore. In almost five years which she afterwards passed there she did but little to enlarge her acquaintance. Of the letters of introduction which she bore, some are found unused among her papers: as one to Arthur Helps, from Emerson; one to Sir Henry Ellis, principal Librarian of the British Museum; one (from Edward Everett) to Mr. A. Panizzi, chief of the Printed Book Department. But she was not long, after going at once to London, in beginning, by the help of one of Emerson's letters, the friendship with Carlyle and his wife, which was to bring her much kindness and comfort in her solitude. This seems to be an answer to the letter of introduction:

5 GT. CHEYNE ROW, CHELSEA, 8 June, 1853.

MY DEAR MADAM, — Will you kindly dispense with the ceremony of being called on (by sickly people, in this hot weather), and come to us on Friday evening to tea at 7. I will try to secure Mr. Spedding at the same time; and we will deliberate what is to be done in your Shakspere affair.

A river steamer will bring you within a gunshot of us. You pronounce " *Chainie* " Row ; and get out at Cadogan Pier, which is your *first* landing place in Chelsea. —— Except Mrs. C. and the chance of Spedding, there will be nobody here.

Yours very sincerely,

T. CARLYLE.

And this followed it at no long interval :

CHELSEA, 14 June, 1853.

MY DEAR MADAM, — Mr. Collier, it seems, does not habitually reside in Town at present; but comes from time to time. If you forward the inclosed Note to him, merely adjoining your own card with your address on it, I am given to expect he will appoint some day to call on you, and have some talk about the Shakspere affair. I do not know Mr. Collier ; the writer of that Note is John Forster (Editor of the "Examiner," &c., &c.), a friend of his and mine.

Richard Monckton Milnes, of whom you may have heard, wishes to see your Paper on Shakspere which is now in my hands; if you give me permission, I will send it to him; not otherwise.

My Wife reports the finding of a beautiful Pockethandkerchief which was left by you here ; she keeps it safe against your return to us, — not a distant date, as we hope. Any day at 3 P. M., (or *most* days), I am to be found here ; my wife,

on fine days, is not certain, I apprehend, after 1
P. M.; and. very generally in the evenings we
are quietly at home.   Believe me, Dear Madam,
        Yours very sincerely,
                        T. CARLYLE.

Some account of the visit invited by Carlyle's
letter of June 8, and referred to in that of the
14th, is given with familiar confidence to her sister, under date of several weeks later.

" My visit to Mr. Carlyle was very rich.   I wish
you could have heard him laugh.   Once or twice
I thought he would have taken the roof of the
house off.   At first they were perfectly stunned —
he and the gentleman he had invited to meet me.
They turned black in the face at my presumption.
' Do you mean to say,' so and so, said Mr. Carlyle,
with his strong emphasis; and I said that I did;
and they both looked at me with staring eyes,
speechless for want of words in which to convey
their sense of my audacity.   At length Mr. Carlyle came down on me with such a volley.   I did
not mind it the least.   I told him he did not know
what was in the Plays if he said that, and no one
could know who believed that that booby wrote
them.   It was then that he began to shriek.   You
could have heard him a mile.   I told him too that
I should not think of questioning his authority in
such a case if it were not with me a matter of

knowledge. I did not advance it as an opinion. They began to be a little moved with my coolness at length, and before the meeting was over they agreed to hold themselves in a state of readiness to receive what I had to say on the subject. I left my introductory statement with him. In the course of two or three days he wrote to me to ask permission to show my paper to Mr. Monckton Milnes, who had expressed a wish to see it, inviting me to come there again very soon. He told me I had left a beautiful handkerchief there which Mrs. Carlyle would keep till I came. He also enclosed to me a letter of introduction to Mr. Collier, which he had taken the pains to obtain for me from another literary gentleman. I have not yet sent it. That was five weeks ago."

[CARLYLE TO D. B.]

CHELSEA, 12 August, 1853.

MY DEAR MADAM, — Here is the Panizzi letter, which I did not shew to Milnes, as quite superfluous in his actual state of knowledge about you; and will now return to avoid risks of losing it.

I yesterday delivered your Paper to Parker the Publisher of " Fraser's Magazine," — with such a testimony about it as you desired; name, country, sex, all is left dark; and Parker's free judgment of the MSS., " Fit for 'Fraser,' or not fit ? " is the one thing he is requested to deliberate upon, and then pronounce to us. —— You, of course, shall

hear of it the instant it arrives here; which ought
to be in some two or three weeks; probably
early next month, for I think the September No.
must be already made up and in the Printer's
hands.   We will not anticipate his verdict; he is a
clever little fellow (*our* " clever," and yours too, I
believe); and his voice will in some considerable
degree represent for us that of the " reading
public" of England.

On Wednesday I forgot to say that the printed
Harley MSS. Catalogue, which I spoke of your
buying, lies for consultation on its table in the
Museum; and that you can examine it to all
lengths, either as a preliminary or as a final measure. —— If you can find in that mass of English
records (the main collection that exists) *any* document tending to confirm your Shakspere theory,
it will be worth all the reasoning in the world, and
will certainly surprise all men.

Finally come and see us, whenever it is not dis-
agreeable, — without misgiving, in spite of nerves!
Almost every evening we are both of us at home
(tea at 7); and at 3 any day I am visible here.

Believe me, Dear Madam,
            Yours very sincerely,   T. CARLYLE.

The impression made by this lonely stranger on
Carlyle is not to be learned from his letters to her
alone.   In September of this year he wrote thus
to her introducer, Emerson: " As for Miss Bacon,

we find her, with her modest shy dignity, with her
solid character and strange enterprise, a real ac-
quisition ; and hope we shall now see more of her,
now that she has come nearer to us to lodge. I
have not in my life seen anything so tragically
quixotic as her Shakspere enterprise ; alas, alas,
there can be nothing but sorrow, toil, and utter
disappointment in it for her! I do cheerfully
what I can, — which is far more than she *asks* of
me (for I have not seen a prouder silent soul) ; but
there is not the least possibility of truth in the
notion she has taken up ; and the hope of ever
proving it, or finding the least document that
countenances it, is equal to that of vanquishing
the windmills by stroke of lance. I am often truly
sorry about the poor lady ; but she troubles
nobody with her difficulties, with her theories ; she
must try the matter to the end, and charitable
souls must further her so far." [1]

There is little among her papers to show where
she was living during this year, 1853, except that
it was in London, and in lodgings to which the
friendly guidance of George Peabody had directed
her. She changed them indeed, as this next letter
shows ; and, with the almost fierce pride which was
innate to her, was so far from presuming upon the
affectionate hospitality which the Carlyles were
urging upon her, that she did not even tell them
of her removals.

[1] *Correspondence of Carlyle and Emerson*, vol. ii. 228-9.

THE GRANGE, ALRESFORD, HANTS,
(The Lord Ashburton's), 10 December, 1853.

DEAR MISS BACON, — We are here since Monday, on a visit, and are not to be in Chelsea again till Christmas pass.

Some days before leaving, I received from Parker a Parcel, with which his man appeared to have tried first at your old Chelsea lodging; my address had then been put upon the cover; it contained your MS. and an open letter to Miss Bacon, full of the due civility, admiring, regretting, &c., and in fine *returning* the offered Paper. As you say, he might have decided sooner! I found that the smallest urging on my part would have made him insert the Piece; but this you had prohibited; nor do I know that it was any way desirable; at any rate, here now is his decision, and with him we have done. Not knowing your new address, I locked the Parcel into a safe place; and there, were Christmas over, it will lie awaiting your convenience, and can be sent at any time.

I am sorry to hear from my wife of your headaches and distresses in that solitary place; I hope you will appear again some morning soon after our return, and shew Chelsea that those were but temporary clouds. Pray be not so shy of us! We cannot much help you, indeed; but there is no want of will, were a possibility offered.

Believe me always,

Yours sincerely,   T. CARLYLE.

On the last day of November, 1853, she took lodgings at St. Albans, attracted, no doubt, by its association with the great Chancellor, to whom it gave a title and a tomb. It was during her stay there that she sought through Sir Edward Bulwer Lytton, as a note from him indicates, an introduction to Lord Verulam. As the bearer of that title was then not a Bacon but a Grimston, there would seem to have been little help from him to be hoped for. Carlyle's friendly mindfulness of her and his keen apprehension of the methods by which she was evolving and maintaining her hypothesis appear from a letter of his to Emerson, April 8, 1854: " Miss Bacon has fled away to *St. Albans* (the *Great* Bacon's place) five or six months ago ; and is there working out her Shakspere Problem, from the depths of her own mind, disdainful apparently, or desperate and careless, of all *evidence* from Museums or Archives; I have not had an answer from her since before Christmas, and have now lost her address. Poor Lady! I sometimes silently wish she were safe home again; for truly there can no madder enterprise than her present one be well figured."[1]

This prolongation of her stay abroad was beyond her own original reckoning, or that of her friends. At midsummer her generous patron put at her disposal a sum ample to pay what she owed and to bring her home. But her work was not

---

[1] *Correspondence, etc.*, vol. ii. 240, 241.

done. At the end of September she wrote from St. Albans to Emerson that her work was prospering, and telling how she managed to stay. " I am enabled to stay here so long, in consequence of having reduced my expenses as soon as I resolved upon this course. The money that I brought with me, which was supposed to be only enough for the first summer, was spun out by this process till the close of the second; and now that I have begun to encroach upon the very ample sum allotted for my return, I am more prudent than ever. But I do not know that there will be any need of it for that purpose, and I am living here as economically as I could in America; and as I think only of finishing my work, and have no other future, and this is enough and more than enough for that purpose, I do not see why I should spend so large a sum merely for the sake of being in America. Not that it is not the best country in the world, — but ' there 's livers out of it,' and I don't forget that I heard Margaret Fuller's friends conclude among themselves that the storm which dashed her on its rocks, and prevented the chance of her landing among them, was a merciful dispensation of Providence. I have some beloved friends there, but my life was finished some time ago in every other respect but this, and as this is the world's work and not mine that I am doing, I suppose the expense of it will have to be paid in some way.

" So I do not trouble myself about it, and am as happy as the day is long, and only wish I lived in Herschel or Jupiter or some of those larger worlds, where it would not be time to go to bed just as one gets fairly awake, and begins to be in earnest a little. I have lived here nearly a year, and have not spoken to one of the natives yet, except by accident, but I have not felt my solitude. It has been a year of sunshine with me; the harvest of many years of toil and weeping. I cannot tell you what pleasures I have had here. This poor perturbed spirit, that had left its work undone, and would not leave me alone till it had brought me here, seems satisfied at last. My work has ceased to be burdensome to me; I find in it a rest such as no one else can ever know, I think, except in heaven. But that is not saying that the world will be pleased with it. I hope it will not disappoint the expectation of those who have made themselves responsible for it, in any manner; and, above all, I hope that you will like it, and will have no occasion to regret the noble concern you have taken in it.

" It has been a great and constant help to me to have two such friends as yourself and Carlyle interested in it. Carlyle is as good and kind as he can be. He is very much troubled about my being here so long alone."

At the time this was written she was again, after an interval, putting herself in communication with the Carlyles, as the following letter shows.

CHELSEA, 4 October, 1854.

DEAR MISS BACON, — We are very glad to hear of you again, and that you are doing well, and getting that wild jungle of sticks victoriously tied into fagots. That is a right success, due to all faithful workers, and which nobody can deprive one of.

My wife cannot by any means recollect the least particular of Mrs. Spring's address at Hampstead, though she was once there, and saw the place with her eyes. However, she assures me it would have done nothing for your present enterprise; it was a place let (*un*furnished with servants) as a whole house; was very dear, and also (as is thought) very dirty, — not at all like what you require. Other lodgings, no doubt, are abundant in Hampstead, especially at this season of the year; but neither of us here knows specially of any, nor can Jane bethink her just at once of any person whom she could confidently consult on the matter. — I myself do, at this moment, call to mind a certain Mrs. Dr. Wilkinson, an accomplished *American* lady withal, and wife of an accomplished and truly superior man, who lives in that neighborhood, not quite *in* Hampstead, but on this side of it, — to whom I would offer you an introduction if you went towards that region. Hampstead is very airy, and has still a set of silent

country walks, though the Bricklayer is fearfully
busy there too in these last years; you could have
no real difficulty in getting a cleanly, honest, and
tolerable lodging there; the worst fault I know is
that of the water; very *hard,* all of it, from the
chalk; which fault, however, applies only to the
Hill, or Old Village, as I suppose? Nay, indeed
there is no pure water to be had in this big Baby-
lon itself, for all its wealth and faculty; the Queen
herself has to drink dirty water (as I often think)
when she favors us with her company, — so extremely wise a set of "successful men" are we
hitherto in these parts. —— Of lodgings about
Chelsea, or indeed, in all quarters urban and sub-
urban, Jane thinks there can be no doubt of ample
choice on every hand; and she will very gladly
give help whenever you embark on such a search.

Her notion, in which I entirely agree, is at present, That whenever you decide on a removal you
are simply to leave your things all *packed* at St.
Albans, and come off at once to the vacant room I
told you of as waiting to welcome you here, —
therefrom to institute whatever search your fancy
and judgment point to, under the favourablest
auspices. This really is the wisest, and also the
easiest; confess that it is, O you of little faith,
and do it. —— I was just going out (by appoint-
ment) yesterday when your letter came; could
not write till now.

Yours very truly, dear Miss B.,
T. CARLYLE.

The letter without date which follows seems to have been written at the holiday season of 1854–5.

DEAR MISS BACON, — I would go, with all the pleasure in life, to answer your letter in person, but the news that you are laid up "*finds me in the same*" (as the maidservants write). I have been having a bad cold, off and on, for the last two months; and gone on trying to put it down *par vive force* till finally *it* put down *me*. These last two weeks I have been confined to my room, and sometimes to bed. —— I am getting better now however, and hope to be what is called "*about*" again next week.

We have not been out of town this season. Mr. C. is dreadfully busy with his " Frederick," who I beg into wish had never been born. —— He, Mr. C., is never out but for a hurried walk after dark ; he declined the usual Christmas visit to the Ashburtons. I was to have gone, however, this very day — to the Grange — on *my own basis* for a month — but the meeting of Parliament has been the means under Providence of putting off the party till the 19th of this month — otherwise I must have given it up altogether. We shall see how the world looks by the 19th — but in any case I hope to see you *here* or *there* before then.

Yours truly,

Saturday.   JANE CARLYLE.

   5 CHEYNE ROW.

These were busy days with her. If nothing else showed it, the paucity of her letters during these many months would. Until late in the following March, this next is the only one which appears, either to her or from her.

CONCORD, MASS., November 20, 1854.

MY DEAR MISS BACON, — I am heartily grieved — but it is past help — at my silence and delays. There can be no forgiveness for it. I have had both your letters, and made ineffectual attempts to answer both. I was very happy to read the good news, which both contained, of your studies and enjoyments. And I heard collaterally from Carlyle, of his goodwill and respect. The statements in your last letter especially engage my interest, and it seems most honorable and most useful, — that which you say, that you can live and study in England for no more than it would cost in America, and that the supplies for one summer can be spun out to serve for two. I can hardly refrain from publishing the fact in the newspapers, for the benefit of all scholars. That your readings prosper, and that you confirm yourself in your conviction, is also good news; for, though I think your hypothesis more incredible than the improbable traditions (and unexplained) it would supplant, yet you cannot maintain any side without shedding light on the first of all literary problems. Carlyle, too, I found, with decided interest and respect, had no faith in the paradox. I went to Phillips & Sampson the last time I was in town to engage their interest in the book. They considered it a promising enterprise, but could not think of it for themselves, and the better the book should be they said the worse for them. For they have several "firstrate" books, as they call them, now in press, or just out of press, and are afraid of a good book as likely to damage these! do not wish to stand in their own light, or overlay their own children. I went to Ticknor & Fields, but with no better success. They are afraid, if I understand it, of a literary book, and answer steadily, "*any time but now,*" as if now nothing but Russia, Australia, and Romance would have any attraction. These two are the best here, and I hesitate a little about the next step; yet shall take another. If you are sure of the book, you may easily be sure of a publisher. I beg you will write me once more (notwithstanding my ill deserts) that it is ready, or that it will soon be, and when and how large it will be. I think of applying to Mr. J. C. Derby, of New York, of whom I hear much good. I meant to print my own tardy MSS. speculations on England in this month, but I doubt and delay. I am however extremely busy. With all congratulation and good hope,

R. W. EMERSON.

For eleven months, until the beginning of November, 1854, she remained at St. Albans, pursuing her work with exhausting eagerness. For the next month she was at Hatfield, redolent of Elizabethan memories, ten miles beyond St. Albans; and thence, at the beginning of December, she returned to London, "driven here," as she wrote to her sister, "by the terrible discomforts of those wretched country houses in winter." At Hatfield, she says (writing January 12, 1855), " I found it was uniformly colder in my room than it was out of doors in the daytime. The thermometer could not have been at all above 50. My hands and feet were aching and stiff with the cold, but since I have been here I have hardly known what the sensation was."

" Carlyle has been here to see me, though I am miles from him, to invite me to his house. I was out when he came, but he left word with the servant, and there was no alternative but for me to go, and it was *very very pleasant.* I went at five o'clock and stayed to dinner and tea, till eleven, and Carlyle spent all the time with us, though he is extremely busy now, finishing his ' Life of Frederic ' the Second, and refuses all invitations. I have real cosy pleasant times when I go there, but I am most heartily glad I have no other acquaintances here ; they would torment me to death."

Then, after some account of the manner in which she had been working, she proceeds: " If

I had known, perhaps, when I was in America, how it would be exactly, and that I should have this book to write first of all, I might have felt tempted to stay with you and try to do it. But I don't think I could ever have written it there. I think the mere fact of my being *here* has had a great deal to do with my success. I have done what it seemed utterly impossible for me to do at home, — what I *tried in vain to do there.* My summer at Cambridge was wasted in vain efforts. I knew not how to relieve myself of this great responsibility. Think, if you can, what it is to feel that I am delivering myself from it at last, that here in this land of my fathers God has at last given me the utterance that I have all my life lacked, and that this great secret, in which the welfare of mankind is concerned, will not perish with me for want of the means of telling it. To go on with it, calmly and patiently, to work away at it, day after day, and year after year, as if it were the merest piece of ordinary drudgery, and without sympathy or counsel, that is what I have had to do, and what I thought I never could do at first. I would have given anything to have had you with me at times; indeed, there have been moments when I have felt that I could not endure it to the end. For you know what kind of health I had to undertake it with."

"On the 16th of this month I shall begin on my last hundred dollars, not without some misgiv-

ings ; and if I were sure of being able to get into
any spot where I should not lose in *time* more than
I should gain in the difference of price I would go
at once to cheaper lodgings. But every change
costs me so much time I am afraid to stir."

The letter which follows is to Emerson; and,
like the one from which these last quotations are
made, is dated at " 12 Spring St., Sussex Gardens,
Hyde Park, London, March " [24, 1855]. It
covers eight pages in her fine, compact, yet very
legible handwriting, and gives a full account of
what she has been doing and what she hopes to do.
" The volume," she says, " which was to have been
finished in December, was merely a history of the
great work I have undertaken to interpret. But
it was a history which contained the key of that
interpretation. The particular application of it,
in the exposition of the plays, was reserved for a
future volume. I intended to have the history in
one book, and the criticism in another." She proceeds to tell how " criticism " had grown and over-
mastered her ; how especially "Coriolanus " had
thrust himself into her work in spite of her; but
also how, although her historical work was thus
diminished in proportion, the criticisms " serve to
put the discovery on the most solid ground, and
leave no room for any doubt in any mind. They
put it where it is henceforth independent of further
historical corroboration."

Then, having thus justified to Emerson what

Carlyle had already written to him of her seeming disdain " of all *evidence* from Museums or Archives," she proceeds to discuss arrangements with publishers in the two countries. As for America, Emerson had undertaken the burden of managing for her, so that the discussion was properly full and detailed. "I cannot satisfy myself," she says, " as to the title. I wish you would help me a little. I send you my last attempt." [It is on a separate leaf:

(Age.)

" Francis Bacon and his (Stage.)

or,

The New Philosophy.

Including also the History of Sir Walter Raleigh and his connection with ' the Globe' Theatre, together with a brief account of Shakspere the Player.

" All *the world's* a stage."]

"If I should call it ' The New Magic' as I should like to, the work would sustain the title, but it might seem fanciful to one who has not read it, or read the ' Advancement of Learning,' and I wish to avoid any appearance of that kind."

It was upon reading this letter that Emerson, on the 17th of April, 1855, wrote thus to Carlyle: [1] "Miss Bacon sends me word, again and again, of your goodness. Against hope and sight she must be making a remarkable book. I have a letter

---

[1] *Correspondence,* vol. ii. 244.

from her, a few days ago, written in perfect assurance of success!"

Nor does any other letter appear before this next one from Carlyle with its enclosure.

CHELSEA, 7 June, 1855.

DEAR MISS BACON, — I am very glad you have got done with your Book, and are secure of an American Publisher on reasonable terms. These are two great points; and we ought to be very thankful for these.

As to an English Publisher, in the present posture of affairs, — at least as to getting any pecuniary profit out of an English Publisher, — I confess I foresee difficulty, and (in my bilious mood) am not without misgivings. This too, however, is part of the problem; this too you must resolutely attempt, and solve to the extent possible.

Of our Publishers here Longman & Co. (Paternoster Row) are probably the *richest;* perfectly respectable men, who publish a great many Books, but have not to my knowledge excelled their contemporaries in detecting *genius* in *MSS.* Murray (Albemarle Street) is also a great Publisher, *son* of the Murray you used to hear of; I find him often connected with scientific, didactic "Serials," as they are called; Travellers' Handbooks, railway reading, and the like. Chapman (Chapman & Hall, 193 Piccadilly), he and Parker are the only two Publishers I have even a slight acquaintance with, who seem likely for you. — On the whole, all, or very nearly *all*, our English Publishers will, if they undertake, behave with perfect (shopkeeper) accuracy to you in fulfilment of their bargain; but beyond the high shopkeeper spirit I do not know any of them that rises very decisively. I have, in late years, had less and less to do with any and all of them; they will *believe* that Paper that I have written by way of testimony — or at least believe it *better* than they would most men's writing (knowing the nature of the beast, that he does not *lie* if he can help it); but that is really pretty much all I can do; that and Emerson's letter (with some *formal* Note of Introduction by anybody acquainted with a Publisher) will pretty much put the man in possession of the case, and enable him to decide with his eyes *open;* which is all we can reasonably want of the poor man. As to the formal " Notes of Introduction," except in the cases of Parker and Chapman, it seems to be probable you are acquainted with persons who can do that more appropriately than I, — though certainly I too can do it, after a sort, and will cheerfully if you find it needful.

In conclusion, I will wish you *well through* this final unpleasant part of the business; and shall be very anxious to hear how you get along in it.

I have been sunk in bottomless " vortexes of Prussian dust " these many months, my very senses almost choked out of me with that and other mani-

fold confusions, — bodily health too in general by
no means *above* par. Hardly once have I been in
any direction as far as your street, — and never
once *there* (as is too plain!) though my wife has
been often urging. She is in distress about an
umbrella of yours which was left here; I could
have *found* your street and house with the eye, but
the *name* of it I could not communicate to the most
urgent Helpmate, having forgotten the name!

The sooner you come down, through the fine
Summer weather, and see my wife and self again,
it will be the better, on several accounts. Except
Sunday she is not certain to be at home *after* 1
P. M.; but in the evening almost always, or *before*
that time in the early day. — Believe me always,
Dear Miss Bacon, Yours sincerely,

T. CARLYLE.

[*Enclosure.*]

Miss Delia Bacon, an American lady, of much
worth and earnestness of mind, has devoted a great
deal of serious study to Shakspere; and believes
herself to have made a singular and important discovery in regard to the history or origin of his
works. To perfect this discovery, she came over
to England about two years ago, introduced and
recommended by some of the best people in America; and here she has been ever since, working
in the most earnest unwearied manner to demonstrate her idea as to Shakspere's works; and has
now completed, after much care and labour, what
she had to say on that subject.

An American Publisher has engaged the volume for America; and Miss B., whose residence gives her copyright here, wishes to find a Publisher for England.

I have not myself examined or seen Miss B.'s present MS.; but I can freely bear witness in general that she writes in a clear, elegant, ingenious and highly readable manner; that she is a person of definite ideas, of conscientious veracity in thought as well as word, and that probably no Book written among us during these two years has been more seriously elaborated, and in all ways made the best of, than this of hers.

T. CARLYLE.

5 GT. CHEYNE ROW, CHELSEA, 7 June, 1855.

Soon after this there begin to come in the returns from the attempts now made to find a publisher. In June, a note from John Murray; in July, one from J. W. Parker; in August, from G. P. Putnam of New York, and from Phillips & Sampson of Boston. These last make definite proposals to publish; but all the rest, with courteous but sufficient excuses, decline. The two from the American publishers were forwarded by Emerson with his letter which follows:

CONCORD, August 5, 1855.

MY DEAR MISS BACON, — I give you joy on the good news you send me of the ending of your work. What if it is only the beginning of another, it is also the pledge of power to do it. I hope and trust it is good news for us and all people also. And to this end I sent your two letters at once to both the Publishers, and enclose to you Mr. Putnam's reply, which, indeed, I anticipated, as knowing he had been long embarrassed in his trade, though retaining, I am told, the respect of his community.

In the shortness of the time we have to act in, I think it best also to send you Phillips & Sampson's letter; of which, otherwise, I should only send you a summary. I failed to see them, though I went to their compting-room. If you go on with them, you had better preserve their letter. They may seem to you timid, but they are as brave as their experience will allow them to be. Such is the advertising system under which they live, and the giving away of copies to every newspaper, that it costs them $150, I think they showed me, — before a single copy is sold, — for that expense alone. And they have been losers by many books.

You will see that P. & S. object to the title. I do not know but I put it in their heads. I think you can easily give the book a simpler name, simply descriptive, the plainer the better, with or without a motto, and let that not be italicized, as, the "Authorship of the Shakspere Plays," or the like. I who do not know the book cannot tell the title, — but wish it to be of stone.

I am just running up to a country college to read a discourse to the Alumni, and therefore hasten to put these two notes together, lest they lose a steamer, and so cut short my billet. The best hap which ever awaits truth await you! And let me hear and convey your decisions to these men. Yours faithfully,

R. W. EMERSON.

Miss D. S. BACON.

It is of little importance that among the men of letters with whom she entered into communication was George Grote, the historian of Greece. Why it should have been thought that his studies or fancies would incline him to consider her speculations cannot now be known; it is only certain that this letter from his wife is all that came of the communication. But it would hardly be right to withhold so stately and sonorous a piece of rhetoric as the answer of Mrs. Grote. One is not a little puzzled to understand that a lady who thus uttered the simplest facts in the most solemn way should have been an intimate friend and correspondent of Sydney Smith; who nevertheless is said to have permitted himself the freedom to remark, as he first saw her entering a drawing-room crowned with a startling scarlet turban, that he now received a new impression of the meaning of the word Grotesque. The handwriting of the letter is as masculine as its style.

LONDON, 5 August, 1855.

MADAM, — On reaching London late yesterday evening from Lincolnshire (where Mr. Grote and I have been all the week on business), I found your letter and enclosures, which I make it a duty to acknowledge without delay.

I gather from the contents of the letters that you desire some counsel and assistance in regard to securing a reputable Publisher for the work which has so long engaged your time and talents — and in this view I should be happy to concur, with Mr. Grote, in rendering such aid as we could furnish towards that desirable object. My own personal arrangements are, however, for this week incompatible with any London business. Intending to stop one or two nights only in town on passing through to my country residence (about 24 miles distant in the County of Buckinghamshire), I have made engagements to receive friends at the latter place for a few days. So that, for the next 10 days it will be out of my power to invite you to meet me at our town residence. But should your affair require speedy agency, Mr. Grote will have much pleasure in seeing you on any forenoon between now and Friday next, before 2 o'clock, and will endeavor to assist you with his experience and discernment towards obtaining the purpose in view.

My presence in town will be needed for a day or two, about the 20th August, to arrange for workmen coming in on the 25th to paint the interior apartments, and if you could do me the honor to propose a day about that period, it will be my study to meet it, with every inclination to serve a lady whose talents and personal merit entitle her to the good offices of such of her own sex, as well as of the other, who value literary tastes and instructed industry in woman. I have the honor to be, Madam,

Your obedient humble servant,

H. GROTE.

In September comes another declination, this time from Chapman & Hall, and without the courteous expressions of sympathy with which every other publisher was kind enough to soften the pain of rejection. These gentlemen alone put themselves on high moral ground. " As they cannot confess themselves converts to her views, they feel that it would not become them to be the instruments for opening an attack upon one of the most sacred beliefs of the nation and indeed of all nations." They would, however, " be much pleased if they could wish her success in her bold and novel undertaking."

All this delay and disappointment meant far more to her than pride abased or ambition discouraged; more even than sorrow that a great discovery was thus withheld from a waiting world. Trusting to the returns which her work, into which

her soul and life had been thrown, was to bring
her, she had gone on consuming, though with hard
self-denying frugality, the little fund given to bring
her home, and she was now at an end of that.
Late in October she wrote, from the same lodgings
in Spring Street, a very long letter to Emerson,
which was not completed until the first of November. On that day she wrote also a short one to
her brother in New Haven. In the two years and
a half of her absence she seems, in her strong sense
of the wrong his want of sympathy with her great
discovery had done her, to have seldom communicated with him. Even now, while the letter
showed that she retained the absolute confidence
in him which was one of the earliest sentiments of
her life, and even had not lost the affection of a
sister, her pride restrained the faintest intimation
of the nature of her work, which was nevertheless
so well known to him that his disapproval of it had
deeply estranged her from him. With it she sent
him, under seal, the letter to Emerson and a packet
of manuscript beside. "You must excuse," she
says, "the liberty I take in sending this packet to
your care. My living depends on my getting an
early answer to it, and I should have to delay it
unless I took just this course." She speaks of the
finished manuscript in her hands "on a subject
calculated to interest the American public very
deeply," and of the hopes she had had of receiving
something for its publication either in a magazine

or as a book. " The first thing now is to provide for my immediate living, for the delay here has been disastrous to me in that respect. My position is better now than it ever has been before, because my work is now *done* instead of being to do. I have found the leisure which I never could find before for it, and I am glad I have used it as I have, let the consequences to me personally be what they may. And serious enough they are, for I do not now know how I am possibly to live, until I can get an answer to this. Unless the letter I have been depending on " [from Putnam the publisher, who she hoped would print one magazine article] " should arrive very soon, I shall be entirely at the end of my credit, as well as means." " I have sealed the pacquet, because I do not wish you to have *any* responsibility for the work — for reasons which you will understand by and by ; — it is better that you should not see a word of it in MS." — " I am sending my work in parcels as fast as I can copy it. But there is enough here to decide the question of its acceptance with Putnam, and if I can live to get a return from this the trouble will be over."

To Emerson, however, she recounts the alarm which fluttered the English publishers upon the mere suggestion to them of her subject, and proceeds : " Perhaps the American publishers may be frightened too, and follow suit, and I may have to bury my work, and bide my time, as my betters have done.

" These articles I enclose with this are properly the first three chapters of my work, or the first *four* rather, including the one I have already sent; but on account of their length I have concluded to subdivide them. I propose now to send it in parcels, as fast as I can copy it, till I get it all over. But if you read it, there is one point to which I beg leave to direct your attention beforehand. When I began to write it, I did not expect to be able to prove the discovery with it. I depended on further evidence for that. But I thought a book might be made of it as it stood then which would command some attention, and perhaps give me the means which I lacked of bringing the research to its proper conclusion ; and that which makes now the whole of the first book was written simply with that view and intention. I illustrated my assertion with quotations from the Plays, which were freely interwoven with the story. But in copying I expanded the quotations and comments into regular criticisms, and took them out of the place to which they belonged, and made a separate book of them ; and it was when I began to do *that*, that the confidence I have since so freely expressed to you took possession of me. It did not, and does not, seem to me possible that any rational person, who will take the trouble to look at that part of the work, could differ from me as to the conclusion. . . . But as for that part of the work which I am now sending you, I have no such confidence. My only object there was to get the discovery fairly down on paper, to define it, to say what it is, not to prove it ; and what little demonstration there was in it has been taken out. And I ask your attention to this point beforehand, because you will be disappointed if you expect to find there that ground of certainty of which I have spoken."

" As to that recent article in ' Fraser ' on the Minor Poems, I can only regard it as a case of judicial blindness and hardening of the sensibilities on the part of the Editor. If that Article which I sent to you some three or four weeks ago has reached its destination, and is likely to get published, I shall be glad to have a few quotations from Mr. Fraser's last inserted in it, and it is perfectly disgraceful to me to have omitted one point which he kindly brings out for me there, and I wish you would insert it somewhere if you can. I mean the consummation of that life which the author of the article in question claims as the true English type, frankly confessing that it is on that very account that the English cling to it so fondly, — the fact that the Poet fell a victim to this national characteristic at last, for his poetry was so successful, and his good things came in upon him so fast, in his retirement at Stratford, and so much beyond his individual faculty of appropriating them, that he sank under it and died of overeating ; actually perished by the judgment of God,

in an attempt to get the worth of his poetry, in
the only shape in which he could appreciate it;
and it is on account of the very quality which
finally assumes this consummate form in him, that
his memory is embalmed in the grateful recollections of his countrymen. So this Fraser man says,
outright. It is not his poetry that they admire, it
is his character. Anacreon died of a grape-stone.
We have not the particulars *here*, but I suppose it
was roast beef probably or plum pudding which
put an end to this god of the English idolatry in
the midst of his career, and prevented our having
any more Macbeths or Lears or Tempests."

"I do not know where I shall be by the time
your answer to this arrives, and if the work were
all in your hands, I should not so much care. I can
only ask you to direct to me here — perhaps you
have already written in reply to my last, — I hope
so ; for a letter on which I have been very much
depending has not come for some reason or other,
and as the month of November is at hand, I may
be in need of all the encouragement which the
case admits of, and the cheer which your good
words have always given me. It would be very
foolish to expect to have anything like this without paying for it, and so long as the demand does
not involve impossibilities, I hope to be able to
meet it. There's something gained at any rate,
and if that is once secured it is not possible for
one life to pay too dearly for it."

Then follows some discussion of other means than magazines — weekly editions of the New York dailies — for getting some of her manuscript before the public, and some compensation for it, — " and that would enable me to retain my connection with this planet, perhaps, till the work is finished, — if that should seem on the whole desirable. However, there is the Atlantic Ocean to fall back upon, in the last resort,[1] and the Providential scheme is not without its provisions for that class of persons that the land refuses to tolerate, — people who were not expected, and for whom there is in two hemispheres no place. I have been doing the very best thing I could, the most honorable, — the only honorable thing I could. And after a deliberate survey of the ground, I have decided to let things take their course. I am not going to abase myself because I have done my duty. I am not afraid to die in the way of it; when the road comes fairly to an end, I shall stop. I will make no further concession to the nonsense of this world. It has nothing to give me. Permission to finish my work is all I want of it."

Before the answer to this letter reached her she must have received news of the relief which was to come from the publication of the first part of her work. Joyful as the respite must have been to her, with such joy as rewards the heroic endur-

---

[1] There seems to be a reproduction here of her grim allusion to Margaret Fuller in an earlier letter (*supra*, p. 68).

ance of a beleaguered garrison in extremity when the siege is raised, this was nevertheless the first and the last return, beyond the consciousness of faithful sacrifice, from the work to which she gave her life. The letter now given must only have confirmed to her the news which one from the magazine publishers had already brought.

CONCORD, 3 December, 1855.

DEAR MISS BACON, — I have only a few minutes, and perhaps no intelligence for you, and yet cannot let another steamer go in silence. I received your first chapter and read it, and sent it immediately to Putnam, with all the Imprimatur I could add. I did not write you, for I have been uncomfortably, nay ridiculously, busy with printing, writing, and a correspondence of absurd extent, which my practice of lecturing creates. I delayed your letter day by day, until now comes your second parcel, and enclosed letter, giving so much to think of — really so much to think of, that I heartily wish the right man were here to think and counsel. Immediately on its arrival, comes at last a letter from Putnam's editor, signing himself Dix Edwards,[1] saying, that he did duly receive the First Chapter, will print it at last as leading article on 1 January, and wishes Miss Bacon will follow it up, in their Monthly, as fast as she can. Mean-

---

[1] Messrs. Dix & Edwards were publishers (not editors) of the magazine.

time, I hoped that you would yet decide to print by Phillips & Sampson, and make the book at once. I ought to have explained to you, whilst their statement was fresh in my mind, that you are not holden to them by publishing by them any longer than you please. At the end of the first, or of the second, or whatever edition, you can take your copyright to a new publisher. Still, there is reason for holding on by them, namely, that they say they spend a great deal of money on each of their books before any remuneration comes. Also, they reply to your feeling of the injustice of receiving only a tenth part of the price of the book to yourself, that they receive still less, unless and until the book is very successful; for it costs no more to produce a book that sells fifty thousand copies than the one that sells one thousand.

Now you leave me, in your last letter, quite too much liberty. You have not said what I shall do. I am going to the Mississippi, as soon as, or before, my little book is out; and am to read lectures in that country for six weeks perhaps, — through dire necessity, and not from any desire to that work. You must choose, then, whether to print the Book by P. & S., as the only offer in that form we have; or, in Articles by Putnam. I much prefer the first mode. If I had my freedom, I should go to Boston or New York and read your letters and chapters to good men, and found a new Shakespeare Society to print the Book, and install the Author. But the mud of the Mississippi forbids ; and though you suggest several good journals, &c., which ought to exist here for us, they do not yet exist. The first chapter was excellent. So is the second. These are all that I have read. I have the other two, and, when I leave home, shall leave my wife charged to obey exactly the instructions you shall send, in case they arrive before my return, which perhaps will not be till 1 February. Still, what you write will be sent to me in the West. I have not time for another line, and only write this that I may not be heinously negligent where your genius and the high Fate that seem to accompany you have right to demand instant service. I shall strive to find a breathing time to say so much to your friends. Respectfully and gratefully,

R. W. EMERSON.

Miss D. S. BACON.

Before this relief, however, small as it was, could be expected, her extremity was already absolute. On the 20th of December an evidently hasty note, written both to her brother and a sister, attests it. She writes asking for special care about her copyright, for which her solicitude has now a pathetic look, and proceeds : " Money from some quarter I must have immediately. A little delay will make the difference between life and death to me, unless for the sake of my work I should conclude to apply to the American minister ; nothing else would induce me to do it.   I am clearly of the opinion that this work is that which is wanting, and I humbly hope that I may live to see it issued safely, but I do not expect the laws of nature to be altered on my account, though they do indeed seem to have been well-nigh miraculously controlled, for I have lived for months in the lions' den, and thus far God has shut his mouth. . . .   The morning of the longest night, and it is a very long one, is at hand."

It was on the 20th of November that dawn began to gleam in the west, in the following letter from Messrs. Dix & Edwards :

10 PARK PLACE, NEW YORK, Nov. 20, 1855.

MADAME : We beg to say that the chapter of your inquiry into the authorship of Shakespeare's plays, with which we were favored through Mr. Emerson, will appear in the January number of "Putnam's Monthly," when it will be paid for at the rate of our most valued contributors, five dollars a page.   We shall take the liberty to express in a note to this article the hope that the series may be continued in our pages, and we trust it may suit your convenience to forward a second chapter without any delay, in order that it may appear in the February number.

Moreover, should you have made no other arrangements, we shall be happy to treat with you for the publication of the whole after so much of it as you may desire shall have appeared in a serial form.

In the number for January, 1856, "Putnam's Monthly" began its seventh half-yearly volume. It was then the chief American magazine of the lighter literature; for the "Atlantic Monthly," which replaced it, did not begin until the following year. The opening article of the January number was that which follows.

X.

WILLIAM SHAKESPEARE AND HIS PLAYS: AN INQUIRY CONCERNING THEM.[1]

How can we undertake to account for the literary miracles of antiquity, while this great myth of the modern ages still lies at our own door unquestioned?

This vast, magical, unexplained phenomenon, which our own times have produced under our own eyes, appears to be, indeed, the only thing which our modern rationalism is not to be permitted to meddle with. For here the critics themselves still veil their faces, filling the air with mystic utterances which seem to say, that to this shrine at least, for the footstep of the common reason and the common sense, there is yet no admittance. But how can they instruct us to take

---

[1] In commencing the publication of these bold, original, and most ingenious and interesting speculations upon the real authorship of Shakespeare's plays, it is proper for the editor of *Putnam's Monthly*, in disclaiming all responsibility for their startling view of the question, to say that they are the result of long and conscientious investigation on the part of the learned and eloquent scholar, their author; and that the editor has reason to hope that they will be continued through some future numbers of the Magazine. [*Editorial Note.*]

off here the sandals which they themselves have taught us to wear into the inmost *sekos* of the most ancient sanctities?

THE SHAKESPEARE DRAMA, — its import, its limitations, its object and sources, its beginning and end, — for the modern critic, that is surely now the question.

What, indeed, should we know of the origin of the Homeric poems? Twenty-five hundred years ago, when those mystic characters, which the learned Phenician and Egyptian had brought in vain to the singing Greek of the Heroic Ages, began, in the new modifications of national life which the later admixtures of foreign elements created, at length to be put to their true uses, that song of the nation, even in its latest form, was already old on the lips of the learned, and its origin a tradition. All the history of that wonderful individuality wherein the inspirations of so many ages were at last united, — the circumstance, the vicissitude, the poetic life, that had framed that dazzling mirror of old time, and wrought in it those depths of clearness, — all had gone before the art of writing and memories had found its way into Greece, or even the faculty of perceiving the actual had begun to be developed there.

And yet are the scholars of our time content to leave this matter here where they find it? With these poetic remains in their hands, the monuments of a genius whose date is ante-historical, are they content to know of their origin only what Alexander and Plato could know, what Solon and Pisistratus were fain to content themselves with, what the Homerids themselves received of him as their ancestral patron ?

No: with these works in their hands to-day, reasoning from them alone, with no collateral aids, with scarce an extant monument of the age from which they come to us, they are not afraid to fly in the face of all antiquity with their conclusions.

Have they not settled among them already the old dispute of the contending cities, the old dispute of the contending ages, too, for the honor of this poet's birth ? Do they not take him to pieces before our eyes, this venerable Homer; and tell us how many old forgotten poets' ashes went to his formation, and trace in him the mosaic scenes which eluded the scrutiny of the age of Pericles ? Even Mr. Grote will tell us now, just where the Iliad "cuts me" the fiery Achilles "cranking in;" and what could hinder the learned Schlegel, years ago, from setting his chair in the midst of the Delian choirs, confronting the confounded children of Ion with his definitions of the term Homeros, and demonstrating, from the Leipsic Iliad in his hand, that the poet's contemporaries had, in fact, named him Homer the Seer, not Homer the Blind One ?

The criticism of our age found this whole question where the art of writing found it two thou-

sand five hundred years ago ; but because the Io-
nian cities, and Solon, and Pisistratus might be pre-
sumed beforehand to know at least as much about
it as they, or because the opinions of twenty-five
centuries in such a case might seem to be entitled
to some reverence, did the critics leave it there ?

Two hundred and fifty years ago, *our* poet —
our Homer — was alive in the world. Two centuries and a half ago, when the art of letters was
already millenniums old in Europe, when the art of
printing had already been in use a century and a
half, in the midst of a contemporary historical illumination which has its equal nowhere in history,
those works were issued that have given our English life and language their imperishable claim in
the earth, that have made the name in which they
come to us a word by itself in the human speech ;
and to this hour we know of their origin hardly
so much as we knew of the origin of the Homeric
epics when the present discussions in regard to
them commenced, *not* so much — not a hundredth
part so much — as we now know of Pharaohs who
reigned in the valley of the Nile ages before the
invasion of the Hyksos.

But with these products of the national life in
our hands, with all the contemporary light on their
implied conditions which such an age as that of
Elizabeth can furnish, are we going to be able to
sit still much longer, in a period of historical
inquiry and criticism like this, under the gross

impossibilities which the still accepted theory on this subject involves ?

The age which has put back old Homer's eyes safe in his head again, after he had gone without them well-nigh three thousand years; the age which has found, and labeled, and sent to the museum, the skull in which the pyramid of Cheops was designed, and the lions which "the mighty hunter before the Lord" ordered for his new palace on the Tigris some millenniums earlier; the age in which we have abjured our faith in Romulus and Remus, — is surely one in which we may be permitted to ask this question.

Shall this crowning literary product of that great epoch wherein these new ages have their beginning, vividly arrayed in its choicest refinements; flashing everywhere on the surface with its costliest wit; crowded everywhere with its subtlest scholasticisms; betraying on every page its broadest, freshest range of experience, its most varied culture, its profoundest insight, its boldest grasp of comprehension, — shall this crowning result of so many preceding ages of growth and culture, with its essential and now palpable connection with the new scientific movement of the time from which it issues, be able to conceal from us much longer its history ? Shall we be able to accept in explanation of it, much longer, the story of the Stratford poacher ?

The popular and traditional theory of the origin

of these works was received and transmitted after the extraordinary circumstances which led to its first imposition had ceased to exist, because, in fact, no one had any motive for taking the trouble to call it in question. The common disposition to receive in good faith a statement of this kind, however extraordinary; the natural, intellectual preference of the affirmative proposition at hand, as the explanation of a given phenomenon, when the negative or the doubt compels one to launch out for himself in search of new positions, — this alone might serve to account for this result, at a time when criticism as yet was not; when the predominant mental habit, on all ordinary questions, was still that of passive acceptance, and the most extraordinary excitements, on questions of the most momentous interest, could only rouse the public mind to assume temporarily any other attitude.

And the impression which these works produced, even in their first imperfect mode of exhibition, was already so profound and extraordinary as to give to all the circumstances of their attributed origin a blaze of notoriety tending to enhance this positive force in the tradition. Propounded as a fact, not as a theory, its very boldness — its startling improbability— was made at once to contribute to its strength; covering beforehand the whole ground of attack. The wonderful origin of these works was, from the first, the predominant point in the impression they made, — the prominent marvel in those marvels around which all the new wonders that the later criticism evolved still continued to arrange themselves.

For the discoveries of this criticism had yet no tendency to suggest any new belief on this point. In the face of all that new appreciation of the works themselves which was involved in them, the story of that wondrous origin could still maintain its footing ; through all the ramifications of this criticism, it still grew and inwound itself, not without vital limitation, however, to the criticism thus entangled. But these new discoveries involved, for a time, conclusions altogether in keeping with the tradition.

This new force in literature, for which books contained no precedent ; this new manifestation of creative energy, with its self-sustained vitalities ; with its inexhaustible prodigality, mocking nature herself ; with its new grasp of the whole circuit of human aims and activities, — this force, so unlike anything that scholasticism or art had ever before produced, though it came in fact with the sweep of all the ages, moved with all their slow accumulation, could not account for itself to those critics as anything but a new and mystic manifestation of nature, — a new upwelling of the occult vital forces underlying our phenomenal existence ; invading the historic order with one capricious leap, laughing at history, telling the

laboring ages that their sweat and blood had been
in vain.

And the tradition at hand was entirely in harmony with this conception. For to this super-
human genius, bringing with it its own laws and
intuitions from some outlying region of life not
subject to our natural conditions, and not to be
included in our "philosophy," the differences between man and man, natural or acquired, would,
of course, seem trivial. What could any culture,
or any merely natural endowment, accomplish that
would furnish the required explanation of this
result? And, by way of defining itself as an
agency wholly supernal, was it not, in fact, necessary that it should select as its organ one in whom
the natural conditions of the highest intellectual
manifestations were obviously, even grossly, wanting?

With this theory of it, no one need find it strange
that it should pass in its selection those grand old
cities where Learning sat enthroned with all her
time-honored array of means and appliances for
the development of mental resource, — where the
genius of England had hitherto been accomplished
for all its triumphs, — and that it should pass the
lofty centres of church and state, and the crowded
haunts of professional life, where the mental activities of the time were gathered to its conflicts;
where, in hourly collision, each strong individuality was printing itself upon a thousand others,

and taking in turn from all their impress; where, in the thick-coming change of that " time-better- ing age," in its crowding multiplicities, and varie- ties, and oppositions, life grew warm, and in the old the new was stirring, and in the many the one ; where wit, and philosophy, and fancy, and humor, in the thickest onsets of the hour, were learning to veil in courtly phrase, in double and triple meanings, in crowding complexities of con- ceits and unimagined subtleties of form, the free- doms that the time had nurtured ; where genius flashed up from all her hidden sources, and the soul of the age — " the mind reflecting ages past " — was collecting itself, and ready even then to leap forth, " not for an age, but for all time."

And, indeed, was it not fitting that this new in- spiration which was to reveal the latent forces of Nature and her scorn of conditions, — fastening her contempt for all time upon the pride of human culture at its height, — was it not fitting that it should select this moment of all others, and this locality, that it might pass by that very centre of historical influences which the court of Elizabeth then made, — that it might involve in its perpetual eclipse that immortal group of heroes, and states- men, and scholars, and wits, and poets, with its enthroned king of thought, taking all the past for his inheritance, and claiming the minds of men in all futurity as the scene and limit of his dominion ? Yes, even he — he whose thought would grasp the

whole, and keep his grasp on it perpetual — speaks
to us still out of that cloud of mockery that fell
upon him when " Great Nature " passed him by
— even him — with his immortal longings, with
his world-wide aims, with his new mastery of her
secrets, too, and his new sovereignty over her,
to drop her crown of immortality, lit with the
finest essence of that which makes his own page
immortal, on the brow of the pet horse-boy at
Blackfriars, — the wit and good fellow of the London link-holders, the menial *attaché* and *élève* of
the play-house, the future actor, and joint pro-
prietor, of the New Theatre on the Bankside.

Who quarrels with this movement ? Who does
not find it fitting and pleasant enough ? Let the
" thrice three muses " go into mourning as deep as
they will for this desertion, — as desertion it was —
for we all know that to the last hour of his life
this fellow cared never a farthing for them, but
only for his gains at their hands ; let Learning
hide as she best may her baffled head in this disgrace, — who cares ? Who does not rather laugh
with great creating Nature in her triumph ?

At least, who would be willing to admit, for a
moment, that there was one in all that contemporary circle of accomplished scholars, and men of
vast and varied genius, capable of writing these
plays ; and who feels the least difficulty in suppos-
ing that " this player here," as Hamlet terms him,
— the whole force of that outburst of scorn inef-

fable bearing on the word, and on that which it represented to him, — who doubts that this player is most abundantly and superabundantly competent to it?

Now that the deer-stealing fire has gone out of him, now that this youthful impulse has been taught its conventional social limits, sobered into the mild, sagacious, witty " Mr. Shakespeare of the Globe," distinguished for the successful management of his own fortunes, for his upright dealings with his neighbors, too, and " his facetious grace in writing," patronized by men of rank, who include his theatre among their instrumentalities for affecting the popular mind, and whose relations to him are, in fact, identical with those which Hamlet sustains to the players of *his* piece, what is to hinder this Mr. Shakespeare — the man who keeps the theatre on the Bankside — from working himself into a frenzy when he likes, and scribbling out unconsciously Lears, and Macbeths, and Hamlets, merely as the necessary dialogue to the spectacles he professionally exhibits ; ay, and what is to hinder his boiling his kettle with the manuscripts, too, when he has done with them, if he chooses?

What it would be madness to suppose the most magnificently endowed men of that wondrous age could accomplish — its real men, those who have left their lives in it, woven in its web throughout — what it would be madness to suppose these men, who are but men, and known as such, could accomplish, this Mr. Shakespeare, actor and manager, of whom no one knows anything else, shall be able to do for you in " the twinkling of an eye," without so much as knowing it, and there shall be no words about it !

And are not the obscurities that involve his life, so impenetrably in fact, the true Shakespearean element ?   In the boundless sea of negation which surrounds that play-house centre, surely he can unroll himself to any length, or gather himself into any shape or attitude, which the criticism in hand may call for.   There is nothing to bring up against him, with one's theories.   For, here in this day-light of our modern criticism, in its noontide glare, has he not contrived to hide himself in the pro-foundest depths of that stuff that myths are made of ?   Who shall come in competition with him here ?   Who shall dive into the bottom of that sea to pluck his drowned honors from him ?

Take, one by one, the splendid men of this Elizabethan age, and set them down with a Ham-let to write, and you will say beforehand, such an one cannot do it, nor such an one, — nor *he*, with that profoundest insight and determination of his which taught him to put physical nature to the question that he might wring from her her se-crets; but humanity, human nature, of course, had none worth noting for him ; — oh no ; he, with his infinite wit and invention, with his worlds of covert humor, with his driest prose, pressed, burst-

ing with Shakespearean beauty, he could not do it,
nor *he*, with his Shakespearean acquaintance with
life, with his Shakespearean knowledge of men
under all the differing social conditions, at home
and abroad, by land and by sea, with his world-
wide experiences of nature and fortune, with the
rush and outbreak of his fiery mind kindling and
darting through all his time; he, with his Shakespearean grace and freedom, with his versatile and
profound acquirements, with his large, genial, generous, prodigal, Shakespearean soul that would
comprehend all, and ally itself with all, he could
not do it; neither of these men, nor both of them
together, nor all the wits of the age together: —
but this Mr. Shakespeare of the Globe, this mild,
respectable, obliging man, this "Johannes Factotum" (as a contemporary calls him, laughing at
the idea of *his* undertaking "a blank verse"), is
there any difficulty here? Oh no! None in the
world: for, in the impenetrable obscurity of that
illimitable green-room of his, "by the mass, he
is anything, and he can do anything, and that
roundly too."

Is it wonderful? And is not that what we like
in it? Would you make a man of him? With
this miraculous inspiration of his, would you ask
anything else of him? Do you not see that you
touch the Shakespearean essence, with a question
as to motives, and possibilities? Would he be
Shakespeare still, if he should permit·you to ham-

per him with conditions? What is the meaning
of that word, then? And will you not leave him
to us? Shall we have no Shakespeare? Have
we not scholars enough, and wits enough, and
men, of every other kind of genius, enough, — but
have we many Shakespeares? — that you should
wish to run this one through with your questions,
this one, great, glorious, infinite impossibility, that
has had us in its arms, all our lives from the beginning? If you dissolve him, do you not dissolve us
with him? If you take him to pieces, do you not
undo us, also?

Ah, surely we did not need this master spirit of
our race to tell us that there is that in the foundation of this human soul, " that loves to apprehend more than cool reason ever comprehends,"
nay, that there is an infinity in it, that finds her
ordinances too straight, that will leap from them
when it can, and shake the head at her. And have
we not all lived once in regions full of people that
were never compelled to give an account of themselves in any of these matters? And when, precisely, did we pass that charmed line, beyond
which these phantoms cannot come? When was
the word definitively spoken which told us that the
childhood of the race was done, or that its grown-
up children were to have henceforth no conjurers?
Who yet has heard the crowing of that cock, " at
whose warning, whether in earth or air, the ex-
travagant and erring spirit hies to his confine " ?

The nuts, indeed, are all cracked long ago, whence of old the fairy princess, in her coach and six, drove out so freely with all her regal retinue, to crown the hero's fortunes; and the rusty lamp, that once filled the dim hut of poverty with Eastern splendors, has lost its capabilities. But when our youth robbed us of these, had it not marvels and impossibilities of its own to replace them with, yet more magical? and surely, manhood itself, the soberest maturity, cannot yet be without these substitutes; and it is nature's own voice and outcry that we hear whenever one of them is taken from us.

Let him alone! We have lecturers enough and professors enough already. Let him alone! We will keep this one mighty conjurer still, even in the place where men most do congregate, and nobody shall stir a hair on his impossible old head, or trouble him with a question. He shall stand there still, pulling interminable splendors out of places they never could have been in; that is the charm of it; he shall stand there rubbing those few sickly play-house manuscripts of his, or a few, old, musty play-house novels, and wringing from them the very wine of all our life, showering from their greasy folds the gems and gold of all the ages! He shall stand there, spreading, in the twinkling of an eye, for a single night in a dirty theatre, "to complete a purchase that he has a mind to," the feasts of the immortal gods; and before our lips

can, by any chance, have reached even the edge of
those cups, that open down into infinity, when the
show has served his purpose, he shall whisk it all
away again, and leave no wreck behind, except by
accident; and none shall remonstrate, or say to
him, "wherefore?" He shall stand there still, for
us all — the magician; nature's one, complete, incontestable, gorgeous triumph over the impossibilities of reason.

For the primary Shakespearean condition involves at present, not merely the accidental absence of those external means of intellectual enlargement and perfection, whereby the long arts
of the ages are made to bring to the individual
mind their last results, multiplying its single forces
with the life of all; — but it requires also the absence of all personal intellectual tastes, aims, and
pursuits; it requires that this man shall be below
all other men, in his sordid incapacity for appreciating intellectual values; it requires that he shall
be able, not merely to witness the performance of
these plays, not merely to hear them and read
them for himself, but to compose them; it requires
him to be able to compose the "Tempest," and
"Othello," and "Macbeth," without suspecting
that there is anything of permanent interest in
them — anything that will outlast the spectacle of
the hour.

The art of writing had been already in use
twenty - five centuries in Europe, and a Shake-

speare, one would think, might have been able to form some conception of its value and applications; the art of printing had been in use on the continent a century and a half, and it was already darting through every civilized corner of it, and through England, too, no uncertain intimations of its historic purport — intimations significant enough " to make bold power look pale" already — and one would think a Shakespeare might have understood its message. But no! This very spokesman of the new era it ushers in, trusted with this legacy of the new-born times; this man, whom we all so look up to, and reverence, with that inalienable treasure of ours in his hands, which even Ben Jonson knew was not for him, " nor for an age — but for all time," why this Jack Cade that he is must needs take us back three thousand years with it, and land us at the gates of Ilium! The arts of humanity and history, as they stood when Troy was burned, must save this treasure for us, and be our means of access to it! He will leave this work of his, into which the ends of the world have come to be inwrought for all the future, he will leave it where Homer left his, on the lips of the mouthing "rhapsodists!"

Apparently, indeed, he will be careful to teach these "robustious, periwig-pated fellows" their proper relations to him. He will industriously instruct them how to pronounce his dialogue, so as to give the immediate effect intended; controlling even the gesticulations, insisting on the stops, ruling out utterly the town-crier's emphasis; and, above all, protesting, with a true author's jealousy, against interpolation or any meddling with his text. Indeed, the directions to the players, which he puts into the mouth of Hamlet — involving, as they do, not merely the nice sensibility of the artist, and his nervous, instinctive, æsthetic acquaintance with his art, but a thorough scientific knowledge of its principles — these directions would have led us to infer that he would, at least, know enough of the value of his own works to avail himself of the printing-press for their preservation, and not only that, they would have led us to expect from him a most exquisitely careful revision of his proofs. But how is it? He destroys, we are given to understand, the manuscripts of his unpublished plays, and we owe to accident, and to no care of his whatever, his works as they have come to us. Did ever the human mind debase itself to the possibility of receiving such nonsense as this, on any subject, before ?[1]

He had those manuscripts! He had those originals which publishers and scholars would give mil-

---

[1] Though the editors of the first folio profess to have access to these very papers, and boast of being able to bring out an absolutely faultless edition, to take the place of those stolen and surreptitious copies then in circulation, the edition which is actually produced, in connection with this announcement, is itself found to be full of verbal errors, and is supposed, by later editors, to have been derived from no better source than its predecessors.

lions now to purchase a glimpse of; he had the original Hamlet, with its last finish; he had the original Lear, with his own final readings; he had them all — all, pointed, emphasized, directed, as they came from the gods; he had them all, all finished as the critic of "Hamlet" and "Midsummer Night's Dream" must have finished them; and he left us to wear out our youth, and squander our lifetime, in poring over and setting right the old, garbled copies of the play-house! He had those manuscripts, and the printing-press had been at its work a hundred years when he was born, but he was not ashamed to leave the best wits and scholars of all succeeding ages, with Pope and Johnson at their head, to exhaust their ingenuity, and sour their dispositions, and to waste their golden hours, year after year, in groping after and guessing out his hidden meanings!

He had those manuscripts! In the name of that sovereign reason, whose name he dares to take upon his lips so often, what did he do with them? Did he wantonly destroy them? No! Ah, no! he did not care enough for them to take that trouble. No, he did not do that! That would not have been in keeping with the character of this most respectable impersonation of the Genius of the British Isle, as it stands set up for us at present to worship. Some worthy, domestic, private, economic use, doubtless, they were put to. For, is not he a private, economical, practical man —

this Shakespeare of ours — with no stuff and nonsense about him — a plain, true-blooded Englishman, who minds his own business, and leaves other
people to take care of theirs? Is not this our
Shakespeare? Is it not the boast of England,
that he is just that, and nothing else? " What did
he do with them?" He gave them to his cook,
or Dr. Hale put up potions for his patients in
them, or Judith, poor Judith, — who signified her
relationship to the author of " Lear " and the
" Tempest," and her right to the glory of the
name he left her, by the very extraordinary kind
of " mark " which she affixes to legal instruments,
— poor Judith may have curled her hair to the
day of her death with them, without dreaming of
any harm. " What did he do with them?" And
whose business is it? Were n't they his own? If
he chose to burn them up, or put them to some
private use, had not he a perfect right to do it?

No! Traitor and miscreant! No! What did
you do with them? You have skulked this question long enough. You will have to account for
them. You will have to tell us what you did with
them. The awakening ages will put you on the
stand, and you will not leave it until you answer
the question, " What did you do with them?"

And yet, do not the critics dare to boast to us,
that he did compose these works for his own private, particular ends only? Do they not tell us,
as if it were a thing to be proud of, and " a thing

to thank God on," with uplifted eyes, and speech-less admiration points, that he did " die, and leave the world no copy " ? But who is it that insists so much, so strangely, so repetitiously, upon the wrong to humanity, the fraud done to nature, when the individual fails to render in his account to time of all that nature gives him? Who is it that writes, obscurely indeed, so many sonnets, only to ring the changes on this very subject, singing out, point by point, not the Platonic theory, but his own fresh and beautiful study of great nature's law, and his own new and scientific doctrine of conservation and advancement ? And who is it that writes, unconsciously no doubt, and without its ever occurring to him that it was going to be printed, or to be read by any one,

> "*Thyself* and *thy belongings*
> *Are not thine own* so proper, as to waste
> *Thyself upon thy virtues*, them on thee " ?

For here is the preacher of another doctrine, which puts the good that is private and particular where the sovereignty that is in nature puts it : —

> " Heaven doth with us, *as we with torches do ;*
> Not light them for themselves. For if our virtues
> Did not go forth of us, 'twere all alike
> As if we had them not. Spirits are not finely touched
> But to fine issues ; nor nature never lends
> The smallest scruple of her excellence,
> But, like a thrifty goddess, she determines
> Herself the glory of a creditor,
> Both thanks and use."

Truly the man who writes in this style, with

such poetic iteration, might put in Hamlet's plea,
when his critics accuse him of unconsciousness: —

> " Bring me to the test
> And I the matter will re-word ; which madness
> Would gambol from."

What infirmity of blindness is it, then, that we
charge upon this " god of our idolatry " ?   And
what new race of Calibans are we, that we should
be called upon to worship this monstrous incon-
gruity — this Trinculo — this impersonated moral
worthlessness ?   Oh, stupidity past finding out!
" The myriad-minded one," the light of far-off futu-
rities was in him, and he knew it not!   While the
word was on his lips, and he reasoned of it, he
heeded it not!   He, at whose feet all men else are
proud to sit, came to him, and found no reverence.
The treasure for us all was put into his hands, and
— he did not waste it — he did not keep it laid up
in a napkin, he did not dig in the earth, and hide
his Lord's money ; no, he used it!   he used it for
his own despicable and sordid ends, " to complete
purchases that he had a mind to," and he left us
to gather up " the arts and fragments " as best we
may.   And they *dare* to tell us this of him, and
men believe it, and to this hour his bones are
canonized, to this hour his tomb is a shrine, where
the genius of the cool, sagacious, clear-thoughted
Northern Isle is worshipped, under the form of a
mad, unconscious, intellectual possession — a do-
tard inspiration, incapable of its own designs, want-

ing in the essential attribute of all mental power — self-cognition.

And yet, who would be willing to spare, now, one point in that time-honored, incongruous whole? Who would be willing to dispense with the least of those contradictions, which have become, in the progressive development of our appreciation of these works, so inextricably knit together, and thereby inwrought, as it were, into our inmost life? Who can, in fact, fairly convince himself, now, that deer-stealing and link-holding, and the name of an obscure family in Stratford — common enough there, though it means what it does to us — and bad, or indifferent performances, at a Surrey theatre, are not really, after all, essential preliminaries and concomitants to the composition of a " Romeo and Juliet," or a " Midsummer Night's Dream," or a " Twelfth Night "? And what Shakespeare critic, at least, could persuade himself, now, that any other motive than the purchase of the Globe theatre, and that capital messuage or tenement in Stratford, called the New Place, with the appurtenances thereof, and the lands adjoining, and the house in Henley Street, could by any possibility have originated such works as these?

And what fool would undertake to prove, now, that the fact of the deer-stealing, or any other point in the traditionary statement, may admit of question? Certainly, if we are to have an historical or traditionary Shakespeare of any kind, out

of our present materials, it becomes us to protest,
with the utmost severity, against the least meddling therewith. If they are not sufficiently mea-
gre already — if the two or three historical points
we have, or seem to have, and the miserable scraps
and fragments of gossip which the painful explo-
rations of two centuries have, at length, succeeded
in rescuing from the oblivion to which this man's
time consigned him[1] — if these points are to be encroached upon, and impaired by criticism, we may
as well throw up the question altogether.   In the
name of all that is tangible, leave us what there
is of affirmation here.   Surely we have negations
enough already.   If he did not steal the deer, will
you tell us what one mortal thing he did do ?   He
wrote the plays.   But, did the man who wrote the
plays do nothing else ?   Are there not some foregone conclusions in them ? — some intimations, and
round ones, too, that he who wrote them, be he
who he may, has had experiences of some sort ?
Do such things as these, that the plays are full of,
begin in the fingers' ends?   Can you find them
in an ink-horn ?   Can you sharpen them out of a
goose-quill ?   Has your Shakespeare wit and invention enough for that ?

But the man was a player, and the manager of
a play-house, and these are plays that he writes.

---

[1] Constituting, when well put together, precisely that historic trail
which an old, defunct, indifferent, fourth-rate play-actor naturally
leaves behind him, for the benefit of any antiquary who may find
occasion to conduct an exploration for it.

And what kind of play is it that you find in them — and what is the theatre — and who are the actors? Has this man's life been all *play?* Has there been no earnest in it? — no acting in his own name? Had *he* no part of his own in time, then? Has he dealt evermore with second-hand reports, unreal shadows, and mockeries of things? Has there been no personal grapple with realities, here? Ah, let him have that one living opposite. Leave him that single shot "heard round the world." Did not Æschylus fight at Salamis? Did not Scipio teach Terence how to marshal his men and wing his words? (A contemporary and confidant of Shakespeare's thinks, from internal evidence, that the patron wrote the plays, in this case, altogether.) And was not Socrates as brave at Potidœa and Delium as he was in the market-place; and did not Cæsar, the author, kill his millions? But this giant wrestler and warrior of ours, with the essence of all the battles of all ages in his nerves — with the blood of a new Adam bubbling in his veins — he cannot be permitted to leap out of those everlasting buskins of his, long enough to have a brush with this one live deer, but the critics must have out their spectacles, and be down upon him with their objections.

And what honest man would want a Shakespeare at this hour of the day that was not written by that same irregular, lawless, wild, reckless, facetious, law-despising, art-despising genius of a

" Will" that did steal the deer? Is not this the Shakespeare we have had on our shelves with our bibles and prayer-books, since our great-grandsires' times? The next step will be to call in question Moses in the bulrushes, and Pharaoh's daughter.

And what is to become, too, under this supposition, of that exquisite specimen of the player's merciless wit, and "facetious grace in writing," which attracted the attention of his contemporaries, and left such keen impressions on the minds of his fellow-townsmen? What is to become, in this case, of the famous lampoon on Sir Thomas Lucy, nailed up on the park gate, rivaling in Shakespearean grace and sharpness another Attic morceau from the same source — the impromptu on " John-a-Combe"? These remains of the poet, which we find accredited to him in his native village, " with likelihood of truth enough," among those who best knew him, have certainly cost the commentators too much trouble to be lightly relinquished; and, unquestionably, they do bear on the face of them most unmistakable symptoms of the player's wit and the Stratford origin.

No! no! We cannot spare the deer-stealing. As the case now stands, this one, rich, sparkling point in the tradition can by no means be dispensed with. Take this away, and what becomes of our traditional Shakespeare? He goes! The whole fabric tumbles to pieces, or settles at once into a hopeless stolidity. But for the mercurial

lightning, which this youthful reminiscence im-
parts to him — this single indication of a sup-
pressed tendency to an heroic life — how could
that heavy, retired country gentleman, late manager of the Globe and the Blackfriars theatres, be
made to float at any convenient distance above the
earth, in the laboring conceptions of the artists
whose business it is to present his apotheosis to
us? Enlarge the vacant platitudes of that forehead as you will; pile up the artificial brains in
the frontispiece to any height which the credulity
of an awe-struck public will hesitate to pronounce
idiotic; huddle the allegorical shapes about him as
thickly as you will; and yet, but for the twinkle
which this single reminiscence leaves, this one solitary " proof of liberty," " the flash and outbreak
of a fiery mind of general assault," how could the
old player and showman be made to sit the bird of
Jove, so comfortably as he does, on his way to the
waiting Olympus?

But, after all, it is not this old actor of Elizabeth's time who exhibited these plays at his theatre in the way of his trade, and cared for them
precisely as a tradesman would; cared for them as
he would have cared for tin kettles, or earthen
pans and pots, if they had been in his line, instead; it is not this old tradesman; it is not this
old showman and hawker of plays; it is not this
old lackey, whose hand is on all our heart-strings,
whose name is, of mortal names, the most awe-
inspiring.

The Shakespeare of Elizabeth and James, who exhibited at his theatre as plays, among many others surpassing them in immediate theatrical success, the wonderful works which bore his name — works which were only half printed, and that surreptitiously, and in detached portions during his lifetime, which, seven years after his death, were first collected and published by authority in his name, accompanied, according to the custom of the day, with eulogistic verses from surviving brother poets — this yet living theatrical Shakespeare is a very different one from the Shakespeare of our modern criticism ; — the Shakespeare brought out, at length, by more than two centuries of readings and the best scholarly investigation of modern times, from between the two lids of that wondrous folio.

The faintly limned outlines of the nucleus which that name once included are all gone long ago, dissolved in the splendors, dilated into the infinities which this modern Shakespeare dwells in. It is Shakespeare the author that we now know only, the author of these worlds of profoundest art, these thought-crowded worlds, which modern reading discovers in these printed plays of his. It is the posthumous Shakespeare of the posthumous volume that we now know only. No, not even that; it is only the work itself that we now know by that name — the phenomenon and not its beginning. For, with each new study of the printed page, further and further behind it, deeper and deeper into regions where no man so much as undertakes to follow it, retreats the power, which is for us all already, as truly as if we had confessed it to ourselves, the unknown, the unnamed.

What does this old player's name, in fact, stand for with us now? Inwrought not into all our literature merely, but into all the life of our modern time, his unlearned utterances our deepest lore, which " we are toiling all our lives to find," his mystic page, the page where each one sees his own life inscribed, point by point, deepening and deepening with each new experience from the cradle to the grave; what is he to us now? Is he the teacher of our players only? What theatres hold now his school? What actors' names stand now enrolled in its illustrious lists? Do not all our modern works incorporate his lore into their essence, are they not glittering on their surface everywhere, with ever new, unmissed jewels from his mines? Which of our statesmen, our heroes, our divines, our poets, our philosophers, has not learned of him; and in which of all their divergent and multiplying pursuits and experiences do they fail to find him still with them, still before them?

The name which has stood to us from the beginning, for all this — which has been inwrought into it, which concentrates it in its unity — cannot now be touched. It has lost its original significance.

It means this, and this only to us. It has drunk in the essence of all this power, and light, and beauty, and identified itself with it. Never, perhaps, can it well mean anything else to us.

You cannot christen a world anew, though the name that was given to it at the font prove an usurper's. With all that we now know of that heroic scholar, from whose scientific dream the New World was made to emerge at last, in the face of the mockeries of his time, with all that appreciation of his work which the Old World and the New alike bestow upon it, we cannot yet separate the name of his rival from his hard-earned triumph. What name is it that has drunk into its melody, forever, all the music of that hope and promise, which the young continent of Columbus still whispers — in spite of old European evils planted there — still whispers in the troubled earth ? Whose name is it that stretches its golden letters now, from ocean to ocean, from Arctic to Antarctic, whose name now enrings the millions that are born, and live, and die, knowing no world but the world of that patient scholar's dream — no reality but the reality of his chimera ?

What matters it ? Who cares ? " What 's in a name ? " Is there any voice from that hero's own tomb to rebuke this wrong ? No. He did not toil, and struggle, and suffer, and keep his manly heart from breaking, to the end that those millions might be called by *his* name. Ah, little know they, who thus judge of works like his, what roots such growths must spread, what broad, sweet currents they must reach and drink from. If the millions are blessed there, if, through the heat and burden of his weary day, man shall at length attain, though only after many an erring experience and fierce rebuke, in that new world, to some height of learning, to some scientific place of peace and rest, where worlds are in harmony, and men are as one, he will say, in God's name, Amen! For, on the heights of endurance and self-renunciation, where the divine is possible with men, we have one name.

What have we to do with this poor peasant's name, then, so hallowed in all our hearts, now, with household memories, that we should seek to tear it from the countless fastenings which time has given it? This name, chosen at least of fortune, if not of nature, for the place it occupies, dignified with all that she can lend it, — illustrious with her most lavish favoritism, — has she not chosen to encircle it with honors which make poor those that she saves for her kings and heroes? Let it stand, then, and not by grace of fortune only, but by consent of one who could afford to leave it such a legacy. For he was one whom giving did not impoverish ; he had wealth enough of his own and to spare, and honors that he could not part with.

"Once," but in no poet's garb, once, through

the thickest of this " working - day world," he
trod for himself, with bleeding feet, " the ways
of glory" here, " and sounded all the depths and
shoals of honor," and, from the wrecks of lost
" ambition," found to the last " the way to rise
in " : —

> " By that sin fell the angels; how can man, then,
> The image of his Maker, hope to win by 't ?
> Love thyself last : cherish those hearts that hate thee ;
> Still in thy right hand carry gentle peace,
> To silence envious tongues.   Be just, and fear not :
> Let all the ends thou aim'st at, be thy country's,
> Thy God's and truth's ; then, if thou fall'st, thou fall'st
> A blessed martyr ! "

Let the name stand, then, where the poet has
himself left it. If he — if he himself did not
scruple to forego his fairest honors, and leave his
immortality in a peasant's weed ; if he himself
could consent to bind his own princely brows in it,
though it might be for ages, why e'en let him
wear it, then, as his own proudest honor. To all
time let the philosophy be preached in it, which
found " in a name " the heroic height whence its
one great tenet could be uttered with such an emphasis, philosophy — " not harsh and crabbed as
dull fools suppose, but musical as is Apollo's lute,"
roaming here at last in worlds of her own shaping ;
more rich and varied, and more intense than nature's own ; where all things " echo the name of
Prospero " ; where, " beside the groves, the foun-
tains, every region near seems all one mutual

cry "; where even young love's own younges
melodies, from moon-lit balconies, warble its argu
ment. Let it stand, then. Leave to it its strang
honors — its unbought immortality. Let it stanc
at least, till all those who have eaten in their yout
of the magic tables spread in it, shall have died i
the wilderness. Let it stand while it will, only le
its true significance be recognized.

For, the falsity involved in it, as it now stand
has become too gross to be endured any furthe
The common sense cannot any longer receive
without self-abnegation ; and the relations of th
question, on all sides, are now too grave and m
mentous to admit of any further postponemer
of it.

In judging of this question, we must take int
account the fact that, at the time when the
works were issued, all those characteristic organ
zations of the modern ages, for the diffusion of in
tellectual and moral influences, which now ever
where cross and recross with electric fibre th
hitherto impassable social barriers, were as ye
unimagined. The inventions and institutions, i
which these had their origin, were then but begin
ning their work. To-day, there is no scholast
seclusion so profound that the allied voice and a
tion of this mighty living age may not perpeti
ally penetrate it. To-day, the work-shop has b
come *clairvoyant.* The plough and the loom are i
magnetic communication with the loftiest soci

centres. The last results of the most exquisite culture of the world, in all its departments, are within reach of the lowest haunt, where latent genius and refinement await their summons; and there is no "smallest scruple of nature's excellence" that may not be searched out and kindled. The Englishman who but reads "The Times," to-day, puts himself into a connection with his age, and attains thereby a means of enlargement of character and elevation of thought and aims, which in the age of Elizabeth was only possible to men occupying the highest official and social position.

It is necessary, too, to remember that the question here is not a question of lyric inspiration, merely; neither is it a question of dramatic genius, merely. Why, even the poor player, that Hamlet quotes so admiringly, "but in a dream of passion," his soul rapt and subdued with images of tenderness and beauty, "tears in his eyes, the color in his cheeks," even he, with his fine sensibilities, his rhythmical ear, with his living conceits, if nature has but done her part towards it, may compose you a lyric that you would bind up with "Highland Mary," or "Sir Patrick Spens," for immortality. And even this poor tinker, profane and wicked as he is, and coarse and unfurnished for the poet's mission as he seems, when once the infinities of religion, with their divine ideals, shall penetrate to the deep, sweet sources of his yet

undreamed of genius, and arous‹
in him, with their terrific struggl
umphs, even he, from the coar
rials which his external experie
him, shall be able to compose a d
mortal vigor and freshness, whe
hear the rushing of wings — the
spheres — in their life's battle;
shall be able to catch voices anc
this shore. But the question is n
yan or a Burns. And it is not ɛ
we have in hand here. The
whether nature shall be able t
without putting into requisition
strumentalities of the ages. It
ferent in kind; how different, in
of our appreciation of the work
cannot be made manifest.

It is impossible, indeed, to pre
to the case in question. For if v
actor, or the manager of a thea
unlearned except by the acciden
begin now to issue out of his bra
his trade, wholly bent on that,
ferent to any other result, and ur
other, a body of literature, so hig
that we now possess, in any or in
so far exhausting the excellency
stitute, by universal consent, *the*
time; comprehending its entire s‹

ubtlest analysis; pronouncing everywhere its final
vord, — even such a supposition would not begin
o meet the absurdity of the case in question.

If the prince of showmen in our day, in that
tately oriental retreat of his in Connecticut, ri-
aling even the New Place at Stratford in literary
onveniences, should begin now to conceive of
omething of this sort, as his crowning specula-
ion, and should determine to undertake its execu-
ion in person, who would dare to question his
ibility?[1]   Certainly no one would have any right
o criticise, now, the motive conceded, or to put
n suspicion its efficiency for the proposed result.
Vhy, this man could not conduct his business a
lay, he could not even hunt through the journals
or his own puffs and advertisements, without com-
ng by accident in contact with means of moral
ind intellectual enlargement and stimulus, which
ould never have found their way, in any form, to
Elizabeth's player.   The railway, the magnetic
elegraph, the steamship, the steam-press with its
ournals, its magazines, its reviews, and its cheap
iterature of all kinds, the public library, the book-
lub, the popular lecture, the lyceum, the volun-
ary association of every kind — these are all but
ι part of that magnificent apparatus and means
of culture which society is now putting in requisi-

[1] It should be stated, perhaps, that the above was written two or
hree years since, and that no reference to Mr. Barnum's recent ad-
lition to the literature of the age was intended.

tion in that great school of hers, wherein the ur
versal man, rescued from infinite self-degradation
is now at last beginning his culture.   And yet a
these social instrumentalities combined cannc
even now, so supply the deficiencies in the ca
supposed as to make the supposition any oth
than a violent one, to say the least of it.

The material which nature must have contri
uted to the Shakespearean result could, indee
hardly have remained inert, under any superi
cumbent weight of social disadvantages.   But tl
very first indication of its presence, under su
conditions, would have been a struggle with tho
disadvantages.   First of all, it would force i
way upward, through them, to its natural el
ment; first of all, it would make its way into tl
light, and possess itself of all its weapons — n
spend itself in mad movements in the dark, wit
out them.   Look over the history of all the knov
English poets and authors of every kind, ba
even to the days of the Anglo-Saxon Adhelm, ai
Cædmon, and, no matter how humble the positic
in which they are born, how many will you fii
among them that have failed to possess themselv
ultimately of the highest literary culture of tl
age they lived in ?   How many, until you come
this same Shakespeare ?

Well, then, if the Genius of the British Isle tur
us out such men as those from her universitie
but when she would make her Shakespeare retre

into a green-room, and send him forth from that, furnished as we find him, pull down, we say, pull down those gray old towers, for the wisdom of the Great Alfred has been laughed to scorn; undo his illustrious monument to its last Anglo-Saxon stone, and, "by our lady, build — theatres!" If not Juliet only, but her author, and Hamlet's author, too, and Lear's, and Macbeth's can be made without "philosophy," we are for Romeo's verdict, "Hang up philosophy." If such works as these, and Julius Cæsar, and Coriolanus, and Antony, and Henry V, and Henry VIII, — if the "Midsummer Night's Dream," and the "Merchant of Venice," and the "Twelfth Night," — if Beatrice, and Benedict, and Rosalind, and Jaques, and Iago, and Othello, and all their immortal company, — if these works, and all that we find in them, can be got out of "Plutarch's Lives," and "Holinshed," and a few old ballads and novels, — in the name of all that is honest, give us these, and let us go about our business; and henceforth let him that can be convicted "of traitorously corrupting the youth of this realm, by erecting a grammar-school," be consigned to his victims for mercy. "Long live Lord Mortimer!" "Down with the paper-mills!" "Throw learning to the dogs! we'll none of it!"

But we are not, as yet, in a position to estimate the graver bearings of this question. For the reverence which the common theory has hitherto claimed from us, as a well authenticated historical fact, depending apparently, indeed, on the most unimpeachable external evidence for its support, has operated, as it was intended to operate in the first instance, to prevent all that kind of reading and study of the plays which would have made its gross absurdity apparent. In accordance with this original intention, to this hour it has constituted a barrier to the understanding of their true meaning, which no industry or perseverance could surmount; to this hour it has served to prevent, apparently, so much as a suspicion of their true source, and ultimate intention.

But let this theory, and the pre-judgment it involves, be set aside, even by an hypothesis, only long enough to permit us once to see, for ourselves, what these works do in fact contain, and no amount of historical evidence which can be produced, no art, no argument, will suffice to restore it to its present position. But it is not as an hypothesis, it is not as a theory, that the truth here indicated will be developed hereafter. It will come on other grounds. It will ask no favors.

Condemned to refer the origin of these works to the vulgar, illiterate man who kept the theatre where they were first exhibited, a person of the most ordinary character and aims, compelled to regard them as the result merely of an extraordinary talent for pecuniary speculation in this man, how could we, how could any one, dare to see what is really in them? With this theory overhanging them, though we threw our most artistic lights upon it, and kept it out of sight when we could, what painful contradictory mental states, what unacknowledged internal misgivings were yet involved in our best judgments of them? How many passages were we compelled to read " trippingly," with the " mind's eye," as the players were first taught to pronounce them on the tongue ; and if, in spite of all our slurring, the inner depths would open to us, if anything which this theory could not account for, would notwithstanding obtrude itself upon us, we endeavored to believe that it must be the reflection of our own better learning, and so, half lying to ourselves, making a wretched compromise with our own mental integrity, we still hurried on.

Condemned to look for the author of Hamlet himself — the subtle Hamlet of the university, the courtly Hamlet, " the glass of fashion and the mould of form " — in that dirty, doggish group of players, who come into the scene summoned like a pack of hounds to his service, the very tone of his courtesy to them, with its princely condescension, with its arduous familiarity, only serving to make the great, impassable social gulf between them the more evident, — compelled to look in that ignominious group, with its faithful portraiture of the players of that time (taken from the life by one who had had dealings with them), for the princely

scholar himself in his author, how could we understand him — the enigmatical Hamlet, with the
thought of ages in his foregone conclusions?

With such an origin, how could we see the subtlest skill of the university, not in Hamlet and Ho-
ratio only, but in the work itself, incorporated in
its essence, pervading its execution? With such
an origin as this, how was it possible to note, not
in this play only, but in all the Shakespeare drama,
what otherwise we could not have failed to observe, the tone of the highest Elizabethan breeding, the very loftiest tone of that peculiar courtly
culture, which was then, and but *just* then, attain-
ing its height, in the competitions among men of
the highest social rank, and among the most brilliant wits and men of genius of the age, for the
favor of the learned, accomplished, sagacious, wit-
loving maiden queen; — a culture which required
not the best acquisitions of the university merely,
but acquaintance with life, practical knowledge of
affairs, foreign travel and accomplishments, and,
above all, the last refinements of the highest Pa-
risian breeding. For "your courtier" must be, in
fact, "your picked man of countries." He must,
indeed, "get his behavior everywhere." He must
be, in fact and literally, the man of "the world."

But for this prepossession, in that daring treatment of court-life which this single play of Hamlet involves, in the entire freedom with which its
conventionalities are handled, how could we have

failed to recognize the touch of one habitually practiced in its refinements? How could we have failed to recognize, not in this play only, but in all these plays, the poet whose habits and perceptions have been moulded in the atmosphere of these subtle social influences? He cannot shake off this influence when he will. He carries the court perfume with him, unconsciously, wherever he goes, among mobs of artisans that will not "keep their teeth clean"; into the ranks of "greasy citizens" and "rude mechanicals"; into country feasts and merry-makings; among "pretty low-born lasses," "the queens of curds and cheese," and into the heart of that forest, "where there is no clock." He looks into Arden and into Eastcheap from the court standpoint, not from these into the court, and he is as much a prince with Poins and Bardolph as he is when he enters and throws open to us, without awe, without consciousness, the most delicate mysteries of the royal presence.

Compelled to refer the origin of these works to the sordid play-house, who could teach us to distinguish between the ranting, unnatural stuff and bombast which its genuine competitions elicited, in their mercenary appeals to the passions of their audience, ministering to the most vicious tastes, depraving the public conscience, and lowering the common standard of decency, getting up "scenes to tear a cat in," — "out-Heroding Herod," and going regularly into professional fits about Hecuba and Priam and other Trojans, — who could teach us to distinguish between the tone of this original, genuine, play-house fustian, and that of the "dozen or sixteen lines" which Hamlet will at first, for some earnest purpose of his own, with the consent and privity of *one* of the players, cause to be inserted in it? Nay, thus blinded, we shall not, perhaps, be able to distinguish from this foundation that magnificent whole with which, from such beginnings, this author will, perhaps, ultimately replace his worthless originals altogether; that whole in which we shall see, one day, not the burning Ilium, not the old Danish court of the tenth century, but the yet living, illustrious Elizabethan age, with all its momentous interests still at stake, with its yet palpitating hopes and fears, with its newborn energies, bound but unconquerable, already heaving, and muttering through all their undertone; that magnificent whole, where we shall see, one day, "the very abstract and brief chronicle of the time," the "very body of the age, its form and pressure," under any costume of time and country, or under the drapery of any fiction, however absurd or monstrous, which this author shall find already popularized to his hands, and available for his purposes. Hard, indeed, was the time, ill bestead was the spirit of the immemorial English freedom, when the genius of works such as these was compelled to stoop to such a scene to find its instruments.

How could we understand from such a source, while that wretched player was still crying it for his own worthless ends, this majestic exhibition of our common human life from the highest intellectual and social standpoint of that wondrous age, letting in, on all the fripperies and affectations, the arrogance and pretension of that illustrious centre of social life, the new philosophic beam, and sealing up in it, for all time, "all the uses and customs" of the world that then was? Arrested with that transparent petrifaction, in all the rushing life of the moment, and set, henceforth, on the table of philosophic halls for scientific illustration; its gaudy butterflies impaled upon the wing, in their perpetual gold; its microscopic insects, "spacious in the possession of land and dirt," transfixed in all the swell and flutter of the moment; its fantastic apes, unrobed for inextinguishable mortal laughter and celestial tears, still playing, all unconsciously, their solemn pageants through; how could the showman explain all this to us — how could the player tell us what it meant?

How could the player's mercenary motive and the player's range of learning and experiment give us the key to this new application of the human reason to the human life, from the new vantage-ground of thought, but just then rescued from the past, and built up painfully from all its wreck? How could we understand, from such a source, this new, and strange, and persevering application of thought to life, not merely to society and to her laws, but to nature, too; pursuing her to her last retreats, and holding everywhere its mirror up to her, reflecting the whole boundary of her limitations; laying bare, in its cold, clear, pure depths, in all their unpolite, undraped scientific reality, the actualities which society, as it is, can only veil, and the evils which society, as it is, can only hide and palliate?

In vain the shrieking queen remonstrates, for it is the impersonated reason whose clutch is on her, and it says, you go not hence till you have seen the inmost part of you. But does all this tell on the thousand pounds? Is the ghost's word good for that?

No wonder that Hamlet refused to speak, or to be commanded to any utterance of harmony, let the critics listen and entreat as they would, while this illiterate performer, who knew no touch of all that divine music of his, from its lowest note to the top of his key, was still sounding him and fretting him. We shall take another key and another interpreter with us when we begin to understand a work which comprehends in its design all our human aims and activities, and tracks them to their beginnings and ends; which demands the ultimate, scientific perpetual reason in all our life — a work which dares to defer the punishment of the crime that society visits with her most dreaded penalties, till all the principles of the human ac-

tivity have been collected; till all the human conditions have been explored; till the only universal
rational human principle is found — a work which
dares to defer the punishment of the crime that
society condemns, till its principle has been tracked
through the crime which she tolerates; through
the crime which she sanctions; through the crime
which she crowns with all her honors.

We are, indeed, by no means insensible to the
difference between this Shakespeare drama, and
that on which it is based, and that which surrounds
it. We do, indeed, already pronounce that difference, and not faintly, in our word *Shakespeare ;* for
that is what the word now means with us, though
we received it with no such significance. Its historical development is but the next step in our
progress.

Yes, there were men in England then, who had
heard somewhat of those masters of the olden
time, hight Æschylus and Sophocles — men who
had heard of Euripides too, and next, Aristopha-
nes — men who had heard of Terence, and not of
Terence only, but of his patrons — men who had
heard of Plato, too, and of his master. There
were men in England, in those days, who knew
well enough what kind of an instrumentality the
drama had been in its original institution, and with
what voices it had then spoken; who knew, also,
its permanent relations to the popular mind, and
its capability for adaptation to new social exigen-

cies; men, quick enough to perceive, and ready
enough to appreciate to the utmost, the facilities
which this great organ of the wisdom of antiquity
offered for effectual communication between the
loftiest mind, at the height of its culture, and that
mind of the world in which this, impelled by no
law of its own ordaining, seeks ever its own self-
completion and perpetuity.

And where had this mighty instrument of popular sway, this mechanism for moving and mould-
ing the multitude, its first origin, but among men
initiated in the profoundest religious and philosophic mysteries of their time, among men exer-
cised in the control and administration of public
affairs; men clothed even with imperial sway, the
joint administrators of the government of Athens,
when Athens sat on the summit of her power, the
crowned mistress of the seas, the imperial ruler of
" a thousand cities."

Yes, Theseus, and Solon, and Cleisthenes, and
Pythagoras, must be its antecedents there ; it
could not be produced there, till all Athena had
been for ages in Athens, till Athena had been for
ages in all: till three centuries of Olympiads had
poured the Grecian life-blood through it, from By-
zantium to Sicily ; it could not be produced there,
till the life of the state was in each true Athenian
nerve, till each true Athenian's nerve was in the
growing state ; it could not begin to be produced
there, till new religious inspirations from the east

had reached, with their foreign stimulus, the deeper sources of the national life, till the secret philosophic tenet of the inner temple had overflowed, with new gold, the ancient myth, and kindled with new fires the hearts of the nation's leaders. The gay summits of Homer's "ever-young" Olympus must be reached and overlaid anew from the earth's central mysteries; the Dionysian procession must enter the temple; the road to it must cross Ægaleos; the Pnyx must empty its benches into it; Piræus must crowd its strangers' seat with her many costumes, before Æschylus or Sophocles could find an audience to command all their genius. Nay, Zeno and Anaxagoras must send their pupils thither, and Socrates must come in, and the most illustrious scholars of the Olympian cities, from Abdera to Leontium, must be found there, before all the latent resources of the Grecian drama could be unfolded.

And there were men in England, in the age of Elizabeth, who had mastered the Greek and Roman history, and not only that, but the history of their own institutions — men who knew precisely what kind of crisis in human history that was which they were born to occupy. And they had seen the indigenous English drama struggling up, through the earnest, but childish, exhibitions of the cathedral — through "Miracles," and "Mysteries," and "Moralities," to be arrested, in its yet undeveloped vigor, with the unfit and unyielding

forms of the finished Grecian art; and when, too, by the combined effect of institutions otherwise at variance, all that had, till then, made its life, was suddenly abstracted from it. The royal ordinances which excluded it, henceforth, from all that vital range of topics which the censorship of a capricious and timorous despotism might include among the interdicted questions of church and state, found it already expelled from the religious sanctuaries — in which not the drama only, but all that which we call art, *par excellence*, has its birth and nurture. And that was the crisis in which the pulpit began to open its new drain upon it, having only a vicious play-house, where once the indefinite priestly authority had summoned all the soul to its spectacles, and the long-drawn aisle, and fretted vault, had lent to them their sheltering sanctities; where once, as of old, the Athenian temple had pressed its scene into the heart of the Athenian hill — the holy hill — and opened its subterranean communication with Eleusis, while its centre was the altar on which the gods themselves threw incense.

And yet, there was a moment in the history of the national genius, when, roused to its utmost — stimulated to its best capability of ingenuity and invention — it found itself constrained to stoop at its height, even to the threshold of this same degraded play-house. There were men in England, who knew what latent capacities that debased instrument of genius yet contained within it — who knew that in the master's hand it might yet be made to yield, even then, and under those conditions, better music than any which those old Greek sons of song had known how to wake in it.

These men knew well enough the proper relation between the essence of the drama and its form. " Considering poetry in respect to the verse, and not to the argument," says one, " though men in learned languages may tie themselves to ancient measures; yet, in modern languages, it seems to me as free to make new measures as to make new dances; and, in these things, the sense is a better judge than the art." Surely, a Schlegel himself could not give us a truer Shakespearean rule than that. Indeed, if we can but catch them when the wind is south-southwest — these grave and oracular Elizabethan wits — we shall find them putting two and two together, now and then, and drawing inferences, and making distinctions which would have much surprised their " uncle-fathers " and " aunt-mothers " at the time, if they had but noted them. But, as they themselves tell us, " in regard to the rawness and unskillfulness of the hands through which they pass, the greatest matters are sometimes carried in the weakest ciphers." Even over their own names, and in those learned tongues of theirs, if we can but once find their stops, and the skill to command them to any utterance of harmony, they will discourse to us, in spite of the disjointed times, the most eloquent music.

For, although they had, indeed, the happiness
to pursue their studies under the direct personal
supervision of those two matchless scholars, "Eliza
and our James," whose influence in the world of
letters was then so signally felt, they, nevertheless, evidently ventured to dip into antiquity a
little on their own account, and that, apparently,
without feeling called upon to render in a perfectly unambiguous report in full of all that they
found there, for the benefit of their illustrious patrons, to whom, of course, their literary labors are
dedicated. There seemed, indeed, to be no occasion for unpegging the basket on the house's top,
and trying conclusions in any so summary manner.

These men distinctly postpone, not their personal reputation only, but the interpretation of
their avowed works, to freer ages. There were
sparrows abroad then. The tempest was already
"singing in the wind," for an ear fine enough to
catch it; but only invisible Ariels could dare "to
play" then "*on pipe and tabor*" (stage direction).
"Thought is free," but only base Trinculos and
low-born Stephanos could dare to whisper to it.
"That is the tune of our catch, played by the pic-
ture of — Nobody."

Yes, there was one moment in that nation's history, wherein the costume, the fable, the scenic effect, and all the attractive and diverting appliances
and concomitants of the stage, even the degrada-

tion into which it had fallen, its known subser-
viency to the passions of the audience, its habit of
creating a spectacle merely, all combined to furnish to men, in whom the genius of the nation had
attained its highest form, freer instrumentalities
than the book, the pamphlet, the public document,
the parliament, or the pulpit, when all alike were
subject to an oppressive and despotic censorship,
when all alike were forbidden to meddle with their
own proper questions, when cruel maimings and
tortures old and new, life-long imprisonment, and
death itself, awaited, not a violation of these re-
strictions merely, but a suspicion of an intention,
or even wish, to violate them — penalties which
England's noblest men suffered, on suspicion only.

There was one moment in that history, in which
the ancient drama had, in new forms, its old
power ; when, stamped and blazoned on its surface
everywhere with the badges of servitude, it had
yet leaping within the indomitable heart of its ancient freedom, the spirit of the immemorial European liberties, which Magna Charta had only recognized, and more than that, the freedom of the
new ages that were then beginning, "the freedom
of the chainless mind." There was one moment
in which all the elements of the national genius,
that are now separated and incorporated in institutions as wide apart, at least, as earth and heaven,
were held together, and that in their first vigor,
pressed from without into their old Greek conjunc-

tion. That moment there was; it is chronicled;
we have one word for it; we call it—Shakespeare!

Has the time come at last, or has it not yet
come, in which this message of the new time can
be laid open to us? This message from the lips of
one endowed so wondrously, with skill to utter it;
endowed, not with the speaker's melodious tones
and subduing harmonies only, but with the teacher's divinely glowing heart, with the ambition that
seeks its own in all, with the love that is sweeter
than the tongues of men and angels. Are we, or
are we not, his legatees? Surely this new summing up of all the real questions of our common
life, from such an elevation in it, this new philosophy of all men's business and desires, cannot be
without its perpetual vital uses. For, in all the
points on which the demonstration rests, these dia-
grams from the dissolving views of the past are
still included in the problems of the present.

And if, in this new and more earnest research
into the true ends and meanings of this greatest
of our teachers, the poor player who was willing
enough to assume the responsibility of these works,
while they were still plays — theatrical exhibitions
only, and quite in his line for the time; who might,
indeed, be glad enough to do it for the sake of the
princely patronage that henceforth encompassed his
fortunes, even to the granting of a thousand pounds
at a time, if that were needed to complete his
purchase — if this good man, sufficiently perplexed

already with the developments which the modern criticism has by degrees already laid at his door, does here positively refuse to go any further with us on this road, why e'en let us shake hands with him and part, he as his business and desire shall point him; "for every man hath business and desire such as it is," and not without a grateful recollection of the good service he has rendered us.

The publisher of these plays let his name go down still and to all posterity on the cover of it. They *were* his plays. He brought them out — he and his firm. They took the scholar's text, that dull black and white, that mere ink and paper, and made of it a living, speaking, many-colored, glittering reality, which even the groundlings of that time could appreciate, in some sort. What was Hamlet to them, without his "inky cloak" and his "forest of feathers" and his "razed shoes" and "the roses" on them? And they came out of this man's bag — he was the owner of the "wardrobe" and of the other "stage properties." He was the owner of the manuscripts; and if he came honestly by them, whose business was it to inquire any further, then? If there was no one who chose, just then, to claim the authorship of them, whose else should they be? Was not the actor himself a poet, and a very facetious one, too? Witness the remains of him, the incontestable poetical remains of him, which have come down to us. What if his ill-natured contemporaries, whose poetic glories he was eclipsing forever with those new plays of his, did assail him on his weak points, and call him, in the face of his time, " a *Johannes Factotum*," and held up to public ridicule his particular style of acting, plainly intimating that it was chargeable with that very fault which the prince of Denmark directs his tragedians to omit — did not the blundering editor of that piece of offensive criticism get a decisive hint from some quarter, that he might better have withheld it; and was it not humbly retracted and hushed up directly? Some of the earlier anonymous plays, which were included in the collection published, after this player's decease, as the plays of William Shakespeare, are, indeed, known to have been produced anonymously at other theatres, and by companies with which this actor had never any connection; but the poet's company and the player's were, as it seems, two different things; and that is a fact which the criticism and history of these plays, as it stands at present, already exhibits. Several of the plays which form the nucleus of the Shakespeare drama had already been brought out, before the Stratford actor was yet in a position to assume that relation to it which proved so advantageous to his fortunes. Such a nucleus of the Shakespeare drama there was already, when the name which this actor bore, with such orthographical variations as the purpose required, began to be assumed as the name and device of that new sovereignty of genius which was then first rising and kindling behind its cloud, and dimming and overflowing with its greater glory all the less, and gilding all it shone on. The machinery of these theatrical establishments offered, indeed, the most natural and effective, as well as, at that time, on other accounts, the most convenient mode of exhibition for that particular class of subjects which the genius of this particular poet naturally inclined him to meddle with. He had the most profoundly philosophical reasons for preferring that mode of exhibiting his poems, as will be seen hereafter.

And, when we have once learned to recognize the actor's true relations to the works which have given to his name its anomalous significance, we shall be prepared, perhaps, to accept, at last, this great offer of aid in our readings of these works, which has been lying here now two hundred and thirty years, unnoticed; then, and not till then, we shall be able to avail ourselves, at last, of the aid of those "friends of his," to whom, two hundred and thirty years ago, "knowing that his wit could no more lie hid than it could be lost," the editors of the first printed collection of these works venture to refer us; "those other friends of his, whom *if we need*, can be our *guides;* and, *if we need them not*, we are able to lead ourselves and others, and such readers they wish him."

If we had accepted either of these two conditions — if we had found ourselves with those who

need this offered guidance, or with those who need
it not — if we had but gone far enough in our
readings of these works to feel the want of that
aid, from exterior sources, which is here proffered
us — there would not have been presented to the
world, at this hour, the spectacle — the stupendous spectacle — of a nation referring the origin of
its drama — a drama more noble, and learned, and
subtle than the Greek — to the invention — the
accidental, unconscious invention — of a stupid,
ignorant, illiterate, third-rate play-actor.

If we had, indeed, but applied to these works
the commonest rules of historical investigation and
criticism, we might, ere this, have been led to inquire, on our own account, whether " this player
here," who brought them out, might not possibly,
in an age like that, like the player in Hamlet, have
had some friend, or "friends," who could, " an' if
they would," or " an' if they might," explain his
miracle to us, and the secret of his " poor cell."

If we had accepted this suggestion, the true
Shakespeare would not have been now to seek.
In the circle of that patronage with which this
player's fortunes brought him in contact, in that
illustrious company of wits and poets, we need not
have been at a loss to find the philosopher who
writes, in his prose as well, and over his own name
also,

> " In Nature's *Infinite Book of Secrecy,*
> A little I can read ; " —

we should have found one, at least, furnished for that last and ripest proof of learning which the drama, in the unmiraculous order of the human development, must constitute ; that proof of it in which philosophy returns from history, from its noblest fields, and from her last analysis, with the secret and material of the creative synthesis — with the secret and material of art. With this direction, we should have been able to identify, ere this, the Philosopher who is only the Poet in disguise — the Philosopher who calls himself the New Magician — the Poet who was toiling and plotting to fill the Globe with his Arts, and to make our common, every-day human life poetical — who would have *all* our life, and not a part of it, learned, artistic, beautiful, religious.

We should have found, ere this, *one*, with learning broad enough, and deep enough, and subtle enough, and comprehensive enough, one with nobility of aim and philosophic and poetic genius enough, to be able to claim his own, his own immortal progeny — undwarfed, unblinded, undeprived of one ray or dimple of that all-pervading reason that informs them ; one who is able to reclaim them, even now, " cured and perfect of their limbs, and absolute in their numbers, as he conceived them."

XI.

THERE are those who can remember how public attention was startled, thirty-two years ago, by this unquestionably bold and brilliant paper. The success which it made, however, was all that ever befell its author from her presentation of these ideas, either in the way of public approval or of the means of living. Even the publishers' purpose, expressed in their letter to her, and announced to the public, to continue a series of like papers, was destined to fail.

Negotiating from over sea, and through Emerson as an intermediary, she had, without knowing it, fallen into embarrassing complications with different publishers. The Boston house of Phillips, Sampson & Co. had expressly agreed in August to publish the entire book when completed. Dix & Edwards, in New York, had undertaken to print the first paper in their magazine, had asked for more, and had declared their desire to treat for the publication of the whole.

From London, therefore, she now sought to adjust her relations to these two, which had been complicated by the circumstance that the Boston house communicated only with Emerson, and the New York house with the author directly. Writing now on the 20th of December to Dix & Edwards, she expresses much regret that the exposition of her views must proceed so slowly through a monthly periodical, and says moreover : " The first five or six articles, which make the first part of the work (four of which I have now sent), are those which I should least rely on for its acceptance." It is not, therefore, to be wondered at, that they answered her that a reading of her second, third, and fourth articles, received from Mr. Emerson, " convinces us that Mr. Emerson is right as to the publication of the work. It should decidedly appear in a complete book, and not in a magazine." These articles " are so general in their nature, and apparently make so little progress in the demonstration of the main proposition, that if given separately they would weaken rather than increase the interest in the subject. Indeed, after having put the second article in type for our February number, we have withheld it for that reason." " If, however, you could furnish for our magazine some of the more advanced chapters without their being injured by being taken out of their proper connection with the others, it would be not only advantageous to us and you, but serviceable to the reception of the work when it comes to be published." But as for making such publication themselves, since Phillips & Sampson had already proposed for it, they preferred not to interfere, and would write to Emerson accordingly.

This, then, was the end to her of all immediate
hope; and upon hope alone, it seems, had she
been for months sustained. There was of course
still the distant expectation — the certainty rather
— of ample means when once the book itself
should be before the world. But how should that
be managed, when civil declination was the very
best that any publisher had been persuaded to
give? And how, even, should she meanwhile " retain her connection with this planet," which she
cared to do only that the work might be done?
She had even brought herself, as she had written
to her brother might be possible, to " apply to
the American minister." That official was later
in the same year chosen President of the United
States, and was very near to being their last President. A dignified note, signed " James Buchanan," informs her that he will do himself the
pleasure of calling upon her; but she could not
bring herself, when he called, to tell him of her
need. To her old friends in Cambridge, however,
she had now, after years of silence, told the story
of her late experience with an unreserve which
she had found impossible with the cold and grave
stranger who made an official call upon her. Late
in December she wrote to them; and her letter
recrossed the ocean to Mrs. Professor Farrar, at
Pau in the Pyrenees. She seems to have asked
for nothing; nor did she need to; but instant
relief came to her without the asking; and, still

better, evidences of the strong affection which it
had always been her fortune to command. What
she wrote in reply is partly preserved in Mrs. Farrar's " Recollections."

" She lived [at St. Albans] a year, and then
came to London, all alone and unknown, to seek a
home there. She thus describes her search after
lodgings: 'On a dark December day, about one
o'clock, I came into this metropolis, intending,
with the aid of Providence, to select, between that
and nightfall, a residence in it. I had copied
from the " Times " several advertisements of lodg-
ing-houses, but none of them suited me. The cab-
driver, perceiving what I was in search of, began
to make suggestions of his own, and finding that
he was a man equal to the emergency, and knowing that his acquaintance with the subject was
larger than mine, I put the business into his
hands. I told him to stop at the first good house
which he thought would suit me, and he brought
me to this door, where I have been ever since.
Any one who thinks this is not equal to Elijah
and his raven, and Daniel in the lions' den, does
not know what it is for a lady, and a stranger, to
live for a year in London, without any money to
speak of, maintaining all the time the position of a
lady, and a distinguished lady too; and above all,
such a one cannot be acquainted with the nature
of cab-drivers and lodging-house keepers in general. The one with whom I lodge has behaved to

me like an absolute gentleman. No one could have shown more courtesy and delicacy. For six months at a time he has never sent me a bill; before this I had always paid him weekly, and I believe that is customary. When, after waiting six months, I sent him ten pounds, and he knew that it was all I had, he wrote a note to me, which I preserve as a curiosity, to say that he would entirely prefer that I should keep it. I have lived upon this man's confidence in me for a year, and this comparatively pleasant and comfortable home is one that I owe to the judgment and taste of a cab-driver. . . . Your ten pounds was brought me two or three hours after your letter came, and I sent it immediately to Mr. Walker, and now I am entirely relieved of that most painful feeling of the impropriety of depending upon him in this way, which it has required all my faith and philosophy to endure, because he can now very well wait for the rest, and perceive that the postponement is not an indefinite one. Your letter has warmed my heart, and that was what had suffered most. I would have frozen into a Niobe before I would have asked any help for myself, and would sell gingerbread and apples at the corner of a street for the rest of my days before I could stoop, for myself, to such humiliations as I have borne in behalf of my work, which was the world's work, and I knew that I had a right to demand aid for it.' " [1]

[1] Mrs. Farrar's *Recollections of Seventy Years*, pp. 323–325.

XII.

In this extremity of hers she did not seek recourse for help to those of her own flesh and blood in her native country. They were very few; and none of them could have helped her much, from their narrow means, and under their own heavy burdens. Besides, the eldest brother, to whom she had looked as to the head of her family, had given her deep offense by his strong disapproval of the purpose for which she had crossed the ocean. Late in April, therefore, her brother had written to Emerson for news of her, since her relatives were " without any recent intelligence of her."

Between these two men there must have been as utter a want of sympathy as can be imagined in the case of two New Englanders of like age, of like descent and education, of like professional and intellectual habits, and of strong intellectual powers. There was hardly so much as personal acquaintance even, though each was well known in some sense to the other. But there was no want of tender appreciativeness on Emerson's part of the natural solicitude of the brother, either in this first response or in the answers which he sent to later inquiries during the short remainder of her life.

CONCORD, 25 April, 1856.

DEAR SIR, — I received your note last night. I am sorry to say that I have not had any letter directly from Miss Bacon since last December. Her publishers have a letter dated 28 February last. Her address at her last writing was still 12 *Spring Street, Hyde Park Gardens, London.* I had no right to expect a letter after December, as I had told her that I was going to Illinois, about Christmas, to be absent six weeks or more ; and she accordingly wrote directly to Dix & Edwards of "Putnam's Magazine." I have regretted much my tasks and preoccupations that forbade my keeping up an active correspondence with her, and reproached myself lately with omissions, which after a few weeks I am hoping to repair : and I hear with the more concern that you have no recent news of her. Her letters are full of confidence and devotion to her task — heroic devotion to it — and repeated expressions of indifference as to what becomes of herself, if only she accomplishes her task. Her latest letters had also some sad allusions, I thought, to disappointment in not receiving expected letters, and some misgivings as to her means for remaining in England to prosecute her studies. Her arrangements for publication had not turned out to my wish. I advised her not to print in Putnam, but to publish her results in a book ; and I communicated to her a proposition from Phillips, Sampson & Co., which, well-explained, was fair and even generous. But she decided to print in Putnam; and the editors, after the first article was printed, refused to print the following ones, and assigned their reasons. This refusal left me in no proper plight to carry the book to Phillips & Sampson again, after it was thus used and rejected.

I have not written to her, as indeed I have laid my whole correspondence on the shelf until certain imperative tasks of my own are ended, which should soon be. Meantime, I shall await with great interest your news from her, and shall be entirely at your service to obtain information respecting her address, etc., if she has changed her place. — With great respect,

R. W. EMERSON.

REV. DR. BACON.

XIII

If Delia Bacon had been herself a dramatic poet she could not have brought more faithfully into action, in this dull tragedy which her life was, the Horatian precept which forbids the intervention of a God into the plot until the fit occasion. That occasion had now come.

Nathaniel Hawthorne was at this time consul for the United States at Liverpool. Years before, he had written " The Scarlet Letter " and " The House of the Seven Gables," and had become famous. In that same village of Concord, which was already renowned through Emerson, he had settled down for the secluded life of a man of letters, when, in 1853, his warm friend President Pierce bestowed upon him this place, so attractive by the great income which then belonged to it that he could not refuse it. At the very time, almost, that Delia Bacon was sailing for England, Hawthorne went to assume his new and not congenial duties. To him and to his wife she was personally unknown, although she had no warmer or more sympathetic friend than Miss Elizabeth Peabody, the sister of Mrs. Hawthorne. And to him, when all other help and hope seemed to have

failed, she addressed herself at last, on the 8th of
May, 1856, from her London lodgings, in a letter,
of which this is only a part:

"DEAR MR. HAWTHORNE, — I take the liberty
of addressing myself to you without an introduction, because you are the only one I know of in
this hemisphere able to appreciate the position in
which I find myself at this moment, and I know of
no one else here at present fully qualified to judge
of the claims of a work which is not hemispherical,
but the work of men whose sign was ' Hercules
and his load too.' . . .

"Of course it is not pleasant to me to bring this
subject to the attention of strangers, as I have
been and still am compelled to, for it seems like
a personal intrusion, and like asking a personal
favor; and though I know well myself what
grounds I have for claiming all the aid I need,
it is not every kind of mind to which I can
make them apparent, perhaps, in the course of a
brief interview. Certainly there is no kind of
honest thing I would not rather do than to ask aid
on its behalf from those who are not able to appreciate it in its present form; but this also has
been laid upon me. I tried long to get the means
of doing it all by myself, without asking any one's
leave or help. But I did not succeed in it. I lost
years in the endeavor; and it would never have
been done at all if some of my friends had not

generously come to my aid. Mr. Emerson is the
one who has from first to last stood by me, and
has never in any instance failed to render me the
assistance I sought of him. And I am greatly indebted to Miss Peabody for her most generous
and active interest in the subject, though it is
now a long time since I have had any communication with her in reference to it.

"If it were anything in the world but what
it is, — a science, — a science that the world is
waiting for, I could not do and suffer what I have
done and suffered on its behalf. I ought not to
hesitate at all to ask for all the help I need in it,
for it is a work which the Providence of this
world has imposed on me, and I have cast into its
treasury not only all the living that I had, such as
it was, but my life also. . . .

"For I want some literary counsel, and such as
no Englishman of letters is able to give me. Mr.
Carlyle has been a most cordial personal friend to
me, but there are reasons why I could not ask this
help from him, which would become apparent to
you if you should look at the work at all. Before
I knew that you were coming to England, and
when I had not yet found the means of coming
myself, I had wished to communicate my discovery to you, and Mr. Emerson had promised me an
opportunity of doing so; but I concluded that
your duties here would be so engrossing that it
would be impossible for you to think about it.

But now that it is certain beyond all possibility of
a doubt, now that there is no shadow of a shade of
uncertainty in regard to it, I feel that I should be
wanting to my position if I allowed the dread I
have of annoying you and intruding on that
leisure which is so precious to you now, to prevent me from taking any step which might possibly tend to effect my object.

"The work admits of publication in separate
portions. What I want is to begin to publish
immediately a part of it, enough to secure the discovery. I suppose there is hardly a doubt that
some American publisher might be found to take
the plates on those terms, for Phillips & Sampson offered last July to advance forty pounds on
the first edition, and all the extra expense of this
arrangement is by this proposal to be subtracted
from my share of the profits. But I should not
dare to begin without some advice. I would not
be willing to print any part of it till some friendly
eye had overlooked it, if there were no other
reason for delay. It is not hard reading. Would
you be willing to take a part of it, a part which
you could read in an evening or so, and tell me
whether it would pay for the cost of the plates or
no? For that is the question. If you should
give your consent to it, I think I would send you
to begin with the very least popular part of it,
which contains the 'Art of Tradition,' which was
not only invented, but *employed* for the Advance-

ment of Learning; because this includes inciden-
tally the whole science which had to be brought
out then in a popular form, in order to answer
the purpose of its founders. It is a science which
naturally requires that form however, and which
could not be adequately exhibited in any other.
But this part contains that scientific abstract of it,
which is the key to the popular theatrical exhibition, and which enables the scholar to comprehend at a glance the whole scope of this discovery.

"And then afterwards, if you were not offended
with that, I should like to send you one of those
Plays unfolded, in which, by means of the Baconian Rhetoric or *illustrated* delivery of sciences, the
Baconian Logic is applied to the delicate subject of
the *Cure* of the Commonweal in the reign of James
the First, or one in which it is applied to the most
important social questions, which are as much in
need of scientific treatment now as they were at
the time when they were first included under the
science of nature in general by its founders. And
perhaps in the end you would be willing to glance
over at your leisure the part which makes the Introduction to the common reader, which contains a
new view of the Life of Sir Walter Raleigh, whose
place in the World's History it is our business to
define. I depend on a series of Articles I have
sent to 'Putnam's,' written in a very different style,
in which I have undertaken to send the old Player
about his business, to make way for this graver

performance, and I think if those should be published, you will find that the boards are cleared
and ready for my new actors. *That* I have just
written, but this part which I wish you to look at
has been ready and waiting here for nearly a year;
but the Atlantic Ocean and the English nation
were too mighty for me, and besides I had to wait
I suppose till this great war[1] was done. I hope
you will understand that I do not speak with any
assurance of my own part in this work. All my
confidence is grounded on the indestructible value
of the discovery. I was not a writer when I
began, I despaired of ever being able to write it;
I had to keep my secret for many years, because I
did not know how to tell it. I came to this country in the hope of escaping from that burthen. I
expected to find here, all ready to my hands, what
would make it unnecessary for me to enter upon
this task. What I expected to find here, I know
to be here now, and the means I need for possessing myself of this support are very simple now.
. . . You see this is a piece of history made by
Poets, and great men, the most magnificent mas-
terly kind of men, and all those miserable little
humdrum people, who think there can't be anything true but the sordid kind of prose and matter
of fact that they are capable of, are going to be
put to confusion with it forever, and they seem to
have an instinctive perception of it.

 "And now, sir, you will begin to perceive, per-

---

[1] The Crimean War.

haps, why it is that I address myself particularly to yourself in this emergency. . . . I am determined it shall not be my fault if this thing is lost to us, and there is nothing else I have left untried, I believe, in my attempts to save it."

This was certainly an alarming appeal to come from an utter stranger to a man of shrinking sensitiveness, overburdened with distasteful official duties, with his full share of private anxieties, with his own literary work hampered and retarded by want of time and by private and public cares. It was an appeal which, upon his responding to it, brought him heavy burdens of many kinds, which indeed he could not have failed to foresee. It would not have been hard for him, had he been as fully endowed with insight as the wise people who have always found the sayings of Delia Bacon to be the palpable vagaries of a disordered mind, to dismiss her and her " work " with a discouraging word or two, and thus to save himself much care and toil and loss in many ways. It is no more than justice to her that men should know what Hawthorne thought of her. But to Hawthorne himself there is nothing in all his life or in all that he wrote more honorable than the noble generosity, the unwearying patience, the exquisite considerateness and delicacy, with which for two years he gave unstinted help, even of that material sort which she would not ask for, to this lonely countrywoman. He never saw her — so he has told the world — but once; and these letters will show how, in the approach of that mental disorder which her intense labors and anxieties were surely bringing on, she returned what seemed ingratitude, and almost outrage, for his patient and tender counsel and aid. If, indeed, there were no other reason for telling her melancholy story, the illumination which it casts upon the figure, already become romantic, of Hawthorne would justify it.

These are the first of the many letters which make up the correspondence.

[HAWTHORNE TO D. B.]

LIVERPOOL, May 12, 1856.

DEAR MISS BACON, — It was quite unnecessary to send me these introductory letters (which I re-enclose) for I have long entertained a high respect for your character, and an interest in your object, so far as I understood it. To be sure, I know very little about it, not having seen the articles in "Putnam," nor heard anything but some vague talk from Miss Peabody, three years ago. Neither do I think myself a very fit person to comprehend the matter, nor to advise you in it; especially now, when I am bothered and bored, and harassed and torn in pieces, by a thousand items of daily business, and benumbed as to that part of my mind to which your work would appeal, and depressed by domestic anxieties. I say this, however, by no means to excuse myself from the endeavor to be of service to you in any and every manner, but only to suggest reasons why I shall probably be useless as a critic and a judge. If you really think that I can promote your object, tell me definitely how, and try me; and if I can say a true word to yourself about the work, it shall certainly be said; or if I can aid, personally, or through any connections in London, in bringing the book before the public, it shall be done.

I would not be understood, my dear Miss Bacon, as professing to have faith in the correctness of your views. In fact, I know far too little of them to have any right to form an opinion: and as to the case of the "old Player" (whom you grieve my heart by speaking of so contemptuously) you will have to rend him out of me by the roots, and by main force, if at all. But I feel that you have done a thing that ought to be reverenced, in devoting yourself so entirely to this object, whatever it be, and whether right or wrong; and that, by so doing, you have acquired some of the privileges of an inspired person and a prophetess — and that the world is bound to hear you, if for nothing else, yet because you are so sure of your own mission.

I gather from your note to Mr. Emerson that you are apprehensive of being anticipated by a work announced for publication in London. I have not seen this announcement; but I would stake my life that you will not find your views trenched upon in the least; although (having made your idea so obvious to yourself) it is natural that you should suppose it as clear as sunshine to any other mind.

I know that you will not take any offense from the frankness with which I write. It is impossible for me to pay any compliments, or to speak anything but the plainest truth (according to my own views), in dealing with the noble earnestness of your character.

Believe me, very sincerely,

and most respectfully yours,

NATH' HAWTHORNE.

P. S. If I had known that you were still in England, I should have tried to meet you before now; but I thought you had long ago returned to America. I shall probably be in London in the course of next month, when Mrs. Hawthorne (whose health is very delicate) will be on her return from Madeira. If your affairs make it desirable, you can bid me come to you then.

N. H.

Your letter to Mr. Emerson was in season for the steamer, and has gone by it.   N. H.

12 SPRING ST., SUSSEX GARDENS, HYDE PARK,
May 18, 1856.

DEAR MR. HAWTHORNE, — I thank you for your manful and whole-souled response to my application for help in my work, and I am not sorry that

I wrote to you, if it were only for the sake of this return. You have quieted my apprehension a little in regard to the book I referred to in my note to Mr. Emerson, although I cannot say that my mind is altogether at rest on that subject. That view which you take of it I understand and appreciate, but still I do not quite like the title of it. And that was the immediate occasion of my writing to you. For though I was aware of your being on this side of the Atlantic, and have often wished that it were possible to communicate with you in regard to my work, I knew how much time a Consul would be likely to have for a business of this kind, and I had not the conscience to ask you to interest yourself in it.

But the discovery of " the Philosophy of Shakespeare " is the real discovery which I pretend to have made, and the other part is of no consequence except as it is connected with that; and it was the necessity of getting my work out before this subject came to be discussed here which impressed me so strongly as to induce me to write to you. And in the interval between the writing of the note to Mr. Emerson and the conclusion to inclose it to yourself, I saw an intimation in another quarter that something is going to be done in that department, and that the time for it has come. The Article in the last " Edinburgh Review " on the Collier controversy contains an intimation that that sort of criticism has had its day here, and that the period for an entirely different kind is now beginning.

I should be very glad to be able to get my book printed here, and to put in circulation as many copies as are necessary to effect a legal publication and no more. I do not care to have any attention directed to it in this country at present. It is not adapted to this hemisphere, and it is better that it should come out in America as an American work entirely. That opinion is however the result of my study of the subject since I came. There has been as yet I believe but one Article of it published in " Putnam's Magazine," and that is one that was written three years ago. But I have just been sending three or four more which I do rely on for introducing the subject properly to the attention of those whom it concerns, and I have concluded to wait now till I hear from those, or until I receive an answer from Mr. Emerson, instead of resorting to any such desperate measures as those which I felt myself capable of when I wrote to you before. Still I should be very glad to avail myself of the kind interest you have expressed in my work as a work merely, to ask you to look over quite at your leisure a part of it which contains the doctrine of the work, that you may see what it is, and whether you approve of it or not, without feeling called upon to express any opinion, or to assume any responsibility in regard to it, which your want of time to consider the subject sufficiently, or the requirements of your public position, may make it unsuitable or inconvenient for you to assume. It is not as if I were asking you to judge of an original work of my own. It does not depend on my powers of composition for its claims, though it does perhaps for its chance of an immediate recognition of those claims. But I am giving you an idea that it is something much more formidable than it is. This book of mine does not require study, though the books to which it is related do. The utmost that I ask for mine is a perusal. I am proposing to send you indeed the very driest part of it, and the one on which I do not rely for an impression with the public generally. But it is all out of that new fountain of philosophy, which is life itself condensed and intensified, — abstracted and cleared and recomposed in forms much more to the purpose than the spontaneous combinations.

The truth is, I should be very glad to have it read, and you are the only person this side of the Atlantic whom I could ask to do it, and I would not urge it upon you, knowing as I do how serious your preoccupations are, if I did not know that you would find it at least an easy task, and for the sake of the good it promises, I hope a pleasant one. If I do send it to you you must take your own time for it, for since I have decided not to attempt to publish it till I am warranted in doing so by what I hear from America, there is no immediate urgency.

I hope I may have the honor and pleasure of seeing both yourself and Mrs. Hawthorne when you come to London, though I have conversed so long with spirits that the idea of seeing any one in the body is quite appalling to my imagination. I am truly sorry to hear that Mrs. Hawthorne's state of health is a source of anxiety to you, and that she has been compelled to seek another climate on that account. Permit me to express my sincere hopes that she may return to you quite well. Though I have never seen her I have heard of her from those who know her well.

Very gratefully yours,

DELIA BACON.

P. S. I am sorry to have hurt your feelings with my profane allusions to the Earl of Leicester's groom, a witty fellow enough in his way. But long familiarity with the facts has produced a hopeless obduracy in my mind on that point. The person that you love and reverence is not touched by my proceeding. I have not hurt a hair of his head. He is the one I am at work for. If anybody boasts of love and reverence, to him I might produce my case, and say with St. Paul '*I* more.' But I do not, of course, expect you to adopt my views until you find yourself compelled to do so, neither do I wish you to give the faintest countenance to them till you know fully what they are and their grounds. And this part of the book

that I propose to send to you does not suffice to
put you in possession of the case entirely, and it
would not be proper to expect from you any
avowal of opinion in regard to the question of
the work based on that alone.   D. B.

[HAWTHORNE TO D. B.]

LIVERPOOL, May 16, 1856.

DEAR MISS BACON, — I am ready to receive the
manuscript, as soon as you please to send it.

I have been looking at the Shakspeare article,
in the Edinburgh Review, and I do not see that it
suggests anything more than a different system
from that heretofore in use for amending the text.

Sincerely yours,

NATH' HAWTHORNE.

[D. B. TO HAWTHORNE.]

12 SPRING ST., SUSSEX GARDENS, HYDE PARK,
May 24 [1856].

DEAR MR. HAWTHORNE, — I most thankfully
avail myself of your kind permission to send you
my manuscript, — a favor which, under the circumstances, I do fully appreciate, and on account
of the gravity of the questions involved in the
work, and the feebleness of the agency employed
in it, I shall have to bespeak your utmost patience.
This is only a part, and a small part, of my book,
and it was never meant to be read by itself.   The
articles sent to the Magazine were addressed to
that violent presupposition which this discovery

has to encounter at the first step, and I have no hesitation in saying that that part of the case which is produced in those articles disposes of the present theory of the authorship of these works. I do not claim anything more for it. But in *the book*, I relied on the historical part of the work, which precedes this, and on the Interpretation of the Plays, which follows it, to interest the general reader, while in this I am obliged to presuppose the attention of a class of readers specially qualified to consider a question of this kind, and who would be best prepared to weigh the kind of evidence which is produced here.

You will see that the mere question of the authorship of the Plays is a secondary question in this inquiry. I *found* this system of philosophy in *the Plays*. They were my study for many years, and I worked it all out of them without knowing that it was that part of the great philosophic system which was brought out in that age, which naturally required this particular form of exhibition, and which could not then be produced in any other, — and moreover that part of it which could not then be claimed by its authors in any form. I had read the " Advancement of Learning " more than once, but I had read it as a book that it was incumbent on me to read, and my only business was to see in it what the critics had told me I was to find there, so that my knowledge of the author and his aims really remained second-handed. I went to the reading of it with the common impression in regard to the aim of this philosophy, and in regard to the personal character of the author, then freshened up by Mr. Macaulay's vivid exhibition of both into a sentiment of absolute detestation, and though I saw some things there which very much surprised me, for I was then studying Hamlet, and I could not conceal from myself the fact that in one or two places this man did seem to be in his secret, and that it was not the man that Macaulay described at all, but one of a very different range of comprehension and doctrine, and though I never did get those glimpses of him quite out of my mind, I could not think of resisting such an authority, and suffered myself to be overwhelmed with the weight of it, — at least I did not .pursue the inquiry any further. But my impression of the character of the man was so strong that I made a personal thing of it, and there was no man, dead or alive, that really on the whole gave me so much cause of offense with his contradictions. He appeared to be such a standing disgrace to genius and learning, that I had not the heart to ask anybody to study anything. And that was the state of my mind exactly when in my study of the Plays, after having worked my way at last to the inmost of those inner readings, which you will find referred to here, I found myself directed to that source for further information in regard to the plan of these works, and particularly for " the table " of them, and I found the authorship of them claimed by this man, and his associates, of whom I then knew nothing; I had always supposed that he was alone in his enterprise, and as to the persons named, and particularly as to his chief partner in his literary undertakings, my knowledge of him then would have led me to think of anything sooner than the possibility of such a thing. But the subsequent investigation shows that that reading was correct. He *was* associated with this man, though the fact of an association was the fact which was most guarded from observation. There was much use for what Lord Bacon calls " color," in those times, and the exigency found or produced persons of great artistic gifts in the management of it. I did not intend to trouble you with this preface, but as I have not even the introductory article which has been published to send to you, and as I have concluded to keep back the historical part of the work, because I think it admits of being very much improved, it is proper perhaps to say as much as this by way of introduction, since I have to put my work to so severe a test as to ask you to begin in the middle of it with your criticism. And as Mr. Emerson has carefully read the " Advancement of Learning " since I brought the subject to his attention, for the sake of one sentence in this letter of his I take leave to inclose it to you; as the subject is so very new, I thought you might like to see that opinion, and Mr. Emer-

son does not object to its being used in that manner. I had a long conversation with Mr. Grote on
the subject last summer. It was impossible for
him to enter on the investigation of the question,
for he was then occupied with his twelfth volume,
and was wholly unprepared to express an opinion
on the subject; he spoke of the immense presupposition to be encountered, but he said distinctly
he could not say it was not so, and when I gave
him an account of the way in which I had arrived
at it, he said, and that was at the close of the conversation, that he was certainly inclined to respect
an opinion based on such an inquiry.

I owe you an apology for sending you such a
patched and scratched and ill-looking manuscript.
I am very much ashamed of it, but I cannot help
it, for I am not strong, and it tires me very much
to write, and it was as much as ever I could do to
make it as good as it is. I looked at the Article in
the " Review," to which I referred, in great haste,
at the London Library, and when I was afraid of
losing the object for which I went there, by stop-
ping to do so, and I had no opportunity to look at
it afterwards to correct my mistake. I suppose it
was because my mind was preoccupied with that
idea; you must not take it for a specimen of my
usual reading. I do not expect you to pronounce
an opinion in regard to the question of the work,
but by the time you have read it through, and I
wish you would do it at your leisure, you will

see, perhaps, why I wished to have it read, and why I feel at liberty to call for help in getting it published.

Very gratefully and truly yours,

DELIA BACON.

[HAWTHORNE TO D. B.]

LIVERPOOL, May 26, 1856.

DEAR MISS BACON, — I have just received the manuscript, and will read it diligently and carefully, and (so far as depends on myself) with a disposition to receive the truth of the matter.

Very sincerely yours,

NATH' HAWTHORNE.

[HAWTHORNE TO D. B.]

LIVERPOOL, June 21, '56.

DEAR MISS BACON, — You will have thought me inexcusably dilatory for not sooner writing to you; but I have been absent from Liverpool a great part of the time — Mrs. Hawthorne having recently arrived at Southampton. I shall establish her near London early in July, and will then hope to meet you personally.

Meanwhile, though I have not had time to read the whole of your manuscript, I cannot refrain from saying that I think the work an admirable one. You seem to me to have read Bacon and Montaigne more profoundly than anybody else has read them. It is very long (it was in my early youth, indeed) since I used to read and re-read

Montaigne; and in order to do any justice to your
views I ought to re-peruse him now — and Bacon,
also — and Shakspeare too.   I cannot say, at present, that I adopt your theory, if I rightly comprehend it as partially developed in this portion of
your work.   We find thoughts in all great writers
(and even in small ones) that strike their roots far
beneath the surface, and intertwine themselves
with the roots of other writers' thoughts; so that
when we pull up one, we stir the whole, and yet
those writers have had no conscious society with
one another.   I express this very shabbily: but
you will think it for me better than I can say it.

But this has nothing to do with the depth and
excellence of your work, and its worthiness to
come before the world.   If I can contribute in any
way to this good end, I shall esteem myself happy.
I am not particularly well off pecuniarily, but can
do somewhat in that way, and perhaps in other
ways.   When I see you (or sooner, if you like) we
can talk of this.

In haste, sincerely yours,
Nath' Hawthorne.

[D. B. to Hawthorne.]

12 Spring St., Sussex Gardens,
H. Park, June 22, '56.

Dear Mr. Hawthorne, — That little piece of
my work which you have in your hands does not
furnish you with the means of coming to any satis-

factory conclusion in regard to it. I wished you
to see in outline the comprehension of it, and I
was afraid of burthening you by putting the whole
in your hands, for it is a formidable undertaking
to read a work in manuscript, I know, under the
most favorable circumstances. But before you say
anything about it, even to yourself, I do most earnestly entreat that you will find time to look over
this tragedy of " Lear," which I send to you " unfolded." I am writing another chapter to bring it
down to the present time, and I think of publishing it by itself, as a Tract, though I do *not* propose
to ask the Tract Society to publish it for me. I
wished very much to send with this also " Coriolanus," which contains the application of the same
method of inquiry and the same art of delivery to
the question of the Cure of the Commonweal. If
you will read these *three* Tragedies which make the
third part of my work, you will be able to judge
then of the claim which I make for it, that it contains, however unworthily set forth, *the* Discovery
of the Modern Science, the buried Discovery which
the necessities of this time have cried to Heaven
for, and not in vain. I see my way much more
clearly now than when I wrote these criticisms.
They have been finished more than a year, waiting
their time. The chapter I am writing now is of
more serious import than anything contained in
them at present. I do not know whether I can get
them published while I live. But if I can finish

the work acceptably to the power that has imposed it on me, and leave it in safe hands, — and for myself personally, if I can avoid the dishonor which the failure in the contracts I have relied on seems likely to involve me in here, at this distance from all my friends, that is all that I ask from God or man in reference to it; at least, that is all I think of for the present.

[Then follows an account, covering many pages of her close manuscript, of the perplexities which had come about her from the cross-purposes and misunderstandings with American publishers, and especially from the refusal of the magazine publishers to accomplish their declared purpose, and what she had considered their formal engagement, to print and pay for successive articles, one of which indeed they had even put completely into type. To repeat the story would indeed illustrate, as hardly anything else could, the gentle patience of her correspondent, who bore with all her excited complaints, though it was not difficult to discern in them the approach of those disturbances which before many months were to become declared insanity; not shrinking, meanwhile, from the various burdens which were offered to his shoulders. She tells how, in utter extremity, she had resorted to General Campbell, the consul in London, who was also a stranger to her; how he had "advanced" her twenty pounds, to be repaid from the proceeds of her successive articles; and how her brother had a few days before sent her ten pounds, which she had immediately enclosed to Mr. Campbell. She asks of Hawthorne, however, absolutely nothing but this :]

The way in which you can help me will be to certify that you have read my book and that it is entitled to a publication. If you can say *that*, it will go far towards making it successful, — and you have said it already. I would not ask you to say it *here*, but to Mr. Emerson, or to the American publishers. It has had to depend on my own certificate of its merits entirely hitherto. Your word with the American public would secure it a reading. There is going to be another kind of demonstration. I want this published first. I know it is a good book because I have tried it. I have read it and been strengthened and made better by it repeatedly. But the publishers, I suppose, would think that that was not the very best testimony in the world, and though Mr. Emerson has been willing to confide in my word for it, I don't doubt he would be very glad to know your opinion of it.

But not to make a book of this, in reference to these immediate difficulties, if you see any way in which you can help me I know you will. General Campbell is entirely a stranger to me ; I had not even an introduction to him. Mr. Buchanan told me he would give me one, but I suppose he forgot to do it. Of course you know if it should come to the worst I have friends who would not suffer me to be indebted to the Consul, though I hope not to have to trouble them, and if those men will send me the money they owe me there will be no trouble at all.

I am heartily glad to hear that Mrs. Hawthorne has safely returned. As for myself I am unfit to see any one. I have given up this world entirely, and if I had my choice, I don't know as I should ever see anyone again while I live. Mr. Campbell has been here to see me three or four times about this business, and I would much rather have given him twenty pounds every time he came than to have seen him, if it had been convenient. And he came out of the purest charity. Still, if you are kind enough to look after me when you come, I shall take it as a very disinterested act of humanity, and will try to look through the grates of my cell to see you.

[HAWTHORNE TO D. B.]

Liverpool, June 25, 1856.

DEAR MISS BACON, — I have just received your last package, and will read it as soon as I can get time, and as nearly as possible in such state of mind as you recommend.

Surely I can say most strenuously that it ought to be published.

As regards your friends, let me say frankly that you shall not suffer from any difficulties, within my power to obviate. And I will write to a friend in New York, who used to be connected with the magazine, to see those people and get them to pay what is due you. As regards the £10 due General Campbell, I will speak to him about it, and make myself responsible; so that there need be no delicacy about letting it stand for the present.

I can entirely sympathize with you in your reluctance; none better than I. To tell you the truth, though I see people by scores, every day, I still shrink from any interview of which I am forewarned; and so, if we can arrange all these matters just as well without meeting, I shall not intrude upon you. But I question whether we can.

I leave Liverpool for Southampton on Friday, and shall bring Mrs. Hawthorne to the neighborhood of London on the first of July.

Truly yours,

NATH' HAWTHORNE.

P. S. I enclose (as, for aught I know, you may have immediate occasion for it) a ten pound note. If you acknowledge the receipt before to-morrow, please to address me here: if afterwards, to the care of Bennoch, Twentyman & Co., 77 Wood Street, Cheapside, London. N. H.

More details of her embarrassments with the American publishers come with the grateful acknowledgment, next day, of Hawthorne's unsolicited and " thoughtful kindness," which had brought to her a relief evidently not easy fully to express; and then she adverts thus to the visit which she hoped for, yet with a certain dread:

" When you come to establish Mrs. Hawthorne here, or whenever you find it convenient to do so, I hope you will call upon me. The reason I shrink from seeing any one now is, that I used to be somebody, and whenever I meet a stranger I am troubled with a dim reminiscence of the fact, whereas now I am nothing but this work, and don't wish to be. I would rather be this than anything else. I have lived for three years as much alone with God and the dead as if I had been a departed spirit. And I don't wish to return to the world. I shrink with horror from the thought of it. This is an abnormal state, you see, but I am perfectly harmless, and if you will let me know when you are coming I will put on one of the dresses I used to wear the last time I made my appearance in the world, and try to look as much like a survivor as the circumstances will permit.

" Truly yours,

"DELIA BACON."

At some time after the writing of this, and before the next letter to Hawthorne was written, there came upon her, in the following letter from Emerson, a blow which would have been enough to break down a mind of less original strength than hers, after the body which enclosed it had been so enfeebled by toil and privation and disappointment. For many months she had subsisted upon the hope, which amounted to an assurance, of some return from the successive packets of manuscript sent to Emerson for the magazine, prepared indeed with exhausting midnight labor, upon something like an express requisition for it. It was grievous enough to learn now that all hope of publication in America, either in serial or in book form, had definitively failed. With that came also the news of the heedless loss of the manuscript itself, into which, even if it had no other value, she had poured such a flood of her own life, as almost to have exhausted its source.

This is the letter that told the story:

CONCORD, 23 June, 1856.

MY DEAR MISS BACON, — I am heartily sorry that after so long a space I should not be able to send you some good news. But this time none at all, and indeed much worse than no good news, namely, the most vexatious. There is nothing for it but the kind of earnest that many serious drawbacks and disasters give to the brave and well-deserving, of new and better turns that must befall. On my going west in December I left the three (?) MSS. chapters with my wife. Putnam already had the first. As I had dissuaded the printing in the magazine, they were not to have

the rest without your express advice. They
printed the first, and then sent to my brother
W. E., in New York, demanding the rest to go on
at once. He sent to my wife for it, and she sup-
posing that this was the contingency I had told
her of sent the three (?) chapters. After reading
them, they refused to go on, and returned them
to W. E. Lately, on receiving your letter of May,
I received soon afterwards what MSS. you sent in
May to Dix & Edwards from them, with word that
they did not find them suited to their purpose.
Then I wrote to W. E. to restore the three (?)
chapters. He wrote me back that he was pained
to say that they were lost. Just before my letter
came, he had given them to Sophy Ripley, who was
coming home to Concord via Springfield, to bring
to me. Miss Ripley had been on a visit at his
house in Staten Island for a day or two; her trunk
was in New York city. She took the sealed parcel
in her hands, and came down to the Staten Island
ferry with my brother in his carriage, one and a
half miles, and just before reaching the boat per-
ceived that she had not the parcel. W. E. was
needed at his office in New York; he sent back the
driver instantly from the boat to find the parcel,
informed the collector at the boat office, and ad-
vertised it, with a reward, at once; the chances
seemed all for recovering it at once, but it has
never appeared! Sophy Ripley has returned
home, and dared not come to see me until her

mother Mrs. Ripley had come to tell me her con-
sternation. They inquire first of all if you have a
duplicate? of which I am not sure. I assure you,
all the parties to this misfortune are very miserable at present. I wish I could relieve this disaster
with some better face of the whole affair. But it
does not yet show its best side. I could not carry
the MSS. if I had them thus far complete to Phillips & Sampson (or to another publisher) and ask
as favorable terms as they had offered me at first,
for the éclat, and what publishers would esteem
the promise of the work, was seriously diminished
by Putnam's publishing and then rejecting. That
is a damage which one would say can only be properly met and overcome by publishing the book at
your own risk, in its mature form.

I have now been trying to read the papers sent
to me by Dix & Edwards, and which they decline
to print. It is very difficult for me to read them,
so small and crowded is the writing, and so much
interlined and corrected. My eyes are very failing
servants in these days, and with glasses I do not
much help them. I have set my daughter and
my wife also to help me, and at last I have mainly
surmounted the difficulty. I hesitate a little to
say that I think the magazine men judged rightly
in asking still another form. The moment your
proposition is stated that Shakspeare was only a
player, whom certain superior person or persons
could use, and did use, as a mouthpiece for their

poetry it is perfectly understood. It does not need to be stated twice. The proposition is immensely improbable, and against the single testimony of Ben Jonson, "For I loved the man, and do honor his memory on this side idolatry as much as any," cannot stand. Ben Jonson must be answered, first. Of course we instantly require your proofs. But instead of hastening to these, you expatiate on the absurdity of the accepted biography. Perfectly right to say once, but not necessary to say twice, and unpardonable after telling us that you have proof that this is not the man, and we are waiting for that proof, to say it thrice. There is great incidental worth in these expatiatings; but it is all at disadvantage because we have been summoned to hear an extraordinary announcement of facts, and are impatient of any episodes. I am sure you cannot be aware how voluminously you have cuffed and pounded the poor pretender, and then again, and still again, and no end. I think too (but this I say with less assurance) that you lean much harder than they can bear on many passages you cite from the plays, as if they contained very pointed allusions which admitted of only one application.

Once more, I am a little shocked by the signature "Discoverer of the Authorship of Shakspeare's Plays," which should not be used one moment in advance. Yes, and welcome, and forevermore, wear the crown, from the instant your fact

is made to appear, not before. Certain great merits which appeared in your first papers mark these
last also, — a healthy perception, and natural rec-
titude, which give immense advantage in criticism,
where they are so rare. The account of Englishmen, and what is servile in them, and the prophetic
American relations of this poetry, struck me much,
and your steadfast loyalty to cause and effect, in
mental history.

What practically should be or can be done, I
cannot see to-day. There is no publisher, because
there is not yet the ready book. If you are to
be anticipated, I think you should write a short
letter announcing exactly your propositions, the
points you are prepared to prove, send it to Fraser,
or any other English journal, though it were the
lowest that will print it; print it also in " Putnam," or the "Tribune," or the "Crayon," here;
and then publish your book containing the full
exposition, whenever you can have it ready. I
have been a much worse agent lately than you
might have found me earlier, — though never a
good one, — but worse now through many causes
weary to tell of, — perhaps another year will set
me on my feet again, and then!

With entire respect,
Yours,
R. W. Emerson.

Miss Bacon.

Perhaps it was Hawthorne's good fortune which kept him unwell at Blackheath in the days when this distress was fresh upon his correspondent, and saved thus his tender and sympathetic soul from the direct communication of her grief. It came to him in writing, however, soon enough, and with more than sufficient amplitude, following close upon this note inviting it, but hardly, it may be surmised, inviting all that came.

[HAWTHORNE TO D. B.]

BLACKHEATH, July 17, '56.

DEAR MISS BACON, — I very much regret that I cannot call on you to-day, according to agreement; but I am not well, and do not feel it safe to venture out.

I have seen General Campbell, and made myself responsible for the balance of the debt.

I must go to Liverpool on Monday, to remain there about a week — perhaps ten days. In the interim, I shall be glad if you will write me, and tell me what you would like to have done in reference to the publication of the work. I cannot but think that it may be effected on terms advantageous to yourself. I think I had better write to Emerson, by next steamer, and get him to see what arrangements can be made.

As soon as I return from Liverpool, I will call.

Sincerely yours,

' NATH' HAWTHORNE.

DEAR MR. HAWTHORNE, — I was very much disappointed at not seeing you on Saturday, and if I had known how to have addressed you in time would have entreated you not to return to Liverpool without giving me an opportunity of speaking to you.

For your assurance in regard to my work, strengthened as it is with the approbation of the lady to whom you give so illustrious a title, I could not properly thank you by word of mouth or pen, and so I will not attempt it. I believe you two are the first readers of those last papers. They have been out of my hands once. But they were returned to me with an accidental proof that they had not been read. The first was perhaps looked into a little at another place where it went by itself as it went to you. You shall have all the details as to what has been done. But I do not think that the book has had any trial at all. The theory as announced beforehand is as you will readily believe not a pleasant one to the conservative mind here, and the publishers who cater for that are so frightened at the suggestion, that they hush it up as quick as possible, and try to forget that it has ever been mentioned to them. But the more I think of it the more I am disposed to make another effort to get it published here, as the articles for the Magazine written after I abandoned that idea are not published and I can keep them back now if I choose. . . .

I have had a letter from Mr. Emerson since I wrote you last, but it is the least pleasant one I have received from him. He appears to be disheartened at the course the thing has taken there, which it need not have taken if there had been anybody there to act for me, and I do not think that he likes the work as well as he expected to, and I ought not to be surprised at that, for if I had known what it was myself I should not have taken it to him any more than I would have taken it to my brother, who is a Doctor of Divinity. It would have been equally improper for me to do so. And perhaps it is just as well, since the motion proceeds from himself, that he should let it go now. "Transcendentalism" is the fatal word which I hear pronounced (by people who are not perhaps quite clear as to what that definition covers) when our two principal philosophers are named. But there is nothing, and there never has been anything in this world since time began, so antagonistic to that very thing which the people mean when they use that word as this philosophy, and it is not right to cast on it beforehand, while it has no name of its own, that shadow. The truth which that so-called philosophy of their contains is here also comprehended in this, but i is here in its place. I went to those two men with

it, because they professed philosophy, and though
I knew that my discovery contradicted in the most
direct manner their own published views on this
particular question of the Plays, I thought them
magnanimous enough to disregard that fact entirely, and I found them so. But it is another
thing to ask them to let me bring the world up to
a summit of knowledge which I have accidentally
discovered here, already built, with the road all
open up to the very top, from which their domain
is all overlooked, and the whole zig-zag of its
boundary defined. They are men of genius, but
they lack the genius of the new logic, which is
only the stronger expression of the genius of the
Moderns, and the world reproves them for it.
Carlyle treated me with an extraordinary personal
kindness, and so did his wife, and it is my own
fault that I have not continued my acquaintance
with them, but Mr. Emerson is a flight higher than
that. He has mastered an intellectual height, from
which he looks down on the human sensibilities.
He has the advantage of me in that respect. I
cannot write to a man as I would to a gale of wind
exactly, and though I know what his theory is,
and that he talks of the ethical principle as he
does of a good ear in music, after all I am taken
a little by surprise, when he comes to give me a
direct practical vindication of his views. He never
pretended to any personal kindness for me, the
idea of my work has always stood on its own

merits with him entirely, and the way in which he disposes of that, and me, and my worldly affairs in his last letter is, as they say in the West, "a caution." He begins by giving me the very pretty piece of information that three very important chapters of the work are lost, tumbled out of a carriage months ago, when some lady was carrying them in her hand, and never heard of since, and for that he does express a strong sense of human regret, as they were lost after they were returned to his brother's custody by those Magazine men. But I don't consider the persons who lost them in the least to blame. After they were taken out of his hands, the Publishers of the Magazine were responsible to me for them, and had no right to send them on that journey. And this reminds me to beg you to be more than usually careful, for I have no duplicates of these papers that I send to you, and that was the reason that I would not send them across the water, and now that I am reminded of the dangers of the land by this accident, I know you will forgive me for this caution. For there seems to be a special antagonism at work here. These are not the first of my papers that have been destroyed. Before I came here, I wrote something on the subject which was received with great approbation. Mr. Emerson said in writing that he had " seen nothing in the United States in the way of literary criticism which he thought so good," but a black waiter finding it one day in his

department and looking it over from his standpoint, could see nothing in it to the purpose, and
threw it into the fire. And that was when it was
in my own keeping.

I have had a letter from the sister, who is my
chief earthly reliance now. She thinks that my
work has failed I believe, poor child, and she
knows that I object to receiving aid from my
brother, though she does not fully know *why.* . . .
She says she wishes she could send me immediately a hundred pounds, but she cannot except on
one condition, but that her husband and my brother
will immediately send whatever I require for my
bills here, and my journey home, if I will *promise*
to come as soon as I have received it. And she
requires in the most urgent manner that I shall
send her that answer by the next steamer. I
would die here before I would give her any such
promise, but I have put in this otherwise impertinent passage, that you may see exactly what my
position is at this moment. My friends think that
I am wasting my life here to no purpose. And
they think from the account I gave to my sister of
my present difficulties that they have now an opportunity of speaking with authority and compel-
ling me to come home. But I will open a "cent
shop" in my House of Seven Gables first. There
is not anything which is honest that I will not do
rather than put the Atlantic Ocean between me
and what I came to find. I would infinitely rather

never go back than do that. It is a moral impossibility. I could no more do it than I could kill
myself. It gives me a sense of suffocation to try
to think of it. It would be an impossible crime.
I am sure that my *Friar Francis*, if I can find his
cell, will be able to give me some better advice
than that. . . .

So you see my case is given up by that Physician. I called you in for a consultation. But he
had pronounced on it before you came, and had
gone, so that alters your position a little. I have
been all these three years writing to somebody
that was not there to get my letters, and the fact
is I begin to think that the person I wish to speak
to so much is not anywhere except in my own
mind, and in these books, or I should have been
apt to think that, if the hand that brought that
letter had not had yours in it of the 10th. Don't
tell me that you were not inspired to write that,
for I know you were. I could not have got through
with that letter of Mr. Emerson's if yours had had
any shade less of goodness in it. It took Mrs.
Hawthorne's word of assurance and all to help me
through it. As it was it made me very ill, and I
have not recovered from it. . . .

I have thought it right to tell you all this, because I have a feeling that the facts make the best
basis after all for any proceeding. But I begin to
think if I had a little more of the art in which
these men whose school I am in were such adepts,

I should manage this affair of theirs rather better.
All this is calculated to annoy and discourage you,
but my feeling is that your judgments are not
very easily biased by extraneous influences. But
perhaps we are none of us altogether independent
of them. I don't know as I could have been true
to my own work, if it had come back to me as it
came to Mr. Emerson in the first place, with the
brand of that rejection on it. And the badness of
the manuscript and the weakness of his eyes and
the vexatious loss of those papers, and the whole
series of untoward circumstances, and the feeling
that the éclat of the work was lost, helped I have
no doubt a little in the summing up of the question. Besides he has never seen the book, he has
only my word for it that there is one, and he has
evidently made up his mind that I am laboring
under an hallucination in respect to its existence.
He has seen only the outside of the preliminary
chapters — one of them he says he read and approved. Under these circumstances I don't consider his decision a final one. I think too he may
have felt unconsciously perhaps the antagonism of
this philosophy, of which there has been no hint
before in what I have written, and of which I am
not the author. He censures the boldness of my
claims, and evidently prefers to have the evidence
in the form of direct historical testimony, and says
that Ben Jonson must be answered first, whereas
he won't be answered till there is no occasion to

answer him. I know all about Ben Jonson. He has two patrons besides "Shakspeare." *One* was Raleigh, *the other* was Bacon. The author of these Plays and Poems was his Patron. It would not have been strange if he had loved and honored his memory on this side idolatry as much as any. But Lord Bacon was a man of art, and he was much in the habit of writing letters for other people, in which he could say some things to the purpose which he could not say as well over his own name. The fact that he was not too scrupulous to employ such arts was betrayed on the trial of Essex. That was not the only time that Mr. Anthony Bacon's name was used to accomplish Mr. Francis Bacon's ends. It was very much used I find. There was a great deal of correspondence that went on in that person's name, which might not have prospered so well in the name of his brother. And it was not dialogues on the stage only that the myriad-minded resorted to, to accomplish his ends. Letters written in the names of various individuals, which were not published at the time, but reserved for future publication, *because they related to recent matters of state, fictitious letters,* form a very important part of this author's works, to which he takes great pains to refer those who care to know more about him.

As to what is to be done, please to look over — *read* as well as you can in this poor form, making due allowance for it, — this play of " The Consulship." It is Lord Bacon's as much as "The Scarlet Letter" is yours. No, I will not say that. These plays passed through the hands of more persons than one. But the Chancellor claims this one. I have seen what he says about it. My interpretation is approved. Do not read it thinking there is no other proof, but merely to see, whether, as it stands there with those other parts of the work that you have, and some preliminary statements, it will make a book that can perhaps be published here. If that feat can be accomplished, there will be no difficulty about the other side. What I wish to know is whether you think it would be possible to get it published here without waiting for that further confirmation that I speak of, which I speak of as assuredly as anything which has been subjected to the contingency of a *trust* can be spoken of. If you could give me a title to it, and write a few lines of Introduction, I think you could make it successful. I would like to have it published without my name, and I would like to have you introduce it to the public, saying just what you are willing to say to the public about it, and no more. Just keep the position that you have already taken in reference to it. Merely say that it is a book that has claims of its own, and is entitled to be read. Give to the anonymous author the authorship of this new Baconian philosophy and the invention of this new Shakspeare, if you choose. If it is an invention, I insist upon it, it is a very fine one, but it would be dishonest in me to take the credit of it. Suppose I was dead and you had this Romance in your hands, the boldest one that was ever invented, what would you do with it? (Call it a Romance if you choose, till I can prove it.) You find it given over, — perishing by inches, for want of a printer, for want of a reader, three chapters of it given to the winds by those to whom I sent it to read and to print. If you can save it, and any good comes of it, the world will owe it to you. You have done more for it already in the weeks that you have had it, with all the cares of your Consulship upon you, and those particular urgent cares which your arrangements for Mrs. Hawthorne's residence here devolved upon you, than others have done in years. You have done what nobody else has done for it before. *You have read it,* as much of it as you had to read. The chapters I took so much pains to send to America, for the purpose of having them read, have not been read yet by any one who knew enough to know what the letters stood for, and never will be now. They were sent on the 1st of *November,* and when they were inquired for in *June,* the news was that they were lost. Mr. Emerson talks about "the ready book." It is well it was not ready for the kind of fate that awaited those *avant couriers* of it. Mr. Emerson is no more to blame for the loss of those papers than I am, but I should have been glad if somebody could have read them before they were destroyed besides that goose of an editor, who can say what he likes about them now, uncontradicted. The reason I did not send any more was, there was nobody there to take them. I sent many appeals out in the name of that which is most commanding with men; but one had gone to his farm, and another to his merchandise, and another had married a wife and could not come. But you had married one, happily, who was able to come with you. I know how much I owe to that "better self" of yours, who ought to be very good to deserve that title. I am thankful that there was one there who was ready to help, instead of hindering you, *not* in your toil through the manuscripts only, but in your detection of what was worth saving under that disguise. I don't like to see people, or I would go and see her. My personal history is concluded; there has been enough of it and to spare. I have had my share of the good things of this life, and I have been ready to go this some time. I only wait to finish this work. Mr. Emerson talks about my "wearing the crown," he says, "yes, wear it and welcome and forevermore, from the instant your fact is made to appear;" but he recommends that I should not put it on prematurely. He was quarreling with my assuming the title of a Discoverer in those anonymous articles. I thought there was no honor in claiming that title now, unless it is an honor to rush on the drawn swords of the world. I meant it for a challenge. I have to begin with an unspeakable audacity. That is a part of the play. Does anyone think that I am not conscious of the position? Mr. Emerson has never been taught, as I have, what the human approbation amounts to. If I thought I had a right to do it, I would take this discovery to my grave with me. As soon as I can get all my duties of one kind and another reconciled and fulfilled, I shall ask leave to retire from this scene for the present, and shall hope to return again when it is in better order.

In the first place I am going to write immediately to my sister, perhaps to my brother D. D., to say that I lose my copyright here by coming home now, and that it will be eventually valuable, and that as my living here is hardly more expensive than it would be in America, as far as they are concerned in that particular, it is better for me to stay here, till I am ready to help myself, than to come home.

And in the second place, I will write to the Editors of the Magazine, and tell them to send me immediately, without any demur at all, the three hundred dollars due for the articles which they engaged to print, and which they caused to be lost instead. I will do it for the benefit of any poor authors who may happen to be at their mercy hereafter, as they thought I was. The loss of those papers through their means, appears to me

to introduce a new element into the question, and they shall answer for them : — that is, if I am not advised to the contrary. I do not like to receive any money from them, as they derived no advantage from the papers, but it is better that *they* should pay it to me, than that I should owe it to others in consequence of their deliberately destroying the provision I had made for my living here. They knew about that contract with the Boston Publishers, and that I was dependent on it, or another as good, and that I had relinquished it to fulfill my engagement with them, and they might at least have answered my letters.

I am thinking a little of asking my brother to get me a publisher in America. He does not know at all what the work is. I did not know, when I came here. My sister says that he thinks the book will be read, whether it is a Discovery or not. He is the first person I spoke to about my Discovery of the philosophy, which was eleven or twelve years ago, and he said " Go on with it," not knowing what he said. But he is a good man, though he has had a bad education and he is in bad company. I have been very careful not to connect him with it at all of late, because his obligations are different from mine. He said to me in his last letter, " Your ' Philosophy of Shakespeare ' will have readers, I dare say." It is death to be charged with being " liberal " in his church, and those who watch for his halting in this respect

would be glad to make him responsible for this book, I know.

I think you will conclude not to write to Mr. Emerson. I have written a letter which passed his on the way, and I shall probably hear from him again. You will not be able to do more than read this in the ten days that you are at Liverpool, and I will not send you my tragedy, though it has been sealed and directed these many days, until I have your orders. *I do very much rely on that,* because it is full of science. I do not know how it is possible ever to shut it up again after it has once been opened. You need not reprove me for this letter and tell me how many pages there are of it. I know, and I am reproving myself. It is not the business of the Consulship that I care for interrupting, because this is the Consulship that we talk of. But how do I know what mystic and delicate processes I am disturbing and what new and beautiful work of art, destined to be a joy forever, is getting hindered with it.

Fresh from such an impressive lesson in chirography, I ought not to make such work as this, but you will forgive it I hope, and I will promise not to trouble you in this way again.

Truly yours,
DELIA BACON.

I have been thinking hard whether to burn this up or to send it. I have had the weakness which

results from a severe attack of neuralgia to struggle with in the writing of it, or it would not have
been so long. You asked me what I wished you
to do. I will answer you as Mr. Emerson has
answered me. I wish you to get the book published by somebody or other on this side of the
water or that, that is if you continue to think it is
fit to be published, when you have heard this story
of the rejection of it without a reading, and besides that I wish you to hear what else I have to
say, for it is very important. I want you to take
charge of this work, in case anything happens to
me, and act as you see fit in reference to it, sup-
press it or publish it, as your judgment and conscience shall guide you. It is not good for anything except as a beginning.   D. BACON.

[HAWTHORNE TO D. B.]

LIVERPOOL, July 21, 1856.

DEAR MISS BACON,—I do not see any use in
writing to Mr. Emerson; in fact, I always wondered at finding him in the position which he has
hitherto held, in respect to your work. I heartily
wish (on your own account) that you had a better
alternative than myself; but I shall do what I can,
and as well as I know how.

It seems to me improbable that John Murray
will be induced to undertake the publication of a
book like this. However, if you judge it important, I will endeavor to have the MS. presented to

him under good auspices — those, for instance, of some respectable English man of letters. My own word would not be worth a farthing with him.

If the book were my own, I should not care who published it, so long as it did really come before the world. Were *that* once accomplished, through whatsoever medium, you would have fulfilled your mission, and would have a right to talk of going hence. If a preacher is inspired, and cannot find a pulpit, he must speak from the top of a barrel. But there are very respectable publishers in London, some one of whom, I hope, would undertake it. Routledge has published about a hundred thousand volumes of my books, and has several times sought to institute personal relations with me. I do not yet know him, but would see him, if you desire it, on this subject; and if any commendation on my part might avail with him, it should not be wanting. It would be in his power to circulate the work widely; and I presume he would deal fairly with you, on the principles of the Trade.

There are other publishers, to whom I should have similar facilities of introducing the book.

I shall be able to return to London the latter part of this week — perhaps not till Saturday. As soon as possible, next week, I will call; and perhaps it is better that I should receive " Coriolanus " from your own hands.

You will not accomplish any good purpose, I think, by writing to those magazine people. They

will pay you nothing, unless on compulsion of law :
and they will consider themselves free from liability, as having returned the papers to an agent
pointed out, I suppose, by your agent, Mr. Emerson. If anything can be done, Mr. E. ought to
feel himself bound to do it, that is, if he were a
man like other men ; but he is far more than that,
and not so much.

With my best wishes,

Very sincerely yours,

Natᴴ' Hawthorne.

The reply to this, two days later, brought to
Hawthorne more and more narrative and discussion — about the loss of the manuscript in America ;
about the responsibility for so heart-breaking a
disaster, whether upon Emerson, or the magazine
publishers, or upon whom ; about past communi-
cations with English publishers, and what should
now be done with them or with others. As for
Routledge, of whom Hawthorne had spoken : " I
should like nothing better," she says, " than to
have him publish it if he will, and if you would
give me a Title for it, — for that is the principal
thing at first, — I think you might make of it a
book for him. I have tried in vain to fix upon so
much as a tolerable one. Mr. Emerson suggested
' The Authorship of Shakespeare's Plays,' or something of that kind, though he said he could not
name it himself, because he had not seen the book,

but would wish to have it ' in stone.' I told him that that was not the true title of the book, and why it was not; but for lack of the true one I concluded to take it, and the copyright of a book with that title has I believe been secured in my name in America. But that is of no consequence I suppose. I have now a chance to begin anew. Let that book go, since they have killed it there amongst them, or voted it dead, and performed the last offices for it. Let us begin with a new one here that nobody has heard of yet. I have thought a little of calling it ' The Baconian Philosophy Illustrated with Plays and Poems,' or ' The Baconian Fables,' (and Aphorisms). Suppose we say nothing about the Actor in the title this time. He has had his name on the title-page of this Philosophy long enough. But I must be careful what I say, for I suppose I must take it for granted there is a great gulf here between us still. I am not fit to speak to any one else on that point, for I have forgotten how to frame the venerable chimera that that name used to stand for. I can hardly persuade myself that there is anybody now alive that really believes in that moon-calf."

Then again recurring to the great grief of the lost manuscript, she submits herself nevertheless, with a docility which certainly does not yet evince complete mental overthrow, to Hawthorne's pacificatory dissuasions, and consents to withhold the sharp complaints she had determined to send. She

does not overlook, indeed, the finely delicate analysis of one illustrious Concord neighbor by another,
in the closing words of the last letter, saying : " As
to Mr. Emerson, he has appeared so much like a
man, and a great man too, in this affair that I
almost forgot he was a 'genius' ! " And she closes
with a reminiscence of words which she must first
have heard in the grievous days of her infancy, in
the Ohio log-cabin : " ' They that wait upon the
Lord shall renew their strength. They shall mount
up with wings as eagles ; they shall run and not
be weary, they shall walk and not faint.' And
since I have heard your voice in this outer darkness reviving the mortal life in me when it was
well-nigh gone, I take it for an omen that there
is something more to be done here yet, and begin
to plan anew."

XIV

It was only by metaphor that she spoke, in closing her letter of July 23, of hearing the " voice
in the outer darkness." A few days afterward she
heard it, in literal truth, for the first time, — and
the last.

Under date July 29, 1856, of Hawthorne's
" English Note-Books," he mentions his visit,
within three days before, to Delia Bacon ; and in
his book, largely made up from those notes, which
he called " Our Old Home," he thus describes the
visit. It is in the chapter entitled, from the subject which so largely occupies it, " Recollections of
a Gifted Woman."

" I should hardly have dared to add another to
the innumerable descriptions of Stratford-on-Avon,
if it had not seemed to me that this would form a
fitting framework to some reminiscences of a very
remarkable woman. Her labor, while she lived,
was of a nature and purpose outwardly irreverent
to the name of Shakspeare, yet, by its actual tendency, entitling her to the distinction of being
that one of all his worshippers who sought, though
she knew it not, to place the richest and stateliest

diadem upon his brow. We Americans, at least, in the scanty annals of our literature, cannot afford to forget her high and conscientious exercise of noble faculties, which, indeed, if you look at the matter in one way, evolved only a miserable error, but, more fairly considered, produced a result worth almost what it cost her. Her faith in her own ideas was so genuine, that, erroneous as they were, it transmuted them to gold, or, at all events, interfused a large proportion of that precious and indestructible substance among the waste material from which it can readily be sifted.

"The only time I ever saw Miss Bacon was in London, where she had lodgings in Spring Street, Sussex Gardens, at the house of a grocer, a portly middle-aged, civil, and friendly man, who, as well as his wife, appeared to feel a personal kindness towards their lodger. I was ushered up two (and I rather believe three) pair of stairs into a parlor somewhat humbly furnished, and told that Miss Bacon would come soon. There were a number of books on the table, and, looking into them, I found that every one had some reference, more or less immediate, to her Shaksperian theory, — a volume of Raleigh's 'History of the World,' a volume of Montaigne, a volume of Lord Bacon's letters, a volume of Shakspeare's Plays, and on another table lay a large roll of manuscript, which I presume to have been a portion of her work. To be sure, there was a pocket-Bible among the books, but everything else referred to the one despotic idea that had got possession of her mind; and as it had engrossed her whole soul as well as her intellect, I had no doubt that she had established subtile connections between it and the Bible likewise.   As is apt to be the case with solitary students, Miss Bacon probably read late and rose late; for I took up Montaigne (it was Hazlitt's translation) and had been reading his journey to Italy a good while before she appeared.

" I had expected (the more shame for me, having no other ground of such expectation than that she was a literary woman) to see a very homely, uncouth, elderly personage, and was quite agreeably disappointed by her aspect.   She was rather uncommonly tall, and had a striking and expressive face, dark hair, dark eyes, which shone with an inward light as soon as she began to speak, and by and by a color came into her cheeks and made her look almost young.   Not that she really was so; she must have been beyond middle age : and there was no unkindness in coming to that conclusion, because, making allowance for years and ill health, I could suppose her to have been handsome and exceedingly attractive once.   Though wholly estranged from society, there was little or no restraint or embarrassment in her manner : lonely people are generally glad to give utterance to their pent-up ideas, and often bubble over with them as freely as children with their new-found syllables.

I cannot tell how it came about, but we immediately found ourselves taking a friendly and familiar
tone together, and began to talk as if we had
known one another a very long while. A little
preliminary correspondence had indeed smoothed
the way, and we had a definite topic in the con-
templated publication of her book.

"She was very communicative about her theory,
and would have been much more so had I desired
it; but, being conscious within myself of a sturdy
unbelief, I deemed it fair and honest rather to
repress than draw her out upon the subject.
Unquestionably, she was a monomaniac; these
overmastering ideas about the authorship of
Shakspeare's plays, and the deep political philosophy concealed beneath the surface of them, had
completely thrown her off her balance ; but at the
same time they had wonderfully developed her
intellect, and made her what she could not otherwise have become. It was a very singular phenomenon : a system of philosophy grown up in
this woman's mind without her volition, — contrary, in fact, to the determined resistance of her
volition, — and substituting itself in the place of
everything that originally grew there. To have
based such a system on fancy, and unconsciously
elaborated it for herself, was almost as wonderful
as really to have found it in the plays. But, in
a certain sense, she did actually find it there.
Shakspeare has surface beneath surface to an im-

measurable depth, adapted to the plummet-line of every reader; his works present many phases of truth, each with scope large enough to fill a contemplative mind. Whatever you seek in him you will surely discover, provided you seek truth. There is no exhausting the various interpretation of his symbols; and a thousand years hence, a world of new readers will possess a whole library of new books, as we ourselves do, in these volumes old already. I had half a mind to suggest to Miss Bacon this explanation of her theory, but forbore, because (as I could readily perceive) she had as princely a spirit as Queen Elizabeth herself, and would at once have motioned me from the room.

"I had heard, long ago, that she believed that the material evidences of her dogma as to the authorship, together with the key of the new philosophy, would be found buried in Shakspeare's grave. Recently, as I understood her, this notion had been somewhat modified, and was now accurately defined and fully developed in her mind, with a result of perfect certainty. In Lord Bacon's letters, on which she laid her finger as she spoke, she had discovered the key and clew to the whole mystery. There were definite and minute instructions how to find a will and other documents relating to the conclave of Elizabethan philosophers, which were concealed (when and by whom she did not inform me) in a hollow space in the under surface of Shakspeare's gravestone.

Thus the terrible prohibition to remove the stone was accounted for. The directions, she intimated, went completely and precisely to the point, obviating all difficulties in the way of coming at the treasure, and even, if I remember right, were so contrived as to ward off any troublesome consequences likely to ensue from the interference of the parish officers. All that Miss Bacon now remained in England for — indeed, the object for which she had come hither, and which had kept her here for three years past — was to obtain possession of these material and unquestionable proofs of the authenticity of her theory.

"She communicated all this strange matter in a low, quiet tone; while, on my part, I listened as quietly, and without any expression of dissent. Controversy against a faith so settled would have shut her up at once, and that, too, without in the least weakening her belief in the existence of those treasures of the tomb ; and had it been possible to convince her of their intangible nature, I apprehend that there would have been nothing left for the poor enthusiast save to collapse and die. She frankly confessed that she could no longer bear the society of those who did not at least lend a certain sympathy to her views, if not fully share in them ; and meeting little sympathy or none, she had now entirely secluded herself from the world. In all these years, she had seen Mrs. Farrar a few times, but had long ago given her up, — Carlyle once or

twice, but not of late, although he had received
her kindly; Mr. Buchanan, while Minister in England, had once called on her, and General Campbell, our Consul in London, had met her two or
three times on business. With these exceptions,
which she marked so scrupulously that it was per-
ceptible what epochs they were in the monotonous
passage of her days, she had lived in the profoundest solitude. She never walked out; she suffered
much from ill health; and yet, she assured me,
she was perfectly happy.

" I could well conceive it; for Miss Bacon imagined herself to have received (what is certainly
the greatest boon ever assigned to mortals) a high
mission in the world, with adequate powers for its
accomplishment; and lest even these should prove
insufficient, she had faith that special interpositions
of Providence were forwarding her human efforts.
This idea was continually coming to the surface
during our interview. She believed, for example,
that she had been providentially led to her lodging house, and put in relations with the good-
natured grocer and his family; and, to say the
truth, considering what a savage and stealthy tribe
the London lodging-house keepers usually are, the
honest kindness of this man and his household
appeared to have been little less than miraculous.
Evidently, too, she thought that Providence had
brought me forward — a man somewhat connected
with literature — at the critical juncture when she

needed a negotiator with the booksellers ; and, on
my part, though little accustomed to regard myself
as a divine minister, and though I might even
have preferred that Providence should select some
other instrument, I had no scruples in undertaking
to do what I could for her. Her book, as I could
see by turning it over, was a very remarkable one,
and worthy of being offered to the public, which,
if wise enough to appreciate it, would be thankful
for what was good in it and merciful to its faults.
It was founded on a prodigious error, but was built
up from that foundation with a good many prodigious truths. And, at all events, whether I could
aid her literary views or no, it would have been
both rash and impertinent.in me to attempt drawing poor Miss Bacon out of her delusions, which
were the condition on which she lived in comfort
and joy, and in the exercise of great intellectual
power. So I left her to dream as she pleased
about the treasures of Shakspeare's tombstone,
and to form whatever designs might seem good to
herself for obtaining possession of them. I was
sensible of a ladylike feeling of propriety in Miss
Bacon, and a New England orderliness in her character, and, in spite of her bewilderment, a sturdy
common-sense, which I trusted would begin to
operate at the right time, and keep her from any
actual extravagance. And as regarded this matter
of the tombstone, so it proved.

"The interview lasted above an hour, during

which she flowed out freely, as to the sole auditor, capable of any degree of intelligent sympathy, whom she had met with in a very long while. Her conversation was remarkably suggestive, alluring forth one's own ideas and fantasies from the shy places where they usually haunt. She was indeed an admirable talker, considering how long she had held her tongue for lack of a listener, — pleasant, sunny, and shadowy, often piquant, and giving glimpses of all a woman's various and readily changeable moods and humors; and beneath them all there ran a deep and powerful under-current of earnestness, which did not fail to produce in the listener's mind something like a temporary faith in what she herself believed so fervently. But the streets of London are not favorable to enthusiasms of this kind, nor, in fact, are they likely to flourish anywhere in the English atmosphere; so that, long before reaching Paternoster Row, I felt that it would be a difficult and doubtful matter to advocate the publication of Miss Bacon's book. Nevertheless, it did finally get published."

Close upon this visit she sends Hawthorne, as she had long been anxious to do, her study of " Coriolanus," or part of it. It brought to her one of the great joys of her fast shortening life ; for it brought her into communication with Hawthorne's wife, whose sister, Elizabeth Peabody, had been almost the first *confidante* of her great secret, four or five years before. This was Mrs. Hawthorne's letter; and it is only justice to her to whom it was addressed that it should be known what not unkindly judgments were in those days formed of the work she was doing, and by what manner of persons : —

MY DEAR MISS BACON, — Mr. Hawthorne wishes me to tell you that your manuscript arrived safely on Saturday evening. He has not read it yet, for the very good reason that he could not, as I have had possession of it ever since it came, and only finished it last evening. My dear Miss Bacon, I feel so ignorant in the presence of your extraordinary learning, that it seems absurd in me even to say what I think of your manuscripts, and yet I cannot help it; for I never read so profound and wonderful a criticism, and I think there never was such a philosophic insight and appreciation since Lord Bacon himself. No subject has so great a fascination for me as " divine Philosophy," this searching into the nature of things, and extracting their essence and discovering the central order, the Law that perpetually is striving to bring Harmony, and which never can be broken — I mean not without a darkening of the Universe. I am one of those who have

> " a credence in my heart,
> An espérance so obstinately strong
> As doth outdo the attest of eyes and ears." [1]

---

[1] *Troilus and Cressida*, Act V., scene 2. " *Invert* the attest " is the original. [T. B.]

(I believe these are the words of the immortal poet whom we have called Shakspere,) and so I am always ready to say " Yes, it may be so," to every new suggestion, however astounding. I have often thought we had effects without cause in those works, if they were written by an uncultivated mind, or rather by a mind not cultivated and educated to the *last* possibility, and I have said " It is a miracle." Yet I could believe in a miracle. To add all these, however, to what Lord Bacon has avowedly done, is to make him such a prodigy as the world never before saw. But this I have room enough for also. What I want now is more and more and more of your detections, your proofs, your criticism. I have an insatiable hunger, and I shall be glad when these and all are in print, for just as sure as there comes a point of trembling interest, you begin to interline and I am driven wild. But this last manuscript is much plainer than the others. Mr. Hawthorne has gone to Routledge this morning to speak about them. I hope that he will have the wit to publish them, for, irrespective of their ulterior purpose, they are wonderful, magnificent.

Sincerely yours,

SOPHIA HAWTHORNE.

August 3 [1856].

Blackheath Park, Mr. Bennock's.

The answer to this is dated August 9. " I was truly glad to hear your voice at last. I have had a kind of image of you for some time in my mind, and now that you draw nearer, I am very glad to identify in the features of your letter the ' soul feminine ' of my so noble friend and helper, whom not seeing I had known also. And yet I think with Carlyle that the least glimpse of a human face, or the poorest portrait, gives one a better idea of the individuality than any other kind of demonstration. But I found such decided and constant features not in Mr. Hawthorne's books only but in his letters, and not in his words only but in his acts, that my confidence in him did not need that confirmation. He has helped me most of all by demonstrating his acquaintance with this human doctrine, a knowledge in which I have found some men of fame and learning wanting. . . .

" I should like very much to see you and those dear little children of yours, that I saw once for a moment. But there is but one thing for me to do at present. If you are able to do so I should take it as a great favor if you would come and see me. But I will not ask it of you, because I know it would be a great deal of trouble, and there would be nothing to pay you for it. My book is all that there is of me now, or rather my *work*, for the book is only the beginning of it. I broke off with the Carlyles (for there are *two* of them) on that account entirely. I did not think I was fit company for any one, and it was a mere imposition on my part to be pretending to it."

LIVERPOOL, August 12, '56.

DEAR MISS BACON, — I had to return hither, some days ago; but I had already gone twice to Routledge's, and, the second time, I saw one of the partners — Routledge himself being absent for a month or two. The partner (the same, perhaps, whom you talked with) suggested the probable unsuitableness of the book to their general line of business; but he desired to see the manuscript, and promised me, in any case, his best advice and utmost aid towards getting the work published. He seemed to think that it would be quite practicable. The second part of Coriolanus had not arrived when I left Blackheath; but I propose to deliver that portion of the work, first and alone, to the Routledges, as being perhaps calculated to make the best impression on their practical minds. I expect, at all events, much benefit from the counsels of these men, and I will not doubt that the world shall be made to hear your voice.

I cannot now say how soon I shall return to Blackheath; but Mrs. Hawthorne will be delighted to receive the remaining part of Coriolanus, in the meantime. I have not yet read the first part; but she, while reading it, kept overflowing into my ears with the many passages that took effect on her.   In haste,

Sincerely yours,

NATH' HAWTHORNE.

No one who knew Hawthorne through his books alone could need evidence of his exquisitely refined delicacy and sensibility. Nor could one who knew him thus imagine that the same man was characterized by the solidest and most substantial good sense, and by a strong intrepidity which would bring him, notwithstanding an almost morbid shrinking from human contact, to confront utter strangers with affairs not at all his own, and even to incur the risk of being thought officious in the business of others. ˙ In all these letters of his, nothing seems better to declare at once his singular good sense and his unselfish generosity than this which follows, addressed to one with whom he had no acquaintance, and venturing advice upon matters in regard to which men are sometimes very sensitive to intrusion. Its manifest kindness, however, was answered with the sincerest thanks, as having " brought some measure of relief to the anxiety of her nearest friends." But it was plain that he already discerned in her extreme exaltation the danger, if not the actual beginning, of that pronounced derangement of mind which was but a few months distant.

U. S. CONSULATE,
LIVERPOOL, August 14, '56.

MY DEAR SIR, — I have recently held some communication with your sister, Miss Delia Bacon, at present residing in London : and, as I believe she

has no other friend in England, you will not think
me impertinent in addressing you with reference
to her affairs.　I understand from her (and can
readily suppose it to be the case) that you are
very urgent that she should return to America;
nor can I deny that I should give her similar advice, if her mind were differently circumstanced
from what I find it.　But Miss Bacon has become
possessed by an idea, that there are discoveries
within her reach, in reference to the authorship of
Shakspeare, and that, by quitting England, she
should forfeit all chance of following up these discoveries, and making them manifest to the public.
I say nothing as to the correctness of this idea (as
respects the existence of direct, material, and doc-
umentary evidence) as she has not imparted to me
the grounds of her belief.　But, at all events, she
is so fully and firmly possessed by it, that she will
never leave England, voluntarily, until she shall
have done everything in her power to obtain these
proofs; nor would any argument, nor, I think, any
amount of poverty and hardship avail with her to
the contrary.　And I will say to you in confidence,
my dear Sir, that I should dread the effect, on her
mind, of any compulsory measures on the part of
her friends, towards a removal.　If I might presume to advise, my counsel would be that you
should acquiesce, for the present, in her remaining
here, and do what may be in your power towards
making her comfortable.

However mistaken your sister may be, she has produced a most remarkable work, written with wonderful earnestness and ability, and full of very profound criticism. Its merits are entirely independent of the truth of her theory about the authorship of the plays. I am in hopes to find a publisher for the work, here in England; and I should judge that there was a fair chance of its meeting with such success as would render her independent of her friends. But this, of course, must be an affair of time.

At the only interview which I have had with Miss Bacon, I found her tolerably well in bodily health, perfectly cheerful, and conversing with great power and intelligence. She lodges in the house of some excellent people, who seem to be attached to her, and who treat her as few London lodging-house keepers would treat their inmates, if suspected of poverty. She is very fortunate in having found such a home; and I submit it to your judgment, on a view of the whole case, whether it will not be more for her well-being to remain here, than (against such strong convictions as actuate her) to return to America. And, as I have already said, it seems to me quite certain that she will *not* return (with her purpose unfulfilled) while she continues to be a free agent.

I write this note of my own motion, being greatly interested by what I have seen of your sister, and feeling, indeed, an anxious responsibility in putting her situation fairly before you.

Pardon me if I have used an undue freedom, and believe me,

Very sincerely and respectfully,
NATH' HAWTHORNE.

REV. DR. BACON.

On the 20th of August she writes briefly to Mrs. Hawthorne, telling of much suffering from sickness and pain, of plans for leaving London, of relief which had come from her friends in America, and of " a very pleasant letter from Mr. Emerson," which she is going to send, and which, having been sent, is not among her papers. But she says that Hawthorne's favorable criticism of such part of her work as he had read had "had a good effect already " on Emerson.

Then follow these two letters ; and after them she left London for the last time. Her work was almost done.

MY DEAR MISS BACON, — I have this moment received your manuscript, and am thankful for such a godsend this dull weather and in the continued absence of my husband. The winter of my discontent will not be made glorious summer till next Wednesday, and so we cannot read it together. I rejoice at all your hopes and assurances, but grieve much over your suffering. I have been waiting for a good day to go and see you, but the weather confines me on account of my throat.

Will you tell me where you shall be after Monday, that I may discover you when I can go to town.

In the greatest haste at present,

I am sincerely yours,

SOPHIA HAWTHORNE.

I send this directly to relieve your mind of anxiety about the manuscript.

BLACKHEATH PARK,
August 21, 1856.

12 SPRING ST., August 26, '56.

DEAR MRS. HAWTHORNE, — I have been trying to be able to write a note either to Mr. H. or yourself ever since I received yours acknowledging the manuscript, but the illness of which I spoke then has proved a very serious one, and if I had thought you were quite well enough to come and see me I should certainly have sent for you. All my arrangements were made to go into the country on Monday, but yesterday I could not sit up, and whether I get off to-day or not is very doubtful. I looked on while the servant packed my trunks for me last night after her fashion, and it nearly killed me. I am dying partly, principally I think, of want of proper food, proper for an invalid. The mercy of the lodging-house keepers, in that respect, is small when the difference in price between the nutritious and the poisonous article goes to them. Just at the moment when it became absolutely necessary that I should make a change on that account I found myself in possession of the means of paying my bill here entirely, leaving a very very small sum over. I hoped I should receive more this week, but it has not come. . . .

Mrs. Farrar sent me some nice things last week, but I think they came too late. They don't revive or strengthen me at all that I can see. The Dr. says that I must go to a farm-house; I told him I was very poor, and he says I can live on almost nothing there, and have the very diet that I require. He recommends the vicinity of Leamington, at least I told him I had been thinking of that, and he says it is the very best I can choose. I shall try to go to-day. I shall take those chapters with me, and write them over at my leisure. I put my book into Mr. Hawthorne's hands to dispose of as he thinks best whether I live or die. I wrote to my friends that I had done so. If he can get it published here or in America, I wish he would. I know he will make the best terms for it that he can, and he need not wait to consult me about it at all.

In great haste.

> Truly and affectionately yours,
> DELIA BACON.

Direct to me at Stratford-on-Avon Post-office. I shall leave my address there for any one who inquires for it.

XV

IN what condition it was that she made alone this last expedition of her life, to Stratford, is briefly told by Mrs. Farrar in the book already quoted.

In London she " had suffered many privations during the time that she was writing her book. She lived on the poorest food, and was often without the means of having a fire in her chamber. She told me that she wrote a great part of her large octavo volume sitting up in bed, in order to keep warm. . . .

" Her life of privation and seclusion was very injurious to both body and mind. How great that seclusion was is seen from the following passage from another of her letters to me : ' I am glad to know that you are still alive and on this side of that wide sea which parts me from so many that were once so *near*, for I have lived here much like a departed spirit, looking back on the joys and sorrows of a world in which I have no longer any place. I have been more than a year in this house, and have had but three visitors in all that time, and paid but one visit myself, and that was to Carlyle, after he had taken the trouble to come

all the way from Chelsea to invite me, and although he has since written to invite me, I have not been able to accept his kindness. I have had calls from Mr. Grote and Mr. Monckton Milnes;[1] and Mr. Buchanan came to see me, though I had not delivered my letter to him.'

"All the fine spirits who knew Miss Bacon found in her what pleased and interested them, and had not that one engrossing idea possessed her, she might have had a brilliant career among the literary society of London.

"One dark winter evening, after writing all day in her bed, she rose, threw on some clothes, and walked out to take the air. Her lodgings were at the West End of London, near to Sussex Gardens, and not far from where my mother lived. She needed my address, and suddenly resolved to go to the house of Mrs. R. for it. She sent in her request, and while standing in the doorway she had a glimpse of the interior. It looked warm, cheerful, and inviting, and she had a strong desire to see my mother; so she readily accepted an invitation to walk in, and found the old lady with her daughter and a friend just sitting down to tea. Happily my sister remembered that a Miss Bacon had been favorably mentioned in my letters from Cambridge, so she had no hesitation in asking her to take tea with them. The stranger's dress was such an extraordinary dishabille that nothing but her lady-

[1] Richard Monckton Milnes, afterward Lord Houghton. [T. B.]

like manners and conversation could have convinced the family that she was the person whom she pretended to be. She told me how much ashamed she was of her appearance that evening; she had intended going only to the door, but could not resist the inclination to enter and sit down at that cheerful tea-table, which looked so like mine in Cambridge.

"The next summer I was living in London. The death of a dear friend had just occurred in my house; the relatives were collected there, and all were feeling very sad, when I was told by my servant that a lady wished to see me. I sent word that there was death in the house, and I could see no one that night. The servant returned, saying, 'She will not go away, ma'am, and she will not give her name.'

"On hearing this I went to the door, and there stood Delia Bacon, pale and sad. I took her in my arms and pressed her to my bosom; she gasped for breath and could not speak. We went into a vacant room and sat down together. She was faint, but recovered on drinking a glass of port wine, and then she told me that her book was finished and in the hands of Mr. Hawthorne, and now she was ready to go to Stratford-upon-Avon. There she expected to verify her hypothesis, by opening the tomb of Shakespeare, where she felt sure of finding papers that would disclose the real authorship of the plays. I tried in vain to dissuade her

from this insane project; she was resolved, and
only wished for my aid in winding up her affairs
in London and setting her off for Stratford. This
aid I gave with many a sad misgiving as to the result. She looked so ill when I took leave of her
in the railroad carriage that I blamed myself for
not having accompanied her to Stratford, and was
only put at ease by a very cheerful letter from
her, received a few days after her departure."

This letter was very like in substance, and almost in terms, to that which follows here.

August 29–30, '56.

MY DEAR MRS. HAWTHORNE, — Twenty-four
hours after I left London — alone, and fearfully ill
— not knowing hardly whither I went, — I found
myself lying on the sofa, in the most perfect little
Paradise of neatness and comfort that you can
possibly conceive of — if it had been invented on
purpose, and dropped down out of the clouds to
receive me at the end of my journey, it could not
have been more exactly the place I wanted, — with
a dear good motherly old lady to nurse me and
take care of me, and no other creature in the
house but her little servant who is all of a piece
with the rest of it. It is not a lodging house.
The owner of it lives on her rents, and never took
a lodger in her life before, but some person had
heard that she thought of taking a friend of hers
for company, and something had happened to pre-

vent it, and she thought if she could find a lady to
her mind, perhaps she would take one. I had stipulated for a place near the church, and this was
mentioned in that connection. The only objects
to be seen from my window as I write are the
trees on the banks of the Avon, and the church
directly before me, only a few yards from here,
though I shall have to go about some to find access to it, I suppose. I took the old lady by storm.
She was not at home when I arrived here. I had
come in a " Fly " from the " Red 'Orse," for I could
just as soon have forded the Atlantic Ocean as to
have walked the short distance from my inn to this
place. You must know I was so deadly ill that I
could not get taken in at an ordinary lodging
house ; they thought from my appearance that I
was going to die directly and that it would not be
worth the trouble. At least there was great hesitation on that account evidently, and I could not
wait for the decision. This old lady had gone to
church — something about the Jews — her little
handmaid said, from which I argued favorably.
The moment I looked into the house I thought I
saw that it was the place appointed for me, and I
ordered the porter to take off my luggage. It
was deposited in the hall, and seating myself in
the room which I intended to occupy, and trying
to get as much life into my face as I could, I
awaited with some anxiety the return of the owner
of the establishment. The little handmaid seemed

to have some misgivings and once she came to the
door and said timidly, "Do you know Mrs. Terrett?"
I told her she need not give herself any trouble, I
would take all the blame of it. The *kitchen* was
what finally decided me to stop; I walked into it,
and I thought it was the prettiest place I ever saw.
The walls were painted cerulean blue, and everything in it shone like gold. The little servant kept
running up stairs and putting her head out of the
window, and finally she reported that the thing was
ended, whatever it was, and that her mistress was
coming. The moment I saw her kind countenance
I was sure that I had not made a mistake. She
was very much surprised of course, — said that she
had thought a little of such a thing, but was not
aware that she had named it to any one. She saw
that I was very ill, and *that* I think decided her not
to send me away, at least till I was better. We
talked about the price. — Two very, very nice
rooms, good sized, and well furnished — the front
room and the room over it. She asked me if I
thought — if she furnished linen, etc. — if *seven*
shillings per week would be too much for rent and
attendance. As I had been paying *eighteen*, for
accommodations very much less to my mind, I told
her I thought it would not. So all was settled,
and she made me lie down on the sofa and covered
me up like a mother, and went off to prepare some
refreshment for me immediately, and there I lay
at two o'clock — (the hour I left London the day

before) looking out on that church spire, and those trees on the Avon, so near, so very near, and yet doubtful whether my feet would ever take me there. For such deathly, deathly weakness no one ever felt before I believe who was able to go about in person to take lodgings. I have scarcely had a thought or an emotion since I left London. I am only an automaton obeying some former purpose, obeying rather the Power above that is working beneficently in all this. I have no anxiety, no care about it. I love to be here. Those beautiful trees and that church spire look a little like dream-land to me, and after the trouble of the journey yesterday I felt almost inclined to pronounce the aspirate as the natives do here; it would not be the first time that that play on the word has been made — 'Avon. I lie here as quiet and as helpless as a baby waiting on the Power that has brought me here, with no fear now that any thing will fail which the opening of this new fountain of blessings for men, requires to be done. I shall be here perhaps for months to come. To recover my health is now my only object. If that *can be* done, this I think is the place for it. The air is as pure as heaven, and the calm after that noise for twenty months soothes me every moment. Yesterday I could not have written a page of this to save my life, but I have had the table drawn up to the sofa and I stop and rest me whenever I am tired. It gives me pleasure to write it to you, and

I think you will like to know what has become of me, though I do not know as you will care for all these details. But I thought you might feel some uneasiness about me, taking *all* the circumstances into the account, and I wished both Mr. H. and yourself to know that I am here for my health, and for the rest I shall wait for clear indications, and I expect help and direction from a power which is not limited to the sphere of my consciousness and volitions. I expect it to work in other minds as well as my own if that should be required, for I do not think that I have been brought here after so long a time for nothing. I had to stop in the midst of a sentence last night for that deathly faintness came over me again and I could not even sign my name to the letter so as to get it to the Post in time. I slept eight hours last night and this morning I begin to feel some faint return of my former self. Till now my mind has instinctively excluded all thoughts of my work and everything connected with it. What I have put on paper here is the most that I have thought on the subject since I left London. There was no vitality to spare, and I suppose it will take many days yet to put me back where I was in health when I planned my journey here.

Most truly yours,

DELIA BACON.

Address at Mrs. Terrett's,
    College St., Stratford-on-Avon.

My dear Miss Bacon, — When I received your very welcome note dated Stratford-on-Avon, I had on my bonnet to go to Oxford with Mr. Hawthorne, or I should have replied to it at once. I have been to Oxford — and when there was hurried from place to place and obliged to sit and be polite part of the time, as we were guests of a gentleman there. On my return I was obliged to spend the very next day in London to see the Doctor and a dentist. The next day I went to Hampton Court, and now this is the first quiet and leisure I have had. I am unspeakably stupid from fatigue to-day, but I cannot allow another mail to pass without telling you what a relief it was to me to have your note, and to hear that you were in such a sweet little quiet place, and under such kind guardianship. May Heaven bless the old lady and her little maid! May the sun ever shine on the cottage! You seem led by the angel of the Lord. I wish very much to know whether you are getting better. If you cannot write, tell the kind old lady to write for you and let me know how you do. We shall leave Blackheath on the Thursday or Friday of this week — and then will you direct to the Consulate till I can tell you where we are at the seaside. It seems to me impertinent to be anxious or careful about you whom the angels guard. Our friend Mr. Bennoch is going to aid us about getting your manuscripts published, but I know nothing to tell you quite yet.

My dear Miss Bacon, I did not know till your note enclosed by Mrs. Farrar that your health was feeble, or that your friends had left you solely to God. Mr. Hawthorne had never informed me of your present needs. I thought you "beyond the utmost scope and vision of calamity," like a disembodied thought. You ought not to be obliged to think of what you shall eat or wherewithal you should be clothed while occupied with your noble work.

With the highest admiration and respect,

I am very sincerely yours,

SOPHIA HAWTHORNE.

7th September [1856].

[HAWTHORNE TO D. B.]

LIVERPOOL, Sept. 24, '56.

DEAR MISS BACON, — I have seen a notice of the publication you tell me about, in the Athenæum; but I have not seen the thing itself, and can not procure it here. The Athenæum refers to your essay on the subject, published in Putnam's Magazine. From the extracts, I should judge that the author of the "Letter" takes hold of the matter externally, without looking inside of the plays for any part of his argument. I will write to a friend in London to send you a copy.

When I was compelled to leave London, I put the affair (of publishing your work) into the hands of a gentleman in whose energy I had all confidence, and who seemed to take hold of it lovingly, for my sake. But I do not yet know what he has done about it. I shall stir him and all other people up about it. I do not know what effect the publication of the " Letter " will have on the minds of booksellers; but, should it draw notice to the subject, I should deem it all the better. Your original property in the idea is sufficiently established.

Mrs. Hawthorne is at Southport, about twenty miles from Liverpool, and is pretty well.

I write in immense haste.

Sincerely yours,
NATH' HAWTHORNE.

P. S. You say nothing about the state of your funds. Pardon me for alluding to the subject; but you promised to apply to me in case of need. I am ready.   N. H.

Two allusions in the last preceding letter are worthy of explanation.

The "publication" which had been noticed in the *Athenæum*, and of which she had evidently written to Hawthorne in some alarm, was a pamphlet by Mr. William Henry Smith, printed in London for private circulation in September, 1856, and entitled, " Was Lord Bacon the Author of

Shakespeare's Plays: A Letter to the Earl of Ellesmere."

Upon this, Hawthorne, in his Introduction to Delia Bacon's book, animadverted with severity, as an unfair assumption of that lady's theory as original with the author of the pamphlet.

This accusation, however, he afterward publicly withdrew, upon sufficient assurance from Mr. Smith that he had " never heard the name of Miss Bacon until it was mentioned in the review of" his pamphlet.

The friend in whose hands Hawthorne had now " put the affair of publishing" was Francis Bennoch, F. S. A., a London merchant, and sometime Member of Parliament. The published " English Note-Books" of Hawthorne show on almost every page how close their friendship was during all his stay in England. He was himself — or he would not have been Hawthorne's friend — a gentleman of fine tastes, which are evinced in a collected volume of his poems.[1]

[1] *Poems, Lyrics, Songs, and Sonnets:* Houghton, Mifflin & Co., 1881.

XVI

WHEN Hawthorne saw his correspondent, on the 29th of July, he recorded in his diary the judgment that she was "a monomaniac." The phrase, which he may have used, as it is used so often, in something less than its scientific sense, was rapidly coming to be strictly exact. The complete significance of these following letters, in showing her increasing mental disturbance, will be made clearer by giving some account of a long and most wise, considerate, and affectionate one from her brother to her, about the 12th of September.

He tells of that "ceaseless pressure of work," known to all who knew him, which had hindered his writing to her very often or very long. "But your last letter," he says, "moves me to seize time from other duties, and to write more at length than I have done heretofore. . . .

"I read with much interest your article in the January number of Putnam's Magazine; and I shared with you — as I believe I have already told you — in the disappointment which followed. The thought of your obtaining for your long labors something which might give you at least a temporary support was one which I entertained the more gladly for its unexpectedness. I will still hope that the materials which you have accumulated as the result of so much toil may be made available for your relief from the troubles that crowd you. Of course, I have no means of judging what those materials are, except from the specimen in the Magazine. If any one can help you in making them available, Mr. Hawthorne is the man. Let me beg you to follow his advice. If he can find a publisher for you, do not hesitate to accept any compensation which he may think reasonable, or (in your circumstances) expedient. As an experienced author, he is competent to advise you on all questions, both as to *what* you will select for publication, and *how* you will publish it. As to the title, I would say, Let him and the publisher agree about that. Their judgment will be worth more than yours and mine together. This, however, I will venture to suggest. Your materials, if I have any idea of them, will be worth more to you in the shape of separate articles for magazines and other periodicals, than if put into one solid volume. And, furthermore, your theory about the authorship of Shakspeare's Plays is worth far less in money value to you or to any publisher, than your exposition of the meaning of those compositions. You know perfectly well that the great world does not care a sixpence who wrote Hamlet. But there are myriads who can read Hamlet with delight, and who will be thankful to anybody that will make their reading of it more delightful or more useful.

"Indeed, my dear sister, if you will but have the courage to fall back on your natural good sense, you will find your way out of ' the enchanted wood ' into which you have been led. Misguided by your imagination, you have yielded yourself to a delusion which, if you do not resist it and escape from it as for your life, will be fatal to you. How to say less than this, I know not. I am not now to inform you that your theory about Shakspeare and Shakspeare's tomb and all that is a mere delusion — a trick of the imagination. For five years you have known that I think so. And — O my dear sister — can you not, in God's name, and in the strength which he will give you, break the spell, and escape from the delusion ? "

Then, after news of many persons in whom she was interested, he resumes :

"I have written this long letter at intervals, snatching a few moments now and then for the purpose of expressing my undiminished brotherly interest in your welfare. Some passages were written with the consciousness that they would be painful to you, but I show you more respect and treat you with more confidence by retaining them, than I could by suppressing them. The friends who humor your delusion, and permit you to be-lieve that they think there may be something in it, may have the kindest intentions, but they have less confidence in you than I have shown by speaking frankly what they think would be lost upon you.   And having returned to this subject, I will make another suggestion.   Your theory about the authorship of Shakspeare's plays may after all be worth something if published *as* a fiction.   You might introduce such things into a romance, and find readers who would accept it respectfully as a work of imagination, and be gratified with it, when if the same things are brought forward with grave argument, as facts to be believed, they will reject the whole work with contempt.   I make this suggestion, not to discourage you, but to encourage you, by showing how all your materials may be turned to good account. . . . I hope to write to you again before long.   Meanwhile commending you to the watchfulness and covenant love of the God of our father and mother, I am your affectionate brother."

This letter was never answered.   Its effect upon her however, so different from that which its wise and solemnly tender remonstrance must surely have had upon her normal mind, is plainly enough shown in that to Hawthorne which follows.   But before giving that there should be mentioned three little notes from the vicar of Stratford.   On the 11th of October he expresses regret at having been unable to call on her that morning, and promises to come on Monday.   That day he again excuses himself on the ground of a forgotten en-

gagement, and proceeds : " As further delay might
cause inconvenience to yourself I shall commit to
paper what I should have preferred to say *viva
voce*, viz., that I regret extremely that I cannot
accede to your request under a sense of the duty
which I owe to others; but I must at the same
time assure you most sincerely that my decision is
not influenced by the least want of confidence in
yourself. I shall however be most happy to find
that I can make such arrangements as will enable
you to accomplish your purpose. If you would
not object to the presence of the Clerk, who I feel
sure would not betray your confidence, or if you
would like better to be accompanied by me, which-
ever you prefer, you have only to intimate your
wishes and I will pay the readiest attention to
them. I need scarcely add that I have complied
with your request not to mention the subject to
any human being." And at last, on the 14th, in
answer, it seems, to further urgency of the sort
disclosed in her letter which follows, he writes
again " to assure you that I am not in the least
disposed to look upon our brothers of the other
side of the Atlantic at all as strangers. The fact
of their coming so long a pilgrimage to the shrine
of Shakspeare would induce me to give them a
greater degree of consideration than my own
countrymen. Having a distinct and plain duty to
perform, I should not, even were Lord Carlisle
to come here and make the same request to me,

grant it to him even, — and he has certainly done much for us in Stratford; and that I do trust you will not conceive I am for one moment throwing the least doubt on your good faith in the decision I have come to."

[D. B. TO HAWTHORNE.]

STRATFORD-UPON-AVON, Oct. 16 [1856].

DEAR MR. HAWTHORNE, — I have not yet tested my belief in regard to the deposit of certain memorials here which may tend to hasten the reception of those new applications of science to practice which the work you have so nobly taken in hand was meant to propound, and which do not depend on any such contingency for their value. Since I have been here I have been in such a state of health that it has been literally impossible for me to make the experiment which I came here to make. I could not bear so much as the thought of it. Even though I had positively known beforehand that I should be successful, I should still have recoiled from it. But I felt that I must not yield to that weakness, and I was constantly watching for the moment when my physical strength would allow me to take the preliminary steps. The week after I wrote you last, I went to the church for the second time since I have been here (I told you of my first visit). I chose the hour at which the clerk told me I should be the least likely perhaps to be interrupted by other visitors, and in the course of that hour, I think he brought in not less than twenty persons. I outstayed them all, but the liability to intrusion at any moment was not favorable to my objects.

" The clerk having locked me in, came for me at six o'clock, by agreement. That was " a *fair* day " he said, but from eight o'clock in the morning there was no hour in the day when I could be sure of being left to myself. I then proposed the evening, and he made no objection, but said he would give me a candle and any assistance that I wanted.

" So the next time I went was in the evening at seven o'clock. He gave me the key, and he was to call for me at ten. It was necessary for me to make a sort of confidant of my landlady, and a very excellent one she is. It happened that I met her as I was going, and I induced her to walk there with me. She shrank very much from going into the church in the dark, but I told her I was not in the least afraid, — I only wanted her to help me a little. So I groped my way to the chancel, and she waited till the light was struck. I had a dark lantern like Guy Fawkes, and some other articles which might have been considered suspicious if the police had come upon us. The clerk was getting uneasy, and I found he had followed us, though he had not proposed to do so, and I was very glad Mrs. ―― was with me, because I made a statement in her presence which reas-

sured him, and they both went off and left me
there. That was the chance that I had desired,
but I had made a promise to the clerk that I would
not do the least thing for which he could be called
in question, — and though I went far enough to
see that the examination I had proposed to make,
could be made, leaving all exactly as I found it, it
could not be made in that time, nor under those
conditions. I did not feel at liberty to make it, for
fear I might violate the trust this man had reposed
in me, and if I were not wholly and immediately
successful I should have run the risk of losing any
chance of continuing my research. I was alone
there till ten o'clock. On my right was the old
Player, I knew, looking down on me, but I could
not see him. I looked up to the ceiling but it
was not visible; there was something that looked
like a midnight sky, and all the long drawn aisle
was in utter darkness. I heard a creaking in it,
a cautious step, repeatedly, and I knew that the
clerk was there and watching me. He told me
when he came in at last, that he had been about
the church all the evening. He evidently felt that
he was doing something questionable at least, in
permitting me to be there under those circumstances, and as I knew that my movements must
seem quite unaccountable to him, I told him then
and there, in general terms, what my objects were,
but that I had respected my promise to him, and
though I might need his aid I would not propose

to him anything inconsistent with his duties, and
that I had concluded to ask the permission of the
Vicar before I proceeded any further. He told me
it would be as much as his place was worth (and
nobody knows how much that is) to assist me
without leave, but if the Vicar would give him leave
he should be very glad to do so. I told him not
to say anything to the Vicar about it until I had
seen him, and though I had not a letter to him I
had some testimonials which would answer my
purpose, and I would introduce myself. That was
rather a premature movement, and I had to stop
to rest upon it."

Then follow many pages — twice as many as
are printed above — telling of the letter from her
brother, with the bitterest complaints of his cold
and deliberate cruelty in writing to her thus. Before this, in the course of this pursuit of hers, she
says, "I have suffered, past the power of tongue
or pen to say how much, from his harshness and
coldness and from his desertion of me, but I have
always apologized for him and my belief in him
and affection for him has always been ready to revive again, and asking leave to heal over all these
wrongs. But I do not think there *is* any healing
for this. . . . He knows how to express himself
according to the prescribed rules of Christian
kindness, when he is most cruel. This is a very
fraternal letter on the surface. . . . He affects to

consider it [the book] a total failure, and suggests
that I might possibly, out of the wreck of my materials, compose a work of fiction which might be
amusing and saleable. I might in that way, he
thinks, avoid the ' contempt ' — that is his word —
which my views in their present form provoke, —
a contempt which he has just been trying to express to me with a refinement of cruelty, which
is calculated to make up for its want of sincerity. . . . I told you my brother was a good man,
and I have always thought him the very very best
man there was, and the people who know him best
are apt to think that of him. And that is what
has given him this power to hurt me. But this
last letter has robbed him of it. It is the last of
many acts of which I have complained to him in
the bitterness of my soul, but now I understand
them and him, and I shall never complain to him
again. But I don't want any one — I don't want
Mrs. Hawthorne to think ill of him, and for that
reason — and for another which is, I think, a good
one — I wish you would not show her this letter
if you can help it. It is necessary that you should
know what fatal misunderstanding this is, that
separates me from my natural helpers. . . . The
case is a very difficult one you see. I have never
written to them for any aid. I would have died
first. . . . I have used the money that my brother
sent me because I could not well help it; but if he
sends me any more, as I suppose from a line at the

end of his letter he expects to, I shall return it to
him. I have not written for any money, but I had
reason to suppose that from one source or the
other I should have some by this time; but it has
not come yet, and I shall have to take your offer,
for the present. It is not much that I want, but
the money I brought with me is gone, — and to
undertake to do what I propose to do here absolutely without money, though I am getting on
without any impediment thus far, is I suppose asking too much of human nature, in a place where
the visits of strangers are calculated on as the
principal means of living. . . .

"I am living now in High Street, in a house not
far from the one that Shakespeare retired to or
rather not far from the site of it, and on the same
side of the street, in a house that was evidently
here then, and one that he has often been in I
suppose, and whether it is the air of the place or
the spirit of that abused individual revengefully
inciting me — even without the means and appliances of the New Place, I would be glad to settle
down here quietly as he did, and mind my own
business for the future. And I am not at all sure
that I shan't do that, if I find I can, and the world
should conclude it does not want any help of mine
— I am a great deal more at home here than I
am in America — I tell all the people here, that I
see, that they need not call me ' a foreigner.' My
fathers helped conquer this country, and I have as

good a right here as they have. I have not definitely decided what I am to do in case all that I
am depending on now, fails, but the conviction that
I shall do something, and not die, is getting strong
in me. I shall be relieved from the necessity of
any future reference to the judgment of the world
on my conduct, though I propose to keep by all
means on good terms with myself. I want you to
help me till I can get over this difficulty. Help
me through this research. I won't ask any one
else. After that if I *do* live I will help myself.
I owe this year of my life to you, and I do not
mean that you, or yours, shall be the poorer for it,
and I say that not for your sake but for my own.
I should have died when Mr. Emerson's letter
came, I think, if it had not been for yours that
came with it, and this *more* cruel one was sheathed
with those two little bits of paper on which you
wrote so much. I had *had* the first when this letter came, and I received the second a few days
after. I have not acknowledged them, but I have
been living on them. I had no heart to go on
till I received the second, after that assault upon
my reason. I knew what fearful risk I was incur-
ring, what my own brother was prepared to say of
me in case I failed, as I expected to, for I began
to take part against myself — it was enough to
drive one mad. But I reviewed all the ground of
my belief, — I summoned to my aid all the faculty
for distinguishing truth from error which God has

given me, and though I could not predict the result, though my belief as to what it may be, and
ought to be, is altogether different from that which
I have in regard to the authorship of the works,
(for that is a scientific certainty, that is knowledge
and not faith,) even under this so fearful penalty,
assured that I *may* find nothing there, — and *that*
that is perhaps the thing most to be expected, —
I have concluded that I should fail in the obligations which have been imposed on me, if I were
to shrink now from this examination for fear of the
personal consequences. That would be base and
cowardly. The inscription speaks of *stones ;* there
may be but one lying directly on the ground, and
if it is only of the usual thickness there is not
likely to be room for my theory in it. I suppose
this to be a *lid*, and that there is one beneath it.
Whether there is, or not, I mean to ascertain.
There may have been one beneath it and it may
have been removed. If it contained anything
valuable, it is the more likely to have been.
There must have been a trust reposed in some
one, — if I positively knew it was there *once*, I
could not be *sure* it is there now. The stones on
either side of it have been put there since. This
very clerk saw the two on the west side of it put
down, but as to the depth of this, he could not
give me any information. If I can ascertain the
depth beforehand, it might save the trouble of
going any further.

"I wanted to have my book published before I made this inquiry, and I never meant to have my belief on this point known until I had had an opportunity of testing it; but some one to whom I told it in the most sacred confidence, and under a solemn promise of secresy, *caused it to be put in the newspapers,* and it has been published all over England and America. My comfort was that a paragraph in the newspapers does not live very long if there is nothing to fan it.

"I want to stay here all winter. I like Stratford. Shakespeare was right. It is a very nice comfortable place to stop in, much better than London for a person of a genial but retiring turn of mind. Some time while I am here I expect that examination to be made. Perhaps no one else but the person who *must* be present (I find) will know *when* it happens. *Three* persons in this town know that it is to be made. They are *the* persons who have the power and right to permit and sanction it; they are sworn to secresy in case of its failure. I have taken the clerk and the *vicar* into my confidence, and the vicar has consulted a friend who is at the same time a lawyer and a Stratford man and the one he would most rely on. I asked the latter for leave to make the examination alone, and the night is the only time possible for it. He took my request into consideration, and the result was that he found it would not be consistent with the solemn obligations he assumed when he took formally the keys of the church from the wardens of it, to allow of *that.* It was no want of confidence in me. If Lord Carlisle should make the same request, and he has certainly done a great deal for Stratford, he could only give him the same answer. He knew *why* I wished for secresy, and he told me if I would not object to the presence of the clerk, who would not, he thought, betray my confidence, or if I preferred that he himself should accompany me, he would make the necessary arrangements for accomplishing my wishes. I have seen him since and told him I would accept his offer, and though I should of course prefer to have him there it might be a tedious operation ; but he says he should not mind that at all, and from his last note I see he has concluded to be there and he only waits now to hear from me. He has been to see me twice about it, and there has been considerable correspondence. He is 'High Church,' but not affectedly or perhaps very zealously religious, and I am glad he is *not.* I would not trust a *very* religious man as I shall have to trust him. What between justification, and free will, and the greatest good of the greatest number, which, practically applied, means number one for the time being, there is quite too large a margin left for a case like this. This man is a gentleman and naturally a fine honorable man, which is much more to the purpose. 'Nature hath meal and bran' in the church and out of it. The arrangements are all

made, but they are made as if I were absolutely
certain of failure. I have found by experiment
that I *can* make the examination thoroughly, and
leave the stone exactly as I find it, and I could do
it alone, weak as I am, now, without any one to
lift a finger to help me. I have promised to perform the experiment without removing a particle
of the stone, or leaving a trace of harm, and what
is very gratifying to me under the circumstances,
neither the clerk nor the vicar appears disposed
to take it for granted that I am insane. I have
told them my reasons for it. The archives of this
secret philosophical society are buried somewhere,
perhaps in more places than one. The evidence
points very strongly this way, it points to a tomb
— Lord Bacon's tomb would throw some light on
it I think. Spenser's *I know* contains, or did when
it was closed, *verses*, ' and the pens that writ
them,' the verses of his brother poets, — the poets
of this school, — Raleigh's school. . . .

"I *am* going to write to Mrs. Hawthorne as soon
as I can. But I cannot speak now, this thing
presses on me so heavily; the terrors of it are
what you see. If I could do it alone it would not
be so fearful. If I had hope enough to justify it,
I would insist on your being here. But I have
not. The conviction that I ought to do it is the
strength in which I go about it. The vicar is very
friendly to me; he has not told ' a human being,'
not even his wife, he says, or he had not until I

gave him leave to take advice confidentially, and
therefore, on his account perhaps, as well as on
account of what I have said about my brother, this
letter ought to be for your eye only.   Don't stop
to answer this letter.   If you will read it that is all
I ask — at present — I have been waiting till the
last moment to write it.   I could not write any
less.   Truly yours,

DELIA BACON."

It is not without doubt and hesitation that it has
been decided to make publicly known these letters
that follow.   But it has seemed right that this part
of the story should be told with the rest; that the
inexhaustible patience, gentleness, and generosity
of Hawthorne should be known, as they could never
be but by showing these shrewd trials to which
they were submitted; while it is not unjust to the
memory of her whose life was now consciously ending, that the approach should be shown of that madness which nevertheless had not yet stricken her.
His intercession for her brother, whom he did not
know, — seeking by gentle words to turn away
from him unjust accusation; his untiring devotion
to the purpose which was all that she was now
living for; only served to involve him, the most
helpful friend, except her brother, whom she had
ever known, in the bitter suspicion and anger
which is so often the earliest sign of coming insanity.   Yet misunderstanding, ingratitude, injustice,

could not turn him back from helping her.   His clairvoyant soul could see through it all the sincere, earnest, truthful spirit which he honored, and would serve, even against its consent.

LIVERPOOL, Oct. 21, 1856.

DEAR MISS BACON, — I send a post-office order for five pounds, payable to you at the Stratford post-office.

I should have had, probably, some decisive intelligence about your book, if my friend Mr. Bennoch had not been called away from London for a few days.   On his return, we shall certainly know about it; and the news *shall* be good — at least, not bad — though all the fiends fight against us.

As regards your brother, it is to be considered that he is, at all events, a brother, and cannot divest himself of the duties of that relation.   And your claims upon him are quite independent of any injustice on his part, and of any delicacy of feeling on yours.   He is bound to help you, and you to be helped by him, just the same as if he had the highest faith in yourself and your deeds.   No stranger has a right to interfere in your behalf, unless constrained by deep interest and respect; but a brother stands on quite different ground.   My conviction is strong that you ought not to return any money that he may remit.   Moreover (taking into consideration as much of his character, and as many of all the circumstances, as I am aware of) I can see that his sympathy was hardly to be hoped for. In short, I mean to think him a good man yet.

I shall not (unless you give me leave) show your letter to Mrs. Hawthorne.

In great haste,

Sincerely yours,

NATH' HAWTHORNE.

[D. B. TO HAWTHORNE.]

STRATFORD-ON-AVON, October 22, '56.

DEAR MR. HAWTHORNE, — I have received your note with its enclosure of five pounds, for which I thank you. As to my last letter, I put it entirely at your discretion. You may publish it in the newspapers if you choose. I gave you two reasons for wishing it to be considered confidential for the present, but of these the first appears to be deprived of its force by your answer, and as to the second I know Mrs. Hawthorne would not betray my confidence — I had no fear as to that — but the fact is it was very foolish for me to write on that subject at all at present, and I am very sorry that I did so, particularly as I have not been able to accept the permission given me, and the probability is that I shall not do so. I may feel that it is better not to make the inquiry at all than to make it under such conditions and liabilities. And I cannot say that I feel at present any strong inclination to pursue my inquiries on this subject any further, and as to the book, my feeling at this moment is that there would be very little use in publishing it at present. All the evidence of my sanity there is, you have, and you are not surprised at the imputations my brother casts on me, and certainly the world is not likely to make any more favorable judgment. If my own household and the world are against me, what else shall we call it? But it cannot be that I am alone, — a creature by myself in my mental constitution, — and if I am out of my way here, it is time that I was looking for my kindred and the place where my judgment of the true, and my feeling of the just, are not insanity. Some such place I believe in.

If I were sure that my brother would send me any money I would send this back to you at once, for I feel that it is a baseness in me to take it, but I am very far from being sure of that, and unfortunately I had encroached on this before it came while hoping to receive some from another source. As to my expectation from my brother, it was only an inference of mine from the fact that he knew exactly my circumstances, and that he spoke of writing again in a few days in a connection which seemed to imply that he would hardly write for any other purpose. In case of any accident to myself, or in case I should not be able to return it very soon, I wish you to call on him for it, and for the rest of the money that I owe you, — and he knows exactly what it is, — and tell him from me that he is bound to pay it; for in defending himself from a charge against which there was no defense, he has not scrupled to deprive me of the resources I had left in the affection and confidence of my family and my friends, and he has not even scrupled to impair the respect which under these hard conditions I had won from strangers. In referring to my delusions he speaks of persons " who *humor* me by *affecting* to *believe* that there may be something in them because they think there would be no use in opposing me "! I supposed he referred to Mr. Emerson. I knew he had had some correspondence with him, and I suppose that Mr. Emerson really thinks now, that that *is* the course he has taken. But I could not understand why your so favorable opinion of the book should be so wholly overlooked — treated as if it had not been expressed — in all that he said on that subject.

But I should be sorry to involve you in any further correspondence on so painful a subject. It was necessary for me to write this. I sincerely hope that you will not think it necessary to reply to it. As to the book, I do not trouble myself much about that now. I have cast it on the waters, and if I do not find it again, the world will.

Truly yours,
DELIA BACON.

You must not answer this. It is a small matter to you. You have nothing at stake. Any one would say that you were perhaps called upon to say exactly what you did, but this I had to write and my life depends now on my not reading any more letters.

That is literally true I believe, and I cannot squander at this fearful rate that which is so precious. I have done with this. I will have no more letters I say from brothers or strangers, friends or foes. My experience for the last few days shows that I am not equal to it, so I am obliged to take this resolution.

October 23, '56.

P. S. This is what I wrote yesterday. But I cannot let it go as it is. It does no justice at all to the feeling with which I have received your letter, or to the position in which I am placed by it. And I cannot return you this money immediately, as of course you thought I would, when you wrote that. Whatever other ill you thought of me you did not think I could keep it, — you did not think me capable of that! — and yet you knew I must. For that letter which it nearly cost me my life to write, put you in possession of the case entirely. But I see how it is. You have heard some bad news about my book. You have ascertained that it has no pecuniary value, and the other part of my work of which I wrote is in that case not available, and you think that I have nothing else to depend on, and that what I said about promptly helping myself as soon as this one more requisition was fulfilled, meant nothing, or that it was only some vague, impracticable purpose that I was weakly relying on. But that you should have thought it necessary to write in that manner to me at just this time, as if I were a person of such hardened sensibilities that something less, or something different, would not have sufficed — that is what I do not understand. I will show you how much of the feeling I have left that you thought me wanting in, — that you must have thought me wanting in, or you could not have written that to me at the moment in which I was asking you for money, and taking it from you. I will tell you exactly how much of that feeling I have left. You cannot help me any more after writing that to me. If you had the keys of heaven you could not. Ay, but I keep this money, — so I do. — You do not understand that, — but you shall. If I do not pay you in one month, — and the chance that I shall is small, but I ask that time — write to my brother for it. He shall know what 't is to have a sister with such a name as I have. I will not take my book out of your hands because I do not know but it may have some pecuniary value after all, and if it has it is properly yours at least until you have been paid for what I owe you. But what I desire is that you should have no more trouble with it.

I will not have a novel made out of it as my brother proposes that I should. I will not have my monomania converted into never so profitable a speculation, and this life and death earnest of mine is not going to be published either for the amusement or contempt of the world. Seal it up and wait till it is true.

Truly yours,
DELIA BACON.

[HAWTHORNE TO D. B.]

LIVERPOOL, October 24, '56.

MY DEAR MISS BACON, — I do not know what reply to make to your last note. Indeed, when people misunderstand me, I seldom take the trouble (and never should, on my own account) to attempt to set them right. I meant, when I began this scrawl, to say something in my own defence; but I find it makes me sick to think of it — so we will let it pass. By telling me what was the state of affairs between yourself and your brother, you made it my duty to give you the best advice I could; and, on further reflection, I find my opinion precisely the same as it was at first. And, seeing with his eyes, I cannot wonder at his acting as he has.

My opinion of the book has never varied; nor have I, up to this moment, spared any effort to bring it before the public, nor relinquished any hope of doing so.

I suppose it would be in vain to tell you that I have never thought, for an instant, of any miserable little interest that I might have, in the success of the book, or in your being on sisterly terms with your brother. But really I don't think you construe me very generously.

However, you will find me always just the same as I have been; and if ever I seem otherwise, the fault is in the eyes that look at me. Nor do I pretend to be very good; there are hundreds of kinder and better people in the world; but such as I am, I am genuine, and in keeping with myself. And, in honest truth, my dear Miss Bacon, I wish to do you what good I can.

Hoping that, one day or other, you will be able to believe this, I say no more.

Sincerely yours,
Nath' Hawthorne.

P. S. Can you possibly have thought that I suggested your brother's advice to turn the book into a novel? I am afraid you did.

[D. B. to Hawthorne.]

Stratford-on-Avon, October 29, 1856.

Dear Mr. Hawthorne, — You did not understand my last letter and I will not undertake to explain it. I supposed that you felt compelled to write as you did. I attributed it to your sense of duty and your view of the proprieties of the case.

I did not call in question a disinterestedness and generosity of character to which I have not found any parallel. I kept your note 24 hours without opening it, because I was literally unable to open it, and I have not answered it, because the explanation which it seemed to require did not appear to me possible. I have written one or two notes denying that I had made any such charge as the ones you attributed to me, but the very denial seemed insulting to you when I saw it on paper, and I would not send them.

I had just prepared an answer however of half a dozen lines or so, that you might not misconstrue my silence, when I received this morning a note from Mr. Bennoch informing me that your efforts and his on behalf of my work had been successful, so I have concluded to send you this that my acknowledgment of what I owe you may accompany what I had said already. My last letter but one, contained allusions to subjects which I am not in the habit of speaking of, confidentially or otherwise, and I shall be glad to know that you have destroyed it.

The fact that these particular publishers undertake the publication of my work happens fortunately to indicate exactly what it owes you. When the subject was first presented to Carlyle three years and a half ago he selected Mr. Parker as the proper person to represent the English public on that question, and proposed to take my article to him, giving me to understand that we were to abide by his decision, which was to determine whether the thing could go on here or not. You know what the fate of the article was, and this very book which he accepts now at your hands and the hands of your friend he refused at mine more than a year ago.

His acceptance of the book is in itself a success which you can hardly estimate though I owe it to you, because it relieves me on the instant from the charge to which my belief on this subject has it seems made me liable. At least that question will now be before the world, and I shall not be any longer at the mercy of men whose mercies, when their own opinions and beliefs are called in question, are so small. But for the sake of all my friends, — for my brother's sake and for your sake, I am glad of this.

And I hope you will not have any occasion to be sorry for your part in it. If any good comes of it, you will know just how much of it is the result of your persevering and most noble efforts on its behalf. For it would have been a private manuscript only and never a book but for you. No one would have dared so much as to read it, no one had dared to read it till it found you. I had exhausted all my means of getting it published, I had tried everything but you. And the reason I had not applied to you sooner was, I did not think it would be possible for you with your official duties combined with your own engagements as an author to give the attention to the work which it would be necessary to give in order to help it at all. I had tried authors who were not consuls, and who were most kindly disposed to me, and who wished to help me, but could not for lack of time. For your sake I hope it will succeed, and that you will not suffer my unfortunate personal relations to you just at this time to detract from the satisfaction that you might otherwise feel in achieving anything so difficult. That Mr. Parker should publish it after all is indeed a proof of what you were able to do for me.

Gratefully yours,
DELIA BACON.

It was on the day of this last date that Mr. Bennoch began his correspondence with her, which was to be for six months so frequent. It can easily be gathered from these letters that it was upon some personal guaranty by Hawthorne himself that the very considerable expense of printing the book was incurred by Parker — whose name, however, was after all not to appear on its title-page.

At the same time with this new life that came to her, she was making one more attempt to explore the secret of the tomb. Another — and the last — note from the vicar, on the 31st of October, tells her: "I shall be happy to accompany you to the Church at any time convenient to yourself, as a preliminary step, and will then arrange a time for further operations when we shall be undisturbed." Whether he was meaning thus to humor the vagaries of an unsound mind — of which the unsoundness certainly had not declared itself to all people — or had really changed his mind, and was willing to take part in examining almost the only famous grave in England which has never been disturbed, is not easy now to tell. But the exploration has, in fact, never yet been made.

Not long after this, too, comes in upon her another kindly breath from the world which she has shut out from herself. In July before, Carlyle had written to Emerson : "I have not seen or distinctly heard of Miss Bacon for a year and a half past : I often ask myself, what has become of that poor Lady, and wish I knew of her being safe among her friends again. I have even lost the address (which at any rate was probably not a lasting one) ; perhaps I could find it by the eye, — but it is five miles away ; and my *non plus ultra* for years past is not above half that distance. Heigho ! "[1] But now, when at last she felt that she was above the need of friends, her pride no longer disdained to speak to them.

[1] *Correspondence of Carlyle and Emerson*, vol. ii. p. 255.

CHELSEA, 14 December, 1856.

DEAR MISS BACON, — I am greatly pleased to hear of you again: my thoughts about you have been many, and my inquiries many in America and here; but nothing would come out of them. Not very long since, — having a House in these days, and your old lodging having thus become accessible to me again, I pulled at the bell of the old House-door (House and Street recognizable to me by eyesight, title of them entirely forgotten), pulled there for several minutes, again and again: but nobody would answer; — I considered withal that probably nobody might in the least *know*.

But now we again hear from yourself; that you are still well; nay more, that you have achieved a manifest success in what has long been the grand Problem of your life. Well done! This must be a greater joy to you than health itself, or any other blessing; and I must say that by your stead-fastness you have deserved it! — You could not have a better Publisher than Parker; I am really thankful, along with you, that your word is at last to go forth.

My incredulity of your Thesis I have never hidden from you: but I willingly vote, and have voted, you should be heard on it to full length; and this, whatever farther come of it, will be a profit to the world, and to yourself — I need not say what profit it will be!

When you return to London let us, so soon as possible, see you again. We are in our old way, except that my Wife is rather poorlier than in common Winters (which are always unkind to her), and that I myself am *sunk* deeper than ever towards the very centre of Chaos, — in fact overwhelmed with such a mud-ocean of confusions and inexecutable businesses, late and early, as are like to drown me altogether, I sometimes think. But they won't either!   Yours always,

T. Carlyle.

During almost four months, from October to February, while Hawthorne was left wholly undisturbed by his importunate correspondent, aggrieved as she was by his very kindness and unselfishness, there raged nevertheless an almost daily storm of letters between her and Mr. Bennoch and the printer. In all Mr. Bennoch's letters there is manifest a lively appreciation of the woman with whose singular work he had been put in charge, and even of the work itself ; and with it all, such keen good sense and judicious tact in dealing with her strong and obstinate temper, as more than justified Hawthorne's choice of his friend for so delicate a service. It is evident that the title of the book was a subject of continual discussion ; on the backs of the letters she received are countless experiments, in her own hand, toward the selection of a title ; and that ultimately adopted, although

with Mr. Bennoch's frank approval, was the result
of mutual concessions on either side.

There arose, however, a trouble of a serious
kind. It was only upon the condition that the
book should have an Introduction by Hawthorne
that Parker had at all consented to publish it; and
such an introduction the author seems to have
determined, at last, not to have. This determination, the cause of which is easy to find in the
offended pride which is discovered in her latest
letters to him, Mr. Bennoch seems in some way to
have succeeded in overcoming; although when at
last it came, she would receive it only upon altera-
tions rigorously insisted upon by her and amiably
yielded by him. But she was not thus prevailed
upon until her refusal of the Preface had brought
Parker, after the printers' work had been almost
completed upon Mr. Bennoch's personal guaranty
of payment, to refuse on his part to publish it.
The best that, upon this grievous failure of plan,
could still be done was done by Mr. Bennoch. He
made new arrangements for the almost completed
work with a house far less known than Parker's
although entirely respectable: the house of Groom-
bridge and Sons, under whose name the book was
not many days after given to the world.

Meanwhile the author had been so far prevailed
upon as to address to Hawthorne this cold and
distant note: —

[D. B. to Hawthorne.]

Stratford-on-Avon, February 10, 1857.

Dear Mr. Hawthorne, — My part in this work is I believe nearly done. I am finishing in great haste a few more pages for the Introduction, which I expect to send to-morrow. The printer writes me to-day that he is now waiting for your preface and wishes me to write to you for it. Of course I understood that you preferred that the correspondence should be conducted through Mr. Bennoch, to whose kind interest in the subject I owe so much, but I have never forgotten on that account what you have done and are doing for the work.

I do not look on it as a private enterprise. I had contributed what I could to it, and I did not call for help till my own power failed. You have caused it to be published, and I hope you will continue to give it whatever aid it may seem to you to deserve and require. I consider that you have a part in the work which is properly yours. As to my own personal obligations to you, I will not now speak of them. I have good hopes of an acquittal that will pay all debts soon, and that you and no one else will have occasion to regret the aid you have given me.

Truly yours,

D. Bacon.

LIVERPOOL, February 11, 1857.

DEAR MISS BACON, — I wrote the Preface yesterday, and am now about forwarding it to Bennoch. It has been delayed by the difficulty of getting a minute's clear space from daily interruptions; and, indeed, ever since I have had your book in hand, my mind has been continually torn in tatters; so that I have had no right to deal with a work demanding, at least, all the mind with which nature gifted me.

My preface comprises extracts from the article which you sent Bennoch, and which he and I thought it better not to publish. I have said all the external things that seemed to me necessary, in order to put you fairly before the public, and have stated what I think as to the merit of the work. It is possible that you may say, in your new Introduction, some things which I have already said for you; but this is no great matter.

Do not consider yourself under any personal obligations to me. I appreciate the spirit in which you sought my assistance, and did not presume to burthen you, even in my secret thoughts, with the imposition of personal favors.

Truly yours,
NATH' HAWTHORNE.

What still harsher and unkinder rebuff may have followed this grave and gentle letter does not

now appear; Hawthorne seems not to have preserved it, perhaps out of consideration for the
writer. But it may be guessed from this which
he wrote in reply.

LIVERPOOL, February 19, '57.

DEAR AUTHOR OF THIS BOOK, — (For you forbid
me to call you anything else), I utterly despair of
being able to satisfy you with a preface. The
extracts which I made from your Introduction were
such as seemed essential to me, and likely to be of
good effect with the Public. It seems to me they
had better remain.

In one of your early letters to me, you said that
I might call the book a Romance, or whatever I
would. I have not called it anything of the kind,
but have merely refrained from expressing a full
conviction of the truth of your theory. But the
book will be in the hands of the public. Let the
public judge; as it must. Nothing that I could
say, beforehand, could influence its judgment; and
I do not agree with your opinion that I have said
anything likely to prevent your cause being heard.

Nevertheless, I am most willing to burn the
Preface at once. I desire quite as little as you do
to be known in reference to this work; and I have
a right not to be known.[1] Pray do not think of

---

[1] Written in the margin, with reference by an asterisk: "I mean,
I have *no right to be* known."

dedicating it to me. You owe me no such acknowledgment; and, under the circumstances, it would not gratify me in the least.

No better method of solving the difficulty occurs to me, than to submit the Preface to Mr. Parker. If he thinks it will do harm, let him say so, as he will do readily enough, being materially interested on that point.

I have no time to write more, but must leave the matter with yourself and Parker and Bennoch, and any other adviser (for instance, Mr. Carlyle) whom you choose to call in.

Truly yours,
Nath' Hawthorne.

Just at this time her brother in America, failing, as she had assured Hawthorne he should fail, to get further news from her, was writing for news to Hawthorne. How sincere and truthful Hawthorne had been, both in his laudations of her work and his admonitions concerning its prospects, may be seen in what he says to her brother, for no one's eyes but his.

U. S. Consulate,
Liverpool, Feb. 26, '57.

My dear Sir, — Your sister is still at Stratford-on-Avon, and was in her usual state of health when I last heard from her, about a week ago. I have forwarded your letter.

Her book is now in print, and will probably be published in this country and in America, within a few weeks. It will undoubtedly do her credit, intellectually, and may perhaps make many converts to her theory; but I do not anticipate a very general success, in this latter respect. Her own anticipations, I believe, are very sanguine. It will, I think, be better received in America than here; and this may perhaps operate as an inducement to her to return home. At all events, she will soon know what her position really is, and will doubtless regulate her proceedings in accordance with it.

Very respectfully yours,

NATH' HAWTHORNE.

REV. DR. BACON,
  New Haven,
    Conn.

XVII

ABOUT the beginning of April, 1857, the book came before the world.

Its title, so long and so laboriously disputed, was this:

" The Philosophy of The Plays of Shakspere Unfolded. By Delia Bacon. With a Preface by Nathaniel Hawthorne, Author of ' The Scarlet Letter,' etc."

Upon the copies sent to the American market the name of Ticknor & Fields, Boston, replaced that of the London publishers.

It was in form an octavo, of about seven hundred pages, including a hundred pages, separately numbered, of the author's " Introduction." This " Introduction," after a statement, not too compact or clear, of " The Proposition," contained a review of " The Age of Elizabeth, and the Elizabethan Men of Letters;" extracts from an altogether separate, and unpublished, Life of Raleigh; " Raleigh's School," and " The New Academy."

The Historical Argument, begun so brilliantly in her *Putnam* article, was expressly omitted here, and its omission announced.

Book I., on " The Elizabethan Art of Delivery

and Tradition," is in two Parts: "Michael de Montaigne's 'Private and Retired Arts,'" and "The Baconian Rhetoric, or The Method of Progression."

Book II., on "Elizabethan 'Secrets of Morality and Policy'; or, The Fables of the New Learning," was also in two Parts: "Lear's Philosopher," and (Part II.) "Julius Cæsar and Coriolanus: The Scientific Cure of the Common-Weal."

To all was prefixed this Preface, which Hawthorne, under so many discouragements, had written for it.

PREFACE.

This Volume contains the argument, drawn from the Plays usually attributed to Shakspere, in support of a theory which the author of it has demonstrated by historical evidences in another work. Having never read this historical demonstration (which remains still in manuscript, with the exception of a preliminary chapter, published long ago in an American periodical), I deem it necessary to cite the author's own account of it : —

"The Historical Part of this work (which was originally the principal part, and designed to furnish the historical key to the great Elizabethan writings), though now for a long time completed and ready for the press, and though repeated reference is made to it in this volume, is, for the most part, omitted here. It contains a true and before unwritten history, and it will yet, perhaps, be published as it stands; but the vivid and accumulating historic detail, with which more recent research tends to enrich the earlier statement, and disclosures which no invention could anticipate, are waiting now to be subjoined to it.

"The INTERNAL EVIDENCE of the assumptions made at the outset is that which is chiefly relied on in the work now first presented on this subject to the public. The demonstration will be found complete on that ground; and on that ground alone the author is willing, and deliberately prefers, for the present, to rest it.

"External evidence, of course, will not be wanting; there will be enough and to spare, if the demonstration here be correct. But the author of the discovery was not willing to rob the world of this great question; but wished rather to share with it the benefit which the true solution of the Problem offers — the solution prescribed by those who propounded it to the future. It seemed better to save to the world the power and beauty of this demonstration, its intellectual stimulus, its demand on the judgment. It seemed better, that the world should acquire it also in the form of criticism, instead of being stupefied and overpowered with the mere force of an irresistible, external, historical proof. Persons incapable of appreciating any other kind of truth, — those who are capable of nothing that does not 'directly fall

under and strike *the senses,'* as Lord Bacon expresses it, — will have their time also; but it was
proposed to present the subject first to minds of
another order.''

In the present volume, accordingly, the author
applies herself to the demonstration and development of a system of philosophy, which has presented itself to her as underlying the superficial
and ostensible text of Shakspere's plays. Traces
of the same philosophy, too, she conceives herself
to have found in the acknowledged works of Lord
Bacon, and in those of other writers contemporary
with him. All agree in one system; all these
traces indicate a common understanding and unity
of purpose in men among whom no brotherhood
has hitherto been suspected, except as representa-
tives of a grand and brilliant age, when the human
intellect made a marked step in advance.

The author did not (as her own consciousness
assures her) either construct or originally seek this
new philosophy. In many respects, if I have
rightly understood her, it was at variance with her
preconceived opinions, whether ethical, religious,
or political. She had been for years a student of
Shakspere, looking for nothing in his plays beyond
what the world has agreed to find in them, when
she began to see, under the surface, the gleam of
this hidden treasure. It was carefully hidden, indeed, yet not less carefully indicated, as with a
pointed finger, by such marks and references as

could not ultimately escape the notice of a subsequent age, which should be capable of profiting by the rich inheritance. So, too, in regard to Lord Bacon. The author of this volume had not sought to put any but the ordinary and obvious interpretation upon his works, nor to take any other view of his character than what accorded with the unanimous judgment upon it of all the generations since his epoch. But, as she penetrated more and more deeply into the plays, and became aware of those inner readings, she found herself compelled to turn back to the " Advancement of Learning " for information as to their plan and purport; and Lord Bacon's Treatise failed not to give her what she sought; thus adding to the immortal dramas, in her idea, a far higher value than their warmest admirers had heretofore claimed for them. They filled out the scientific scheme which Bacon had planned, and which needed only these profound and vivid illustrations of human life and character to make it perfect. Finally, the author's researches led her to a point where she found the plays claimed for Lord Bacon and his associates, — not in a way that was meant to be intelligible in their own perilous times, — but in characters that only became legible, and illuminated, as it were, in the light of a subsequent period.

The reader will soon perceive that the new philosophy, as here demonstrated, was of a kind that no professor could have ventured openly to teach

in the days of Elizabeth and James. The conclud-
ing chapter of the present work makes a powerful
statement of the position which a man, conscious of
great and noble aims, would then have occupied;
and shows, too, how familiar the age was with all
methods of secret communication, and of hiding
thought beneath a masque of conceit or folly. Ap-
plicably to this subject I quote a paragraph from a
manuscript of the author's, not intended for pres-.
ent publication : —

"It was a time when authors, who treated of a
scientific politics and of a scientific ethics inter-
nally connected with it, naturally preferred this
more philosophic, symbolic method of indicating
their connection with their writings, which would
limit the indication to those who could pierce
within the veil of a philosophic symbolism. It was
the time when the cipher, in which one could
write '*omnia per omnia*,' was in such request, and
when 'wheel ciphers' and 'doubles' were thought
not unworthy of philosophic notice. It was a
time, too, when the phonographic art was cultivated, and put to other uses than at present, and
when a *nom de plume* was required for other purposes than to serve as the refuge of an author's
modesty, or vanity, or caprice. It was a time
when puns, and charades, and enigmas, and anagrams, and monograms, and ciphers, and puzzles,
were not good for sport and child's play merely;
when they had need to be close; when they had

need to be solvable, at least, only to those who should *solve* them. It was a time when all the latent capacities of the English language were put in requisition, and it was flashing and crackling, through all its lengths and breadths, with puns and quips, and conceits, and jokes, and satires, and in-lined with philosophic secrets that opened down ' into the bottom of a tomb ' — that opened into the Tower — that opened on the scaffold and the block."

I quote, likewise, another passage, because I think the reader will see in it the noble earnestness of the author's character, and may partly imagine the sacrifices which this research has cost her : —

" The great secret of the Elizabethan age did not lie where any superficial research could ever have discovered it. It was not left within the range of any accidental disclosure. It did not lie on the surface of any Elizabethan document. The most diligent explorers of these documents, in two centuries and a quarter, had not found it. No faintest suspicion of it had ever crossed the mind of the most recent, and clear-sighted, and able investigator of the Baconian remains. It was buried in the lowest depths of the lowest deeps of the deep Elizabethan Art : that Art which no plummet, till now, has ever sounded. It was locked with its utmost reach of traditionary cunning. It was buried in the inmost recesses of the esoteric

Elizabethan learning. It was tied with a knot
that has passed the scrutiny and baffled the sword
of an old, suspicious, dying, military government
— a knot that none could cut — a knot that must
be untied.

"The great secret of the Elizabethan age was
inextricably reserved by the founders of a new
learning, the prophetic and more nobly gifted
minds of a new and nobler race of men, for a research that should test the mind of the discoverer,
and frame and subordinate it to that so sleepless
and indomitable purpose of the prophetic aspira-
tion. It was 'the device' by which they under-
took to live again in the ages in which their
achievements and triumphs were forecast, and to
come forth and rule again, not in one mind, not in
the few, not in the many, but in all. 'For there
is no throne like that throne in the thoughts of
men,' which the ambition of these men climbed
and compassed.

"The principal works of the Elizabethan Philosophy, those in which the new method of learning was practically applied to the noblest subjects,
were presented to the world in the form of AN
ENIGMA. It was a form well fitted to divert inquiry, and baffle even the research of the scholar
for a time ; but one calculated to provoke the philosophic curiosity, and one which would inevitably
command a research that could end only with the
true solution. That solution was reserved for one

who would recognize, at last, in the disguise of the great impersonal teacher, the disguise of a new learning. It waited for the reader who would observe, at last, those thick-strewn scientific clues, those thick-crowding enigmas, those perpetual beckonings from the 'theatre' into the judicial palace of the mind. It was reserved for the student who would recognize, at last, the mind that was seeking so perseveringly to whisper its tale of outrage, and 'the secrets it was forbid.' It waited for one who would answer, at last, that philosophic challenge, and say, 'Go on, I'll follow thee!' It was reserved for one who would count years as days, for the love of the truth it hid; who would never turn back on the long road of initiation, though all 'THE IDOLS' must be left behind in its stages; who would never stop until it stopped in that new cave of Apollo, where the handwriting on the wall spells anew the old Delphic motto, and publishes the word that '*unties* the spell.'"

On this object, which she conceives so loftily, the author has bestowed the solitary and self-sustained toil of many years. The volume now before the reader, together with the historical demonstration which it presupposes, is the product of a most faithful and conscientious labor, and a truly heroic devotion of intellect and heart. No man or woman has ever thought or written more sincerely than the author of this book. She has given nothing less than her life to the work.

And, as if for the greater trial of her constancy,
her theory was divulged, some time ago, in so partial and unsatisfactory a manner — with so exceedingly imperfect a statement of its claims — as to
put her at a great disadvantage before the world.
A single article from her pen, purporting to be the
first of a series, appeared in an American Magazine; but unexpected obstacles prevented the further publication in that form, after enough had
been done to assail the prejudices of the public,
but far too little to gain its sympathy. Another
evil followed. An English writer (in a " Letter to
the Earl of Ellesmere," published within a few
months past) has thought it not inconsistent with
the fair-play, on which his country prides itself, to
take to himself this lady's theory, and favor the
public with it as his own original conception, without allusion to the author's prior claim. In reference to this pamphlet, she generously says : —

" This has not been a selfish enterprise. It is
not a personal concern. It is a discovery which
belongs not to an individual, and not to a people.
Its fields are wide enough and rich enough for us
all; and he that has no work, and whoso will, let
him come and labor in them. The field is the
world's; and the world's work henceforth is in it.
So that it be known in its real comprehension, in
its true relations to the weal of the world, what
matters it? So that the truth, which is dearer
than all the rest — which abides with us when all

others leave us, dearest then — so that the truth, which is neither yours nor mine, but yours *and* mine, be known, loved, honored, emancipated, mitred, crowned, adored — *who* loses anything, that does not find it." " And what matters it," says the philosophic wisdom, speaking in the abstract, " what name it is proclaimed in, and what letters of the alphabet we know it by? — what matter is it, so that they *spell* the name that is *good* for ALL, and *good* for *each*," — for that is the REAL name here?

Speaking on the author's behalf, however, I am not entitled to imitate her magnanimity; and, therefore, hope that the writer of the pamphlet will disclaim any purpose of assuming to himself, on the ground of a slight and superficial performance, the result which she has attained at the cost of many toils and sacrifices.

And now, at length, after many delays and discouragements, the work comes forth. It had been the author's original purpose to publish it in America; for she wished her own country to have the glory of solving the enigma of those mighty dramas, and thus adding a new and higher value to the loftiest productions of the English mind. It seemed to her most fit and desirable that America — having received so much from England, and returned so little — should do what remained to be done towards rendering this great legacy available, as its authors meant it to be, to all future time.

This purpose was frustrated; and it will be seen in what spirit she acquiesces.

"The author was forced to bring it back, and contribute it to the literature of the country from which it was derived, and to which it essentially and inseparably belongs. It was written, every word of it, on English ground, in the midst of the old familiar scenes and household names, that even in our nursery songs revive the dear ancestral memories; those 'royal pursuivants' with which our mother-land still follows and re-takes her own. It was written in the land of our old kings and queens, and in the land of *our own* PHILOSOPHERS and POETS also. It was written on the spot where the works it unlocks were written, and in the perpetual presence of the English mind; the mind that spoke before in the cultured few, and that speaks to-day in the cultured many. And it is now at last, after so long a time — after all, as it should be — the English press that prints it. It is the scientific English press, with those old gags (wherewith our kings and queens sought to stop it, ere they knew what it was) champed asunder, ground to powder, and with its last Elizabethan shackle shaken off, that restores, 'in a better hour,' the torn and garbled science committed to it, and gives back 'the bread cast on its sure waters.'"

There remains little more for me to say. I am not the editor of this work; nor can I consider myself fairly entitled to the honor (which, if I deserved it, I should feel it to be a very high as

well as a perilous one) of seeing my name associated with the author's on the title page. My
object has been merely to speak a few words,
which might, perhaps, serve the purpose of placing my countrywoman upon a ground of amicable
understanding with the public. She has a vast
preliminary difficulty to encounter. The first feeling of every reader must be one of absolute re-
pugnance towards a person who seeks to tear out
of the Anglo-Saxon heart the name which for ages
it has held dearest, and to substitute another name,
or names, to which the settled belief of the world
has long assigned a very different position. What
I claim for this work is, that the ability employed
in its composition has been worthy of its great
subject, and well employed for our intellectual interests, whatever judgment the public may pass
upon the question discussed. And, after listening
to the author's interpretation of the Plays, and
seeing how wide a scope she assigns to them, how
high a purpose, and what richness of inner meaning, the thoughtful reader will hardly return again
— not wholly, at all events — to the common view
of them and of their author. It is for the public
to say whether my countrywoman has proved her
theory. In the worst event, if she has failed, her
failure will be more honorable than most people's
triumphs; since it must fling upon the old tombstone, at Stratford-on-Avon, the noblest tributary
wreath that has ever lain there.

NATHANIEL HAWTHORNE.

XVIII.

The reception which this volume was to meet
from the English public and English critics had
been, indeed, pretty well apprehended in advance
by some of those few who were admitted to its
author's confidence, and were suffered to advise
her. Perhaps, nevertheless, they were right, these
men of philosophic insight and wide experience in
letters — Carlyle, Emerson, Hawthorne — in de-
claring that, whatever might come of it, it was a
work so full of truth and wisdom that the world
ought by no means to be deprived of it. At any
rate, here at last it was; and what did in fact
come of it Hawthorne himself has told.

"Without prejudice to her literary ability, it
must be allowed that Miss Bacon was wholly unfit
to prepare her own work for publication, because,
among many other reasons, she was too thoroughly
in earnest to know what to leave out. Every leaf
and line was sacred, for all had been written under
so deep a conviction of truth as to assume, in her
eyes, the aspect of inspiration. A practised book-
maker, with entire control of her materials, would
have shaped out a duodecimo volume full of eloquence and ingenious dissertation, — criticisms

which quite take the color and pungency out of other people's critical remarks on Shakspeare, — philosophic truths which she imagined herself to have found at the roots of his conceptions, and which certainly come from no inconsiderable depth somewhere. There was a great amount of rubbish, which any competent editor would have shoveled out of the way. But Miss Bacon thrust the whole bulk of inspiration and nonsense into the press in a lump, and there tumbled out a ponderous octavo volume, which fell with a dead thump at the feet of the public, and has never been picked up. A few persons turned over one or two of the leaves, as it lay there, and essayed to kick the volume deeper into the mud; for they were the hack critics of the minor periodical press in London, than whom, I suppose, though doubtless excellent fellows in their way, there are no gentlemen in the world less sensible of any sanctity in a book, or less likely to recognize an author's heart in it, or more utterly careless about bruising, if they do recognize it. It is their trade. They could not do otherwise. I never thought of blaming them. It was not for such Englishmen as one of these to get beyond the idea that an assault was meditated on England's greatest poet. From the scholars and critics of her own country, indeed, Miss Bacon might have looked for a worthier appreciation, because many of the best of them have higher cultivation, and finer and deeper literary sensibilities, than all but the very profoundest and brightest of Englishmen. But they are not a courageous body of men; they dare not think a truth that has an odor of absurdity, lest they should feel themselves bound to speak it out. If any American ever wrote a word in her behalf, Miss Bacon never knew it, nor did I. Our journalists at once republished some of the most brutal vituperations of the English press, thus pelting their poor countrywoman with stolen mud, without even waiting to know whether the ignominy was deserved. And they never have known it, to this day, and never will. . . .

"I believe that it has been the fate of this remarkable book never to have had more than a single reader. I myself am acquainted with it only in insulated chapters and scattered pages and paragraphs. But, since my return to America, a young man of genius and enthusiasm[1] has assured me that he has positively read the book from beginning to end, and is completely a convert to its doctrines. It belongs to him, therefore, and not to me, — whom, in almost the last letter that I received from her, she declared unworthy to med-

---

[1] This "young man" (it was in 1863 that Hawthorne was writing) was Mr. William D. O'Connor, now of the Life-Saving Service, Washington, and author of *Hamlet's Note-book*: Houghton, Mifflin & Co., 1886. The task which Hawthorne, in the passage quoted, seems to lay upon him, failing strength has forced him to abandon. Materials, however, furnished to him by Hawthorne for such a purpose, he has kindly put at my disposal. — [T. B.]

dle with her work, — it belongs surely to this one individual, who has done her so much justice as to know what she wrote, to place Miss Bacon in her due position before the public and posterity." [1]

[1] *Our Old Home:* chapter, " Recollections of a Gifted Woman."

XIX

WHEN this work of hers, for which alone she had for years been willing to live, was done — and failed — her life was ended too.

Before this time in all that she wrote or did there was nothing to mark a disordered intellect, unless her disbelief in the accepted authorship of the Plays was itself proof of insanity. Even her curious haunting of the Stratford church and grave seems not to have been proof of derangement, to the minds of the vicar and the few other Stratford people whom she had come to know, or even to the marvelous instinct of Hawthorne himself. What he says of her in these last days, indeed, is at once so kind, so just, and so wise, that it ought to be reproduced for the mere value of its judgment of her, even though there appear in it her own phrases from her letters already printed above. Nor can one refrain from thinking how apt to the genius of the author of the "Scarlet Letter" must have been the scene which, out of her own description, he presents here, of the night in the ancient church, with the "Old Player's" grave beneath her feet, and his image, unseen, looking down upon her from the darkness. It seems as if only

the tender reverence which he avows for the great
and true soul which was on the verge of distraction could have restrained him from making of it
a chapter in a romance.

" Months before that [the publication of the
book] happened, however, Miss Bacon had taken
up her residence at Stratford-on-Avon, drawn
thither by the magnetism of those rich secrets
which she supposed to have been hidden by
Raleigh, or Bacon, or I know not whom, in Shakspeare's grave, and protected there by a curse, as
pirates used to bury their gold in the guardianship
of a fiend. She took a humble lodging and began
to haunt the church like a ghost. But she did not
condescend to any stratagem or underhand attempt
to violate the grave, which, had she been capable
of admitting such an idea, might possibly have been
accomplished by the aid of a resurrection-man.
As her first step, she made acquaintance with the
clerk, and began to sound him as to the feasibility
of her enterprise and his own willingness to engage
in it. The clerk apparently listened with not un-
favorable ears; but, as his situation (which the
fees of pilgrims, more numerous than at any Catholic shrine, render lucrative) would have been forfeited by any malfeasance in office, he stipulated
for liberty to consult the vicar. Miss Bacon requested to tell her own story to the reverend
gentleman, and seems to have been received by

him with the utmost kindness, and even to have
succeeded in making a certain impression on his
mind as to the desirability of the search. As their
interview had been under the seal of secrecy, he
asked permission to consult a friend, who, as Miss
Bacon either found out or surmised, was a practi-
tioner of the law. What the legal friend advised
she did not learn ; but the negotiation continued,
and certainly was never broken off by an absolute refusal on the vicar's part. He, perhaps, was
kindly temporizing with our poor countrywoman,
whom an Englishman of ordinary mould would
have sent to a lunatic asylum at once. I cannot
help fancying, however, that her familiarity with
the events of Shakspeare's life, and of his death
and burial (of which she would speak as if she had
been present at the edge of the grave), and all the
history, literature and personalities of the Elizabethan age, together with the prevailing power of
her own belief, and the eloquence with which she
knew how to enforce it, had really gone some little
way toward making a convert of the good clergyman. If so, I honor him above all the hierarchy
of England.

"The affair certainly looked very hopeful.
However erroneously, Miss Bacon had understood
from the vicar that no obstacles would be inter-
posed to the investigation, and that he himself
would sanction it with his presence. It was to
take place after nightfall; and all preliminary

arrangements being made, the vicar and clerk professed to wait only her word in order to set about
lifting the awful stone from the sepulchre. So, at
least, Miss Bacon believed; and as her bewilderment was entirely in her own thoughts, and never
disturbed her perception or accurate remembrance
of external things, I see no reason to doubt it, except it be the tinge of absurdity in the fact. But, in
this apparently prosperous state of things, her own
convictions began to falter. A doubt stole into
her mind whether she might not have mistaken the
depository and mode of concealment of those historic treasures; and after once admitting the doubt,
she was afraid to hazard the shock of uplifting the
stone and finding nothing. She examined the surface of the gravestone, and endeavored, without
stirring it, to estimate whether it were of such
thickness as to be capable of containing the archives
of the Elizabethan club. She went over anew the
proofs, the clues, the enigmas, the pregnant sentences, which she had discovered in Bacon's letters
and elsewhere, and now was frightened to perceive that they did not point so definitely to Shakspeare's tomb as she had heretofore supposed.
There was an unmistakably distinct reference to
a tomb, but it might be Bacon's, or Raleigh's, or
Spenser's; and instead of the 'Old Player,' as she
profanely called him, it might be either of those
three illustrious dead, poet, warrior, or statesman,
whose ashes, in Westminster Abbey, or the Tower

burial ground, or wherever they sleep, it was her
mission to disturb. It is very possible, moreover,
that her acute mind may always have had a lurk-
ing and deeply latent distrust of its own fantasies,
and that this now became strong enough to restrain
her from a decisive step.

" But she continued to hover around the church,
and seems to have had full freedom of entrance in
the day time, and special license on one occasion
at least, at a late hour of the night. She went
thither with a dark-lantern, which could but
twinkle like a glow-worm through the volume of
obscurity that filled the great dusky edifice. Groping her way up the aisle and towards the chancel,
she sat down on the elevated part of the pavement
above Shakspeare's grave. If the divine poet
really wrote the inscription there, and cared as
much about the quiet of his bones as its depreca-
tory earnestness would imply, it was time for those
crumbling relics to bestir themselves under her
sacrilegious feet. But they were safe. She made
no attempt to disturb them ; though, I believe, she
looked narrowly into the crevices between Shakspeare's and the two adjacent stones, and in some
way satisfied herself that her single strength would
suffice to lift the former, in case of need. She
threw the feeble ray of her lantern up towards the
bust, but could not make it visible beneath the
darkness of the vaulted roof. Had she been subject to superstitious terrors, it is impossible to con-

ceive of a situation that could better entitle her to
feel them, for, if Shakspeare's ghost would rise at
any provocation, it must have shown itself then;
but it is my sincere belief, that, if his figure had
appeared within the scope of her dark-lantern, in
his slashed doublet and gown, and with his eyes
bent on her beneath the high, bald forehead, just
as we see him in the bust, she would have met
him fearlessly and controverted his claims to the
authorship of the plays to his very face. She
had taught herself to contemn 'Lord Leicester's
groom' (it was one of her disdainful epithets for
the world's incomparable poet) so thoroughly, that
even his disembodied spirit would hardly have
found civil treatment at Miss Bacon's hands.

"Her vigil, though it appears to have had no
definite object, continued far into the night. Several times she heard a low movement in the
aisles: a stealthy, dubious footfall prowling about
in the darkness, now here, now there, among the
pillars and ancient tombs, as if some restless in-
habitant of the latter had crept forth to peep at
the intruder. By and by the clerk made his appearance, and confessed that he had been watching her ever since she entered the church.

"About this time it was that a strange sort of
weariness seems to have fallen upon her: her toil
was all but done, her great purpose, as she believed, on the very point of accomplishment, when
she began to regret that so stupendous a mission

had been imposed on the fragility of a woman. Her faith in the new philosophy was as mighty as ever, and so was her confidence in her own adequate development of it, now about to be given to the world ; yet she wished, or fancied so, that it might never have been her duty to achieve this unparalleled task, and to stagger feebly forward under her immense burden of responsibility and renown. So far as her personal concern in the matter went, she would gladly have forfeited the reward of her patient study and labor for so many years, her exile from her country and estrangement from her family and friends, her sacrifice of health and all other interests to this one pursuit, if she could only find herself free to dwell in Stratford and be forgotten. She liked the old slumbrous town, and awarded the only praise that ever I knew her to bestow on Shakspeare, the individual man, by acknowledging that his taste in a residence was good, and that he knew how to choose a suitable retirement for a person of shy but genial temperament. And at this point, I cease to possess the means of tracing her vicissitudes of feeling any further. In consequence of some advice which I fancied it my duty to tender, as being the only confidant whom she now had in the world, I fell under Miss Bacon's most severe and passionate displeasure, and was cast off by her in the twinkling of an eye. It was a misfortune to which her friends were always particularly liable ; but

I think that none of them ever loved, or even respected, her most ingenuous and noble, but likewise most sensitive and tumultuous character, the less for it." [1]

It was on the 12th of June that Mr. David Rice, surgeon and Mayor of Stratford, wrote in terms of great kindness and respect for his patient, to the American consul at Liverpool, asking for " advice or suggestions " in regard to an American lady whom he had seen that afternoon. His report was: " She is in a very excited and unsatisfactory state, especially mentally, and I think there is much reason to fear that she will become decidedly insane." Hawthorne instantly replied, thanking the surgeon " for your kind attention to my countrywoman "; authorizing all suitable expenditure (for it was also reported that her means were exhausted) that might be necessary for her comfort, and twice over promising to be personally responsible for it. At the same time he transmitted to her brother in America the news he had received.

There was for a few days much improvement in her condition, and " good reason to believe that the equilibrium both of her mental and bodily health will be happily restored, and at no very distant period." She was troubled to learn that both Hawthorne and her brother had been told of her illness, yet grateful to hear of the former's

---

[1] Hawthorne: *Our Old Home.*

generous and instant response. To him she sent immediately a long letter, clear, vigorous, and coherent, yet displaying, for the first time, hallucinations other than that, if it were one, concerning the authorship of the Plays. To her brother she wrote a shorter one, with no word of complaint, and with warm expressions of the old affection which she had thought was gone forever. "Having fulfilled my work as I thought, I have been quietly waiting since the publication of my book, to be informed as to the next movement, — if movement was indeed the word. I have not cared to know the result. Since the day I heard it was published I have made no inquiry on the subject. . . . I am calm and happy. Never happier, — never so happy. I do not want to come back to America. I *can* not come. I pay seven shillings a week for my rooms and it takes very little to keep me alive. I do not want any luxuries. But I think this is the place for me at present.

"Your ever affectionate sister,

DELIA BACON."

Since the purpose of this sketch is simply to furnish, to those who care for it, accurate knowledge and the means of judging justly about her, it is right not to withhold some passages from the grateful answer which her brother wrote to Hawthorne, on receiving his announcement of her prostration.

"The crisis at which my sister's case has arrived,

requires me to say, plainly, that in my opinion
her mind has been ' verging on insanity' for the
last six years.   She knows that since 1851 I have
habitually distrusted the soundness of her judgment.   She knows that I have all along regarded
her darling theory as a mere hallucination.   She
therefore distrusts me.   When she went to England she was very careful to conceal from me the
object of her going and the resources on which she
depended.   Indeed, none of her family friends, as
I understand, had the opportunity of helping her
in that enterprise.   Mr. Emerson, I believe, fitted
her out with some credentials and valuable letters
of introduction — partly, I doubt not, in that wonderful ' good-nature' which is so prominent a feature in his character — partly, I suspect, in the
special sympathy which he has in whatever is unbelief. : . . My fear has been, all along, that whenever and wherever her book might be published,
the disappointment of that long and confident expectation would be disastrous if not fatal to her."

For month after month, notwithstanding intermittent lifting of the cloud which had settled
about her, it became more and more evident that
the cloud was the darkness of night.   There is letter after letter of Hawthorne, showing his unceas-
ing care for the distracted woman whom he had
already so much befriended, and who had seemed
to requite his kindness with distrust and thankless-
ness.   Down to his surrender of the consulate and

his departure from England in October, his correspondence with her surgeon at Stratford and her brother in America was incessant. He had even been able to arrange, difficult as such an arrangement must have been, for her transportation, under suitable care, to her native land; but a new access of violent mania compelled the abandonment of the plan. When, about October, he passed over to the continent, his brief and strange relation to her, which had served at least to illustrate so exquisitely the qualities of that rare character which sought nothing more earnestly than to withdraw itself from admiration, was wholly at an end.

When Hawthorne was gone, there was no longer an American friend left to her in England. Every one in Stratford was kind to her — more kind even than she knew. Even the shoemaker's family, with whom she lodged, and whom in her increasing derangement she sorely tried, were patient and considerate as if she were of their own kindred. One Stratford family too, having many American acquaintances, and who had received her hospitably before this great misfortune came upon her, seems to have done what little could be done for her. But the only American who saw her in Stratford was Miss Maria Mitchell, the eminent astronomer, who, being casually there in October, visited her and reported the visit to the sick woman's friends. But there was not one of those to whom her sad condition brought the deepest distress, for whom it was possible to cross the Atlantic to her relief.

In December, under the stress of her heightening malady, she was removed to an excellent private asylum for a small number of insane persons at Henley-in-Arden, — in "the forest of Arden," — eight miles from Stratford. While she was there, Emerson was advised of her condition; and the terms in which, even in this eclipse of her intellect and after the failure of her work, he still expressed himself concerning her, are worth preserving.

CONCORD, MASS., 18 February, 1858.

DR. LEONARD BACON.

DEAR SIR, — I have just received from Mrs. Flower of Stratford-on-Avon the enclosed note, which I hasten to forward to you. I could heartily wish that I had very different news to send you of a person who has high claims on me and on all of us who love genius and elevation of character. These qualities have so shone in Miss Bacon, that, whilst their present eclipse is the greater calamity, it seems as if the care of her in these present distressing circumstances ought to be not at private, but at the public charge of scholars and friends of learning and truth. If I can serve you in any manner in relation to her, you will please to command me. With great respect,

R. W. EMERSON.

CONCORD, 25 February [1859].

DEAR SIR, — I received this morning your note, and I think it proper to forward to you also this second note from Mrs. Flower, because it seems as if the apology it offers were meant to you. It also gives you perhaps later notices, if you have not yourself letters by the same arrival.

With great respect, yours,

R. W. EMERSON.

REV. DR. BACON.

She was not long in " the forest of Arden." Yet to withdraw her from its seclusion, and to restore her at last, after the five years of her separation from home and friends, to her native land, to find there only a grave, there seems to have been needed an incident as dramatic as many that had marked her life. There came to England late in March, on his rapid way homeward by what was called the "Overland Route," from a two years' cruise in an American frigate in the China Seas, one of the sons — the one best beloved by all who knew him — of her eldest brother. He was a young man not yet twenty-two years of age; and as he hurried in the eagerness of youthful home-sickness, unwilling to spare an hour even for the delights of the England which he had never seen, he remembered nevertheless the relative whom he had, heard to be somewhere there, alone, but of whose sickness and distraction he had heard noth-

ing. Finding that she had been at Stratford, he
hastened there, and was shocked to learn where
she was, and in what condition. Without opportunity to consult those who had authority to act or
advise, the young man[1] assumed the responsibility
which rested nowhere else in England. He surrendered the passage homeward already engaged
for himself; delayed his departure a week, and took
with him, when he embarked for home, the un-
happy woman who had known him in childhood,
and to whom, when he appeared to her at Henley,
a thousand pleasant recollections of her earlier
years came up to dispel the hallucinations which
had possessed her.

On the 13th of April, 1858, five years, wanting but a few days, after she had sailed from New
York upon her enthusiastic quest, she reached
her native land. She did not linger there long.
Her distraction was complete, and hopeless; so
complete that only the care and restraint of an
institution designed for the treatment of the insane was adequate to control her and to provide
for her needs. She was brought very soon to the
" Retreat " at that city of Hartford where so
many years of her childhood had been spent, and
there she remained until the end.

Late in August, 1859, there were brought to her
bedside the two sisters and two brothers who still

[1] Afterward the Rev. George Blagden Bacon, D. D., of Orange,
New Jersey, who died September 15, 1876.

survived of their parents' children. A violent di<del></del> ease had brought her down into extreme debility, and its fatal termination was plainly at hand. For a few days the violence of her mania was abated ; even her hallucinations seemed to be lifted from her mind; she knew those who surrounded her, and received with joy the evidences of their life-long love for her, which was no longer repelled, or requited with suspicion or anger. She recognized, and said so, that she had been under delusions ; although, in these solemn hours of meeting and final parting, what some have thought the great delusion of her life was neither spoken of nor thought of. But the bitterness of her soul against those who had loved her most and longest was all gone, and instead there was peace, and the tender affection of the early days of hardship and struggle. "Stronger by weakness," she was able at last to see what for years had been dark to her : —

"The soul's dark cottage, battered and decayed,
  Let in new light through chinks that Time had made."

Thus attended, on the second day of September, 1859, as her brother then wrote, "she died, clearly and calmly trusting in Christ, and thankful to escape from tribulation and enter into rest." In the old burying-ground at New Haven she was laid, in the parcel of ground with her brother's family. A cross of brown stone, set there by some of the ladies who remembered the love and admiration with which they had received her instruction in history, bears simply the record of her birth and death, and the words:

"*So He bringeth them to their desired haven.*"

No one, of all that cared most for her, could wish to have her judged of more kindly or justly than in the closing words that Hawthorne wrote of her:

"What she may have suffered before her intellect gave way, we had better not try to imagine. No author had ever hoped so confidently as she; none ever failed more utterly.　A superstitious fancy might suggest that the anathema on Shakspeare's tombstone had fallen heavily on her head in requital of even the unaccomplished purpose of disturbing the dust beneath, and that the 'Old Player' had kept so quietly in his grave, on the night of her vigil, because he foresaw how soon and terribly he would be avenged.　But if that benign spirit takes any care or cognizance of such things now, he has surely requited the injustice that she sought to do him — the high justice that she really did — by a tenderness of love and pity of which only he could be capable.　What matters it though she called him by some other name?　He had wrought a greater miracle on her than on all the world besides.　This bewildered enthusiast had recognized a depth in the man whom she decried, which scholars, critics, and learned societies devoted to the elucidation of his unrivalled scenes, had never imagined to exist there.　She had paid

him the loftiest honor that all these ages of renown
have been able to accumulate upon his memory.
And when, not many months after the outward
failure of her lifelong object, she passed into the
better world, I know not why we should hesitate
to believe that the immortal poet may have met
her on the threshold and led her in, reassuring
her with friendly and comfortable words, and
thanking her (yet with a smile of gentle humor in
his eyes at the thought of certain mistaken speculations) for having interpreted him to mankind so
well." [1]

[1] Hawthorne : *Our Old Home.*

INDEX.

www.ingramcontent.com/pod-product-compliance
Lightning Source LLC
Chambersburg PA
CBHW020944030726
47496CB00005B/1346